Harbored Desires

THE HAZELBY SISTERS
BOOK ONE

SHANNON FRANCES JAMES

Cover design: Dar Albert at Wicked Smart Designs
Developmental edit: Lesley Marshall at Editline
Copy edit: Danielle Line
Formatting: Selina Shapland at Empowered Words

Get in touch with Shannon Frances James, read her stories and join her newsletter, The Drawing Room Whispers, for upcoming releases and more!

For Ryan,
The hero of our love story.

Chapter One

SPRING 1810

HARRIET HAZELBY LEANED FORWARD in the saddle, squeezing her buckskin-clad thighs harder and rising in time with each thrust of the stallion's pounding legs. Sweat ran down the back of her neck despite the crisp morning air whipping against her skin. The stallion snorted, his brown ears twitching, and shifted into a gallop. His hooves beat a steady path through the field of her aunt and uncle's estate, Balmaine.

"Is that as fast as you can go?" Harriet called. Her older sister didn't stand a chance even if she had also donned men's clothing for their morning race.

Millie's tinkling laugh was soon lost in the wind as Harriet flew past her.

Clear blue skies spanned the horizon, the sun making its slow creep upward. Morning rays kissed every surface, from the budding tips of wheat to the lines of trees running parallel on either side. A significant improvement on the previous days of rain.

Harriet reached the stables, Millie arriving seconds behind her. Every second counted in a race between them, and she'd won by at least three. That would settle their debate for today. They slid to the ground, ignoring the mounting blocks, boots squelching in the mud.

"I could have won," Millie said. Her shining green eyes, sparkling in the sunlight, matched her voice.

"If you say so." Harriet flashed her sister an affectionate smile. "What next? We could settle who can swim the length of the lake fastest. Or who can climb highest up that tree." She pointed to an ancient oak behind the grand estate home. "We have time before we meet Uncle Frederick for the tenant visits."

Millie tugged at the reins in Harriet's hand. "We both know I can make it much farther up that tree than you." Her smile softened, and her delicate eyebrows drew together. "Besides, I believe the rest of your day will be occupied with Eliza."

Harriet let the leather reins slip through her fingers. Being chaperoned by their eldest sister until their parents arrived in Hull had ruined her peace. Millie wasn't under Eliza's scrutiny, despite this being her third season. Were Harriet's prospects for her first season truly so dismal?

She sighed. Marrying a peer of the realm seemed impossible, but she must try. As the third daughter of an earl without sons, her value lay in marriage, not in acting as an aspiring land steward on her father's estate in Selby.

"It might not be so bad," Millie said, drawing Harriet's gaze from her boots. "She's trying to help."

"I know," Harriet admitted, burying her hands in her pockets, "but there's only so much she can improve with determination alone."

Nothing could change her unfashionable height,

athletic figure, and aversion to society, no matter how much Eliza tried. Only her father's rank and money made her a desirable prospect. She didn't dare dream of meeting a man who looked at her the way their father looked at their mother.

Millie squeezed her shoulder. "I'm going to help with the horses."

With another heavy sigh, Harriet started toward the house alone. Currying the horses or mucking out the stalls would have been preferable to whatever Eliza had planned.

"There you are!" Eliza Malstern, Duchess of Eldon, stood tall and foreboding at the main entry of the house looking as regal as ever. The timber door framed her among the large rectangular sandstone blocks. Her gaze raked over Harriet, lingering on the muddy breeches and riding boots. "Oh, you are positively filthy."

Harriet groaned. "Must you start at me so early?"

Eliza, ever composed, proceeded without a flicker of emotion crossing her face. "You and I have been invited to tea with the Duke of Ailesbury."

Harriet stared at her sister. "We have?"

If anyone should receive an invite to tea with a duke, it was Millie.

"An introduction to a gentleman before your presentation to society won't hurt you. And you never know..." Eliza trailed off, her gaze roaming over Harriet's shoulder.

A gentleman was one thing. A duke was something else entirely. Harriet was *not* duchess material. One look at her in her current state should confirm that.

"What the hell did you tell the man to convince him to meet me?" Or... Her gaze narrowed. "How old is the Duke of Ailesbury?" Older than her father and in dire need of an heir? Her stomach roiled.

Eliza didn't answer. Instead, she swept her hands over her meticulous pink skirts.

How many suitors had her sister arranged to meet prior to the season? The entire eligible cohort of Hull?

Heat radiated up Harriet's neck, spreading across her cheeks, and her hands balled into fists. She stormed the front steps two at a time, reaching her sister on the landing.

"I won't go," Harriet said, grappling for a suitable reason. "It isn't proper. I haven't been presented in society yet."

"Oh"—the dismissive *pff* noise Eliza made was as uncharacteristic as the careless wave of her hand—"would it be so bad if you found a husband before the season? I know you wish not to partake in social gatherings."

"I will not meet my husband before, during, or after the season. I will not find a husband at all. Look at me." Harriet waited for her sister to meet her eye. "No one wants this for a wife. They want a placid, house-trained mouse with wide hips, not someone with a functional brain or understanding of land management. Admit that is why you are taking me to meet the duke before I'm drowned out by more amenable women."

Eliza huffed, blocking the door. "I will do no such thing. Mama and Papa were generous delaying your first London season, but you are nearly nineteen. You still have much to learn, but you *are* ready. Please don't remind me that you can thatch a roof and assist a horse during foaling, among everything else at which a lady should not be proficient. Those are not the things of which I speak." Her tone softened. "We are visiting the duke. Go upstairs and change."

"I am not meeting the duke today, or any day I reside in Hull." Harriet pushed past her sister and thrust the door open.

Mrs. Brinley, the housekeeper, took one look at her muddy attire and swatted her back to the doorstep. "I cannot allow you in the house in this state, my lady. Down to the scullery."

Harriet obliged, stomping behind Mrs. Brinley down the stairs and ignoring her sister. It wasn't the first time she'd been brought inside through the servants' entrance, here or at her own home. They rounded the house, their feet scuffling across the gravel, and descended into the scullery, the narrow stairs creaking with each step.

"Boots off before you take another step," Mrs. Brinley said, her brown heels clicking across the stone floor. "Unless mopping is a skill you wish to practice today."

Harriet grinned and reached for the mop hanging on the wall. "I'll clean the mud from the entryway."

"You'll go straight to your room, and I'll arrange a bath." Mrs. Brinley lifted a dressing gown off a peg and held it open.

Harriet untied her laces and toed off her boots. She shrugged into the dressing gown and slipped out of her breeches.

Mrs. Brinley held out her hand. It must have taken a valiant effort to keep the disapproval from her face as the muddy garment slapped into her hand, but the old woman succeeded.

"I'll clean your boots if you wish," Mrs. Brinley said.

Harriet smiled and turned away. "Thank you, but there's no need." They wouldn't remain clean for long.

She raced upstairs through the servants' internal staircase without passing another soul. In the safety of her third-floor bedroom, Harriet shimmied out of the dressing gown and glared down at her tightly bound torso hidden beneath a loose linen shirt.

"Dratted thing," she mumbled, reaching under her shirt for the ribbons. Removing the corset would have been preferable, but she hadn't mastered the skill required for this newer design, and she didn't have time. If she wanted to make it off the estate, she had to hurry. After some twisting, jumping, and wiggling maneuvers, she could stand more comfortably without the cursed contraption thrusting her barely-there breasts into existence. She reached into the depths of her trunk and dug out her spare breeches, completing the ensemble with her worn walking boots.

Dressed, she glanced at her reflection in the mirror perched atop the dresser. Small flecks of mud dotted her shirt and face. She wiped her hand over her cheeks, smearing the dirt and making her look as though she had been working in the yard.

A resigned chuckle escaped her lips. No amount of time in the bath would make her presentable for a duke—this morning or ever.

Running her fingers through her thick brown hair, she unraveled the double braids and twisted the mass into a tight knot at her nape. A convincing young stable boy stared back at her. She wished hiding her unremarkable features wasn't so easy, but the disguise was effective. No one would recognize her once she made it into town, and she would have the day to explore.

Satisfied, Harriet crept out of her room, pausing at the top of the stairs. This was the only way out unless she climbed through a window, and she was risking enough without courting significant injury or death. She tiptoed down the stairs, her heart pounding.

Quick footsteps clipped toward her. She darted around the newel post, pressing herself against the wall in the shadow under the stairs. Mrs. Brinley bustled past and started up the steps, followed by footmen carrying the copper bath and jugs of water.

Harriet sprinted for the rear door, running through the kitchen garden until she reached the gate.

Captain Alexander Ordell yanked the halyard, pulling the sail into place and tying it off. He glanced over the taffrail and down at the dock master. Still not their turn. He couldn't wait to be away from Hull, and he would make a point of staying away this time.

He sighed and ran his fingers through his hair, pushing it away from his eyes. Despite his parents having died seven years ago, visiting his ancestral home always made him uneasy. The heavy weight of guilt descended each time he walked through those doors. If he hadn't left when he was fourteen, or had done more to protect his mother, would she still be alive?

"I almost forgot. How was your meeting this morning?" Samuel Wethering asked.

Alexander glanced at his closest friend and the first mate on the *Seren*, who had paused his inspection of the rigging. A sail flapped above their heads. The sun shone behind Sam, and Alexander squinted against the glare. He'd thought their conversation would stick to lighter topics since joining the other sailors on deck. *Apparently not.*

"It was horrid, and you know it," Alexander said, lacking the vocabulary to describe the visit with his brother. A breeze blew across the deck that he'd have liked to blame for the shiver that raced up his spine. At last, they were preparing to sail, much later than intended. The tide was almost too low, but this ship was small and fast. They would soon be out on the river, and he'd breathe easily again. He hated visiting George. Each time he saw his brother, he couldn't ignore the sharp cut of his chin and the bright blue eyes reflecting his own. Both a stark reminder of their father, though neither of them were like the man.

"So, he's not letting it go?" Sam asked.

"You have known my brother since we were in leading strings. Do you think he is the type to let something go?" Alexander raised his eyebrows. He lifted a hand, shielding his eyes from the sun, and met Sam's gaze. People had mistaken them for brothers at times, though less so as they'd grown into adulthood. Their similar build and brown hair had once been enough for any passing sailor to draw a connection between them. Had they looked closer, they'd have seen how Sam's rounder face contrasted Alexander's severe jaw, and that Sam's brown eyes held a kindness that escaped Alexander's icy blue. Those differences were clearer now, at the somewhat mature age of twenty-four.

Sam shrugged. "S'pose not." An intrigued look filled his eyes, but he didn't say more.

Alexander hesitated, unsure how much of George's words to share, but he could trust Sam more than anyone. The three of them had grown up together, but Sam and Alexander had run away from home at fourteen, leaving George behind.

"He asked me not to sail today," Alexander admitted, turning back to the mast. He couldn't keep dwelling on the past and the mistakes he'd made.

"He what?" Sam exclaimed.

Alexander glanced over his shoulder with a sheepish grin and kept his voice low. "He said he would speak to *whoever it was who employed me* and demand I be released from service." Years of practice had made his impression of his brother close to perfect, and it brought a smile to Sam's face.

"Pompous ass," Sam muttered, crossing his arms over his chest. "I knew he had connections, but I didn't think the King would be one of them."

Alexander couldn't help but laugh. Trust Sam to lift his spirits. "It would seem George is of the opinion that my time would be better spent in London finding a wife." He rolled his eyes, though the gesture was hollow. He couldn't admit how much that prospect terrified him, and his brother had been incredibly determined in his efforts of persuasion. "George is the one who should be looking for a wife, though we both know that will never happen."

A meaningful glance passed between him and Sam. His brother had been hopelessly in love with a woman for the past four years and devastated that he hadn't married her before another man did. Alexander heard about it every time he returned home, and today had been no exception, only this time, his brother had added a proposal into the mix.

Marriage? Alexander resisted the shiver that tingled at the base of his spine. *Never.* And he certainly wouldn't be marrying a woman to give his brother an heir because the man was too lovesick to do it for himself. Alexander spent ninety percent of his life at sea, and the other ten percent wasn't exclusively in England. While that could be considered a benefit for some women, he refused to enter into a breeding arrangement. That had happened to his mother, and the woman George was in love with, both of whom suffered at the hands of their husbands. What did his brother expect him to do? Impregnate the woman, *his wife,* and leave? He'd witnessed the hell a loveless marriage could cause. Worse, he'd seen what damage *love* could do, what it had done to his brother, and it wasn't pretty. Best to live his life as he was and never submit himself or another person to such pain.

Sam sighed, the sound pulling Alexander from his thoughts.

"Not a productive exercise in the end," his friend said. It wasn't a question. Their hope that George would have answers had been unfounded.

Alexander shook his head, and his thoughts returned to the contents of his pocket.

"Can you cover for me?" he asked, patting the small hidden box. The crew would hold a meeting before they sailed, but his attendance wasn't a necessity.

"Yes," Sam replied with a tilt of his head. "Shall I inform them that you'll be leaving us on our return to London to find a bride?"

"If I have to go, you're coming with me," Alexander threatened, turning toward the stairs. The temptation to fling that box into the water was strong, but after all these years, he couldn't bring himself to do it. *Damn George.* He knew how to get to Alexander, the right strings to pull. Well, his effort would be in vain.

Chapter Two

THE FAMILIAR BUSTLING streets of Hull greeted Harriet, and joy thrilled through her. The River Humber teemed with more activity than she'd seen on previous visits. Ships sailed out of the dock at incredible speed, heading downriver toward the coast.

Her disguise and the growing crowds helped hide her as she approached the town, steadfastly ignoring the shop windows. Men didn't browse, she reminded herself, and her aunt was in town. Aunt Amelia had seen her dressed this way enough times to recognize her should they cross paths. Though her aunt would likely turn a blind eye to Harriet's escapades, she didn't want Eliza to discover how she'd spent her day.

Harriet followed the foot traffic over North Bridge to the old dock where moored ships bobbed and swayed, their sails fluttering in the gentle wind. She continued along, savoring the breeze on her cheeks, until the path veered away from the dock and into the marketplace. The calls of street vendors echoed off the stone walls as they thrust their wares in front of her. Harriet ignored the colorful lengths of silks, miracle balms, bottles with mysterious contents, and heady spices, hurrying forward until she reached the new dock. This was the part of Hull she had been most eager to explore since spying it on the walk into town.

Cargo nets laden with barrels and crates swung overhead, and fish and sweat overpowered the sweet, salty air of Hull. Enormous ships towered over her, their grand shapes and intricate details even more impressive up close. Men moved loads up and down the gangplanks that dotted the timber platform, shouting orders through the crowd.

Head down, Harriet ducked and weaved between the sailors. At the end of the dock, she tucked herself behind three barrels, welcoming the fresh coastal wind that cleansed her nose.

A tall ship glided out of the dock and into the river through an opening that seemed far too narrow. Harriet tipped her head back, taking in the sight, its expansive shape and full sails momentarily blocking out the sun. The ship sailed past, the cacophony of shouts and creaking of masts almost drowning out the groaning timbers.

Long fingers wrapped around Harriet's elbow, and she flinched.

"Don't turn around, lad." The low, hoarse voice was hot on her ear and prickled over her skin. The man's body blocked the breeze, and a putrid stench filled her nostrils. Every muscle in her body tensed, and a wave of shock pulsed from her neck to the tips of her fingers and toes. The grip on her arm was too tight, and fear held her still. A scream might make things worse, though she doubted she could muster a sound with her mouth suddenly so dry.

"I have a message for the captain of that ship," the man rasped. He lifted a grimy finger and pointed at a small ship.

Unlike the others, it sat quiet and calm. No one loaded or unloaded cargo or moved about the deck at all. "I need you to deliver it, sailor," he said.

She wasn't a sailor, and she wouldn't board a ship. Harriet protested, but his grip tightened, his nails digging further into the soft flesh of her inner arm. He leaned closer and his lips were at her ear. Bitter, rancid sweat overwhelmed her. Bile rose in her throat, and she swallowed against it, suppressing a tremble.

"The change of tide will be reflected in the orange moon," he said, repeating the message in a gravelly whisper. Before she could process the request, he spoke again. "Now, lad, you're to deliver my message. And don't think of running, or there'll be trouble. Understood?"

She nodded.

His fingers loosened, and she wrenched her arm free, stumbling forward. She straightened and walked to the gangplank.

The threat rang in her ears, but that message couldn't possibly be intended for a ship's captain. It was nonsense. Was she walking into a trap?

She drew in a breath and frowned up at the ship. How long should it take to deliver a message to a ship's captain? She couldn't seek out the captain or repeat those words, but she could hide on the ship for a few minutes and then return to Balmaine.

Mustering the nonchalant air of a sailor going about his duties, she ascended the gangplank, not stopping until she reached the rail. Some men huddled together near the back of the ship, the rest of the deck clear of people. She stilled. Had they noticed her?

Her lithe movements made no sound on the timber deck when she stepped down from the gangplank. She glanced back toward the men, still absorbed in their meeting, and searched the deck for a place to hide. It was clean and neat, despite the array of barrels and crates. A faint hint of oil mixed with the rich timber. She darted around a tower of crates and waited. One minute had passed by her estimate, not quite long enough yet.

Unable to remain still for long, she continued along the deck toward the front of the ship. The smooth, oiled timber of the rail was exposed as she ran her hand through its salty coating. The dockside noises faded into the silence. Ropes tangled and coiled above her head and around almost every surface in sight.

A gull's sharp cry pierced her musings, spurring her along. Almost three minutes now. She could leave soon. Harriet's foot dropped, and she grappled for the railing. She glared down at the offending hole, an entrance to a staircase. Should she go down? *No*, she couldn't be so reckless. Then why wouldn't her deceitful feet let her turn around?

A shout from behind startled her, the sailor coming her way.

Harriet's brief burst of confidence evaporated. She gathered herself and hurried down the stairs. If she hid until the sailor passed, she could return and disembark the ship. The staircase opening illuminated a small square in the almost pitch black of the lower deck. She strained her eyes in the darkness. Which way to go?

Boots thumped across the deck above.

She gasped.

They were on the stairs.

With no idea which direction would be best, she continued down the next staircase and into the belly of the ship. The deck below was darker again, with little light filtering through from the opening in the main deck. She hurried along, chill seeping into her bones, searching for a place to hide. The footsteps thundered above.

Harriet tripped on a rope and flew forward. Arms outstretched, and eyes squeezed closed, she braced herself for the impact of hitting the deck.

Something was wrong.

The timber's aroma was intense, and now it smelled… warm, somehow, and with a hint of ginger.

Solid arms wrapped around her, and big, strong hands stretched across her back.

ALEXANDER HAD LOCKED the chest and been careful to stand slowly, ducking to avoid the low beam above his head. He'd turned around, his mind still occupied, and a body slammed into him. His arms instinctively shot around the boy, and now he held him steady.

The boy let out a feminine squeak of surprise.

Alexander slid his hands across the boy's back, keeping him close as he regained his balance. He froze. The laces of a corset were unmistakable through the shirt, and her breasts thrust into his chest. Alexander blinked, momentarily lost for words. What was a woman doing here, deep inside the ship, on the orlop deck? Female sailors were rare, and there were none in his crew.

A few strands of silky hair brushed Alexander's cheek, and a sweet floral fragrance enveloped his senses. A hint of mint among a bouquet of gardenias. An exotic scent for a woman in Hull, yet somehow familiar. The women at the docks seldom smelled this intoxicating, and even they wore dresses.

He cleared his throat. "What the hell are you doing

here?" The words came out level, not betraying the uneasiness that had settled in the pit of his stomach.

Her body stiffened, but Alexander made no move to release the woman. Not until he knew more. Through his shirt, her lips moved against his shoulder. The sensation was strange, and it seemed to quiver through him.

"Let me go," she mumbled.

He loosened his hold now that she was steady again. Her hands came between them, and she pushed against his chest, but Alexander didn't budge. Not until her palms glided down to his hips. The shove lacked enough force to move him, but at the sudden jolt from her touch, he stepped away. He moved his hands to her shoulders, keeping a gentle but firm hold of her, and studied her face. His eyes had adjusted well to the dark, but her features weren't clear in the dim of the orlop deck. All he could discern was a deep scowl. If it weren't for the gravity of the situation, he might have laughed. Few stowaways possessed her confidence.

"Who are you?" Alexander asked.

"I—I shall not say."

He narrowed his eyes. Neither her manner nor her tone belonged on the docks. This woman had connections, though he couldn't imagine who that would be in Hull. Women like this didn't appear on ships without a reason, and their reason was rarely good. He must get her off the *Seren* as a matter of urgency.

"What is it you're running from?" His whisper was desperate. If he couldn't facilitate the woman's escape from Hull, the least he could do was leave her on the dock with some direction. "Are you with child?"

She scoffed. "I am not with child, *sir*. And I am not running from anything."

"Then what in the devil are you doing here?" His voice grew brusque. "Posing as a sailor, I might add."

Her lips pressed together into a tight line that complemented her frown. She tried to wriggle away, and Alexander tightened his grip. He didn't want to hurt her, but he had to know what she was planning.

"I'll only ask once more," he said. "Who are you, and what are you doing on this ship?"

"I'll only tell you once more, let me go," she snapped.

Whatever she was running from must be a damn sight worse than the reality of life as a stowaway.

He chuckled at her stubbornness, but the sound lacked humor. "All I am asking is your name and your purpose. Then I will see you safely off this ship." He had a few sovereigns in his pocket from this morning, she could have those. There wasn't time to give her much else when he left her on the docks.

"You promise to let me go?" Despite the glare, her voice faltered. Perhaps she wasn't resolved to stowaway on the ship. Why was she here?

"I will escort you off this ship myself," he assured.

"I was sent to deliver a message to the captain."

"Go on."

"Are you the captain of this ship?" she asked, one eyebrow arching.

He cocked his head, considering her. "I'll see that he gets the message." What did it matter who he was? She would be off his ship in a matter of minutes.

"Fine." She huffed. "The change of tide will be reflected in the orange moon."

Alexander's stomach twisted. Whatever he'd expected her to say, it wasn't that. That changed everything. The young woman's expectant stare bore into him, and he fought to keep his tone even. "Where did you hear that?"

"A man on the dock."

"A man on the dock," he repeated dumbly. "Do you know this man?"

"No. I never saw his face."

"Who *are* you?"

Her brows knitted. "Does it matter? I have delivered the message. It might not have been directly to the captain, but I have every confidence you'll see to that. So, I shall be on my way."

"No." Alexander released her but moved between her and the stairs, blocking the exit.

"No?" That well-bred voice rose several notches. "You said you would let me go if I told you why I was here. Now get out of my way!" Her hands whacked against his chest, and he grabbed her wrists.

"Keep quiet. There are sailors right above us." He inclined his head toward the deck above. In the silence, the muffled conversations were more discernible.

She closed her mouth and stilled.

"You cannot leave the ship." His words were firm, but he was full of regret.

"What?" The confidence in her voice gave way to panic.

"You must stay," he said. "There is no other choice."

"You can let me go, as you promised."

If only it were that simple. Letting this woman leave would be easier, but Alexander couldn't do that now. It was his fault she'd been sent onto his ship. He'd been distracted and careless. If she returned to the dock, the man who passed on the message could kill her. And while Alexander didn't know who she was, he refused to have her death on his conscience.

"I am sorry," he said, and he meant it. He would have done anything to avoid this, but it was too late. "Now, if I let go of you, do you promise not to run?"

"No," she hissed. "I haven't done anything wrong. You have no reason to keep me here."

At least she was honest. Unfortunately, he *did* have a reason, a good one. But it would be better if she didn't know the details. The truth would not make her journey any more bearable. Why should she believe him if he told the truth? He'd already broken the one promise he'd made.

Moving her wrists together, he captured them both in one hand, holding her tight.

"That's hurting me," she said, her words weak and shaky. The sound twinged at something in his chest, and he loosened his grip.

Guiding her along the deck beside him, he searched for a thick rope, but there were hundreds of them, and they were all tangled.

Was he truly considering tying the woman up? And then what was he going to do with her?

"My hands," she whispered, wriggling her fingers.

He couldn't see her tears, but they made her voice thick. With a rope secured in his hand, he relented, loosening his grip once more.

The woman yanked her wrists free of his grasp, pushed past him and dashed toward the stairs.

Alexander stumbled but regained his footing. He chased her up the stairs, grabbing her hips before she'd made it halfway up. One arm snaked around her waist, and he bound the other over her arms, pinning them to her sides. Her strength was remarkable, and he'd likely suffer one hell of a beating if he made the smallest mistake and gave her the freedom to hit him. He dragged her back down the stairs and found the rope he'd dropped. Releasing his hold on her waist, he slung the rope over his arm, took hold of her shoulders and spun her to face him. What choice did he have now? He must tie her up, otherwise, she'd try to run again. Reaching the dock would be worse than a few weeks on the *Seren*, he could give that assurance.

"Do not do that again," he warned. "You won't make it off the ship, and if you do, the man who gave you that message will kill you. Slowly. Taking as much care to make you give him a message you never received. Do you understand?"

"Give me the message, then," she said.

Alexander shook his head. "He'll kill you regardless. You've been a short-term pawn. Whoever he is, that man has no use for you if you return to the docks. You're nothing but a liability to him now."

Chapter Three

MINT AND GARDENIA filled the cool, damp space and made Alexander's head spin. He inched closer to the woman and his jaw tightened. Keeping hold of her shoulders, he backed her toward the mast. A shiver ran through her slender frame. She was scared, and he hated doing this, but his threat must have been sufficient. She didn't make another sincere attempt to escape his grasp.

In his ten years of working for the Crown, he hadn't been responsible for a single murder. This woman would not be the first. His mother's death already weighed too heavily. George had never spoken of their parents' deaths, occurring mere weeks apart, but Alexander had long suspected she'd died at the hands of their father. If only he'd been there to stop it instead of ignoring everything from the other side of the world. He had a chance to save this woman. He wouldn't send her back to the dock and hope for the best.

"I never saw the man," the woman said, the fear in her voice tugging at something deep within him. "I'm not going to tell anyone."

The idea of escorting her home briefly crossed his mind. If not home, perhaps far enough away from the docks that she would be safe. But he didn't have time. They were due to sail any minute, and they couldn't miss this tide, especially not now. She had to stay.

"I know you won't," Alexander said, unsure where that certainty had come from, "but he won't believe anything you say."

"What is this about? I demand you tell me." She stood tall, the top of her head almost reaching his. The details of her face remained swathed in darkness, but she pinned him with an unfaltering glare. Bright white rimmed her dark irises. What color would they be?

Alexander stopped that line of thought and guided her two more steps backward. Her back bumped into the mast, and she gasped. He tried to ignore the sound. The urge to explain everything overwhelmed him, but he kept his mouth shut. There wasn't enough time to explain the events of the past month, nor would they paint him in any better light. He and Sam were on the run for a murder they didn't commit. How could he tell her that and expect her to stay willingly?

Waves lapped at the timber hull, softening once more to silence. Another ship had left the dock. The *Seren's* departure must be imminent.

He braced himself with a slow breath and held her against the mast with his body. He tried to ignore her hair's delicious fragrance and the way her breath whispered across his neck, sending gooseflesh down his arms. Stretching his arms behind her, he unraveled the rope and cast it around the mast, catching the other end. Her hands were on his hips, pushing again and causing a stirring in his abdomen that quivered to his groin. Alexander ignored that too. Well, he did his best.

He brought the rope between them, crossed it over, and stepped back. She made to move with him, but he pulled it tight around her waist, and over her arms. Hopefully, one day he could explain why he'd done this and she would understand, perhaps even forgive.

"What are you doing?" she asked.

"Tying you to the mast," he replied, letting sarcasm drip over his words and hide his fears. "I thought that was obvious." He wrapped the rope back and forth around her and the mast, keeping the thick strands as loose as possible. A surgeon's knot over her ribs finished the bonds. "Can you move?"

She thrust her right shoulder forward, but the parts of her body restrained under the rope didn't move away from the mast. Had he tied it too tight?

"No!" she said, tacking on a colorful choice of words. She'd found her tongue again.

"Good. Are you able to breathe?" He might have tied her up, but he didn't want her to be in any pain while she awaited his return. In his own depraved way, he'd done this for her benefit. Was there a better solution?

She scoffed, and her dark eyes rolled skyward. "Your skills at taking my breath away are hardly a match for my maid tying my corset."

Perhaps tying her up *had* been his best course of action.

Alexander turned away, biting back a smile. "I'll return before we sail."

"You're going to leave me here?"

"Of course I'm going to leave you here," Alexander said, walking over ropes toward the stairs. "Do you think I tied you up to practice my knots?"

"You promised to let me go," she said, her words catching in her throat. "I will leave immediately. Believe me, I have no desire to spend one more moment on this ship. I can make it past that man on my own."

Alexander had promised to let her go, but that promise was broken the instant he'd made a new vow—that he would not allow any harm to befall her. She'd saved his life by delivering that message. Saving hers was the least he could do in return.

"You promised." Her voice was a mere whisper in the darkness. "I trusted your word."

"Something I never asked for," he said roughly. Or would ever earn. "I will return later. It would be in your best interest to keep quiet." He started up the stairs, his hand wrapping around the key in his pocket.

THERE HE LEFT HER, alone in the darkness. Harriet cursed the sailor with a range and fluency that would have shocked a stable hand. She cursed him for tying her up, and for touching her. Where had he gone? What if he was now delivering the message to the captain, and they both returned to deal with her?

Harriet wriggled against her bonds. With each wrap around the post, and her, he had alternated the rope over and under her arms. It would be slow and painful to get herself out, but not impossible. The ship didn't seem to be moving, still tied as firmly to the dock as she was to the post. They hadn't sailed yet.

Her eyes had finally adapted to the darkness, and she glared at the knot below her breasts. The memory of his hands, carelessly grazing her as he'd tied it intruded on her focus.

With slow and careful movements, she stretched her right arm back. He'd underestimated her, as most people did, and neglected to tie her hands together. The rope was loose enough for her to inch her hand through one strand, then another. Freeing her right arm loosened the rope enough to untangle her left. She made quick work of the surgeon's knot, and the ends of the rope fell to the floor with soft thumps. Why hadn't the remaining rope fallen with it? Under the loosened bonds, she slid around the post.

She groaned and cursed the sailor again. On her left, he had tied a hitch into each alternate crossing of the rope, further restricting her chances of escape. He had made quick work of it too. How hadn't she realized what he was doing, when every touch was seared into her memory?

Harriet forced that thought from her mind and began the tedious process of untying the knots.

Thudding footsteps overhead made her pause. Would anyone else come down here? The only thing on this deck was rope, as far as she could tell, but *he* had been here.

She returned to the knot in her hands, tugging at the rope. The hitches were simple, but the rope was thick and coarse. With broken nails and aching fingers, she pulled at one knot after another.

At last, the final one came apart, and Harriet was free. She picked a cautious path over the ropes and raced up the stairs, toward the light of the upper deck. She grabbed the rope banister of the final staircase and hurtled toward the opening at the top of the stairs.

"Get tha' gangplank up now!" a gruff voice called.

Harriet took a step back, keeping herself hidden in the shadows.

"Sorry, sir," another man answered in a thick Cockney accent. "It's coming up now. We'll be sailing in no time."

Sailing? This ship was ready to sail? Harriet's mind raced, but her body remained immobile. Shock, fear, and disbelief settled in her chest.

Sailors jostled about the deck above, shouting back and forth, and their shadows flitted around the entry of the staircase. Harriet pressed herself back into the darkness. Where could she go? She pivoted and ran back down the stairs, searching for another exit, a porthole, a lower gangplank opening, *anything*.

Her chest tightened. There was no way out, and they would soon be away from the dock. She had to return to the main deck and hope she could make for the gangplank before anyone stopped her. Fear spurred her on, and she flew back up the stairs. She stepped onto the main deck and froze.

The deck had been cleared of the remaining cargo, and sailors swarmed between her and where the gangplank should be. Some moved the last of the crates from the deck, others tugged and tied the rigging. A shout from above drew her eyes upward. More men climbed the nets and rope ladders. Beyond the sailors, the buildings of Hull bobbed up and down.

Her stomach lurched. The ship was already away from the dock. Should she jump into the water? She was a competent swimmer. Surviving the dive into the water and avoiding the ships moving within the dock? Another problem entirely. The possibility of being dragged under the hull and drowned did not appeal any more than the thought of being stuck on this ship. What other options did she have? She could sneak back below deck and find a nice Harriet-sized hole to hide in. Even waiting for the sailor to return to her, untied on the orlop deck, was offering better prospects than what she might face from the captain or the rest of the crew. But how would her family react if she didn't return home? They would wait for her, then search for her, and she would be gone.

Gone... *where?*

She *had* to get off the ship.

"Oi!"

She tensed, her body screaming to run, but she had nowhere to go. Holding her breath, she turned slowly toward the gruff voice and came face to face with a short man with wrinkled leather skin. Under a worn brown cap, his thick brows formed a frown. More incoherent grumbles came from his puckered mouth. Was he speaking English?

Harriet stood, awaiting clarification.

He spoke again, his tone firm. "Capt'n. Quarterdeck. Now."

Oh, that she understood. Mostly. What did the captain do to people on the quarterdeck? And where was it? She took a tentative step forward but he spun her around with his large, rough hand on her shoulder.

"Tha' way," Leatherface grumbled, coupled with a jab of his finger at the stairs near the rear of the ship. He turned away, mumbling to himself. "What does he think he's doing, sending me a greenhand right before we sail..."

Puzzled, Harriet shuffled across the deck. What punishment would be in store for a stowaway, especially when that stowaway was a woman? Her feet were heavy, and she dragged them up the stairs. Was she still a stowaway if she had been on board the ship involuntarily when it set sail? How would she explain *that* to the captain? That one of his sailors had found her below deck and tied her up after she delivered a message intended for him. The man would think her deranged. Or perhaps he was her key to leaving this ship before it sailed. If all else failed, she could beg him to take her back to Hull. Her family was wealthy—a bribe might smooth matters over.

Goodness! She had woken this morning as the youngest daughter of the Earl of Selby, and within a few hours, she had been kidnapped and was considering bribing a ship's captain. She glanced out over the rail and cursed. They had already sailed out of the dock and were on the River Humber, heading east toward the sea. The water below was smooth and quiet, and the ship sliced through it. Her heartbeat drummed in her ears, and her heart threatened to leap out of her chest and dive into the water without her.

A movement on the quarterdeck caught her eye, and she turned toward it.

Oh dear.

Now she really had a problem. Her pulse quickened until it became one long, deafening, continuous thrum.

Chapter Four

ALEXANDER STOOD at the rear of the quarterdeck watching the town of Hull grow smaller, though his uneasiness didn't subside as it usually did when he sailed away from his family home. The timber creaked above his head, holding the sails steady in the wind. Shouts drifted up from the deck below, where the sailors worked as an ordered crew. The sounds of the ship helped calm his mind, but it didn't settle. He'd avoided visiting his mother's grave today. Perhaps his problems lay there, but he couldn't bring himself to go after talking to George. He wrenched his mind back to the present conversation, turning to Sam.

"At least you had a more fruitful morning," Alexander said.

Sam nodded. "Fortuitous as it was, I—"

Alexander followed Sam's incredulous gaze to the stairs.

The crown of her head appeared first. Untamed wisps of brown hair blew in the wind, throwing out subtle hints of gold where the sunlight caught them. They had tickled his cheek earlier, and their scent was etched in his memory. Her downcast eyes hid their true color from him once more. She took the final few steps at a crawl, stopping on the edge of the quarterdeck. Her gaze lifted, settling on Sam at the helm.

Alexander cursed. He'd neglected to mention her. How had the wench freed herself? And why had she left the orlop deck? Her presence on the *Seren* could have been concealed.

He shot a peek at Sam, trying to gauge whether he'd seen through her disguise. Though it occurred to Alexander, he hadn't *seen* through her disguise so much as *felt* through it. He returned his attention to the woman, surveying her tall figure and trying to ignore the memory of her curves that still lingered in inconvenient places.

"What do you want?" Alexander kept his words rough and turned away, facing the bow.

"I was—"

He snapped his head in her direction, eyes wide and silently begging her to stop speaking. Thankfully, she possessed enough sense to heed a warning when she saw one. Five long strides took him across the deck, and he stood before her, arms crossed. This mystery woman had better be prepared for the broadside she was about to receive. The sailors on the main deck had slowed, and a few glanced in his direction. Alexander ignored their attention. He regarded the woman, intent on a thorough and intimidating inspection of the newest sailor, before he spoke. That's what she was now, whether they liked it or not, and he did not.

Despite her slender figure and masculine disguise, she had an entirely feminine curve about her. He already knew that, having been intimately introduced to her curves. He couldn't deny himself a lingering glance over her hips and regarded her legs. Long, and wrapped in breeches that fitted her form too well.

Alexander clenched his fists and counted to five on a breath. A hard stare was supposed to intimidate her, not leave him wanting.

Her chin jutted toward him, forcing him to meet the full force of her glare. Framed with thick lashes, her almond-shaped eyes pierced him. The emerald irises were the darkest he'd ever seen, and he lost himself in their depths.

He shook his head and cleared his throat. Perhaps his brother was right. He had spent a long time at sea. Too long. He had never been overcome by a woman's eyes.

His hushed question was quiet enough for her ears alone. "What are you doing here?"

So much for his intended broadside.

"I was told to see the captain," she said, her voice a whisper louder than the wind blowing across the deck. Her head inclined toward Sam, who stood at the ship's wheel.

"The captain, you say? Well, here I am."

Her mouth opened with a pop, and her brow furrowed. "You?" It was closer to a growl than a question. She might fare better on this voyage than he'd anticipated.

"Yes, me," he said, quirking a brow. "Perhaps I should have been clearer. What are you doing up here on deck instead of tied to the mast where I left you?"

"How dare —"

"Uh-uh." He interrupted her with a shake of his head. Her scowl deepened, and he winked. If she could spit fire at him, he had no doubt she would have. He shrugged his shoulders loose and stared at her, keeping his arms crossed.

"So, sailor, am I to understand you are a useless addition to my crew?" He spoke louder and harsher this time. That would appease any sailors within earshot.

She didn't answer, though her thoughts danced across her face. The little spitfire.

Knowing she couldn't refuse him now, he asked, "What is your name?"

"Harr—" She cleared her throat and her gaze flashed up to the sail above his head, then back to his face.

Alexander smirked, biting the corner of his lip. "What sort of name is *Harr*?"

"It's Harry," she replied. Her attempts to deepen her tone did not mask her femininity. Though her composure under the circumstances was admirable.

"Harry," he repeated. "Welcome aboard the *Seren*. I am Captain Alexander."

Miss Harry opened her mouth, but he cut her off. "We're on a tight schedule. I hope you know how to sail." The sailors on the main deck had returned to their tasks, but he had to ensure they would be happy with anything they overheard. A soft captain only made more work for himself. "I also hope you have good sea legs. It will be three weeks before you set foot on land again." He didn't know what he'd do if she couldn't make this work.

Her eyes widened, and her lips parted. She hadn't expected that, but he had no way of getting her back to Hull now. All he could do was hope the land she set foot on was England, but there was no guarantee.

Without waiting for a response, Alexander said, "Speak to Groves." He pointed to the quartermaster on the main deck. "He'll know you are a greenhand, no doubt that's why he sent you to me. Groves will task you appropriately." Alexander didn't take his eyes from hers, and her glare bored into him, the urge to retaliate clear on her face. He shook his head, willing her to wait. She deserved an explanation, to rip him to shreds, but this wasn't the time.

Her mouth snapped shut, and she started back down the stairs. Those tight breeches that matched her skin tone did nothing to help his focus. He would need to find another pair, but given her height, the only other clean clothes that would fit were his, and that would be even worse.

Alexander waited until Miss Harry was back on the main deck and took control of the ship's wheel. Sam busied himself with his maps and compass, though his friend didn't need to navigate until they were out of the river.

The sun bore down steadily, and the silence dragged on. What had Sam noticed?

Alexander couldn't stand it any longer, and he turned to his friend. "Sam?"

Sam stared at him with a blank expression, looking in pain with the effort. The man had the patience of a saint, but at times, he wasn't the best at concealing his true feelings, or in this case, fears.

"You noticed that, er, feminine presence, I take it?" Alexander asked.

Sam blinked. "Only if you did."

"Oh, I did," Alexander said, looking out over the main deck. "I'm the reason she's here."

"What do you mean, Alexander?" Sam's voice was strained, and Alexander glanced in his direction. His friend's mask of indifference crumpled as he assessed the implications of this unplanned addition to their crew.

An uncomfortable twinge tugged at Alexander's chest. "Come on, Sam, you know me better than that. I ran into her on the orlop deck. Well, she ran into me." None of this had been of his choosing.

"What is she still doing here?" Sam paced across the quarterdeck.

"I, er, unfortunately..." Alexander covered his face with his hand, stroking his brow. "I tied her to the mast." That snap decision had seemed the sole rational option at the time, but now Alexander questioned what had possessed him to do it. Might he have come to a reasonable arrangement with the woman if he'd spent a few more minutes trying? He looked at Sam through his fingers, and his friend frowned.

"Why the hell did you do that?"

"She tried to run off the ship." Alexander realized a second too late how incriminating that sounded. He raised his hands, the gesture half surrender and half question, and relayed the events of the morning. "I couldn't leave her in Hull," he finished.

Sam's eyes widened. "You didn't think to tell me that message earlier?"

"I'm sure you can appreciate why it escaped my mind. I was a little preoccupied with getting the ship the hell out of Hull. And your morning was a bit more interesting. Wouldn't you say?"

"You tied up a woman, left her below deck, forgot about her, and you think my morning was more interesting?" Sam threw up his hands and continued pacing through the long, irregular shadows cast by the sails.

"I didn't forget about her," Alexander replied. His grimace reached further than his face, settling deep in his gut. "I simply hadn't told you yet."

Sam stilled, considering him, and rolled his eyes. "You said you tied her up?"

"Yes. I planned to return to her once we were in the harbor." Alexander followed Sam's gaze to one of his knots.

His friend's alarmed expression from a moment earlier changed to one of mockery. "Are you losing your touch?"

"We could test the theory?" Alexander threatened, seizing the opportunity to divert attention from his actions and their implications. "I tied a hitch in every second turn and finished it with a surgeon's knot, as well as threading it over and under her arms. I'd very much enjoy watching you try to get yourself out of it."

"Impressive." Sam's response seemed genuine.

"Hardly," Alexander said. "She untied herself or cut herself free. Either is a concern."

If she had a hidden knife, he needed to know.

"What are we going to do with her?"

"Thanks to her insistence on leaving the orlop deck, she'll have to be part of the crew." Alexander glanced down at the deck, spotting her instantly. He shook his head. "She's a spitfire. I hope it's enough to hold her own down there. What gave her away?"

"It's a convincing disguise. I doubt I'd have realized if I'd come across her on my own. She looks ordinary enough to pass as a young sailor, and Jacob's voice isn't much deeper than hers..." Sam trailed off.

"You're not answering my question." Alexander said. Her disguise wasn't that convincing, was it? Nor could he agree that she was ordinary. He'd been unable to drag his eyes off her, and then that sweet face... He cleared his throat. "What was it about her, Sam? We'll need to help her continue the ruse now."

Sam frowned, pinning him with an accusing stare. "It was you."

"*Me?*" Alexander crossed his arms. The ship's wheel in front of him didn't shift. "What did I do?"

"I don't know exactly. You were different."

"Different how?" Alexander growled. Cryptic clues weren't getting him anywhere.

Sam shrugged. "I can't pinpoint it."

"Exceptionally unhelpful, Sam. Thank you."

"You should keep your distance until we figure out what to do, at least while there are this many sailors around. They won't look twice at her."

Alexander scanned the deck. Miss Harry had already assumed her role among the sailors. Her clothes' cleanliness alone distinguished her from the rest of the crew, and that wouldn't last long. A sailor had clean clothes for the first day or so of a voyage, and the *Seren* had been sailing for weeks, their stop in Hull only overnight. The rest of the crew were a shabby sight, except for Sam and him. Being the captain had its perks, as did having a cabin with storage. And keeping a stash of clean clothes at his brother's country estate had been valuable on more than one occasion.

"You know this means we can't stop in London now," Sam said.

Alexander had known as much when he neglected to send Miss Harry back with a reply. "I know. I don't know who he was, or where he got the message, but if she went back there alone... if he had realized she was a woman when she returned to the dock..."

"He might have killed her," Sam finished the sentence Alexander couldn't voice.

"I know it's reckless, but I couldn't risk her life. She's innocent in all of this, I'm certain." As inconvenient as it was having her on his ship, Alexander didn't regret the decision. He couldn't change what had happened to his mother, but he could atone for his failings in other ways. Protecting Miss Harry and saving her life was a start.

"I would have done the same." Sam's hand clapped Alexander on the back. "We'll figure it out. She'll be safe here." Something in his friend's tone didn't match his words.

"What's the problem, Sam? I never took you to be the superstitious type."

"I don't mind having a woman on board. We're already on the run for a murder neither of us committed. How much worse could our luck get?" Dark humor laced Sam's chuckle. "Don't answer that. It's just that I suspect we'll be in for trouble on our return to England."

"In what way?" With the morning they'd had, there wasn't much time for planning ahead. Alexander had given little thought to how he would deal with their return. And if they couldn't find Harvey, they wouldn't return to England at all. Though what that meant for Miss Harry, he wasn't yet certain. "It shouldn't matter that we're sailing without the guise of trading cargo."

"No, it's not that. We took this woman from Hull, and if we do manage to find Harvey and things go to plan, we'll be sailing back into London." Alexander only had a moment to absorb that before Sam continued. "That might be an issue if she's the daughter of a peer. And I suspect she is, given she's so well-spoken and genteel."

"*Genteel?*" Alexander exclaimed. "Are we discussing the same woman?" He ignored the suspicions that had crept up on him earlier. He had noticed the respectable tenor of her voice, and the way she held herself. But the woman had freed herself from bonds that should have held her until he'd untied them.

A call on the main deck drew their attention down.

"Someone will miss her," Sam said, "and you'll have hell to pay if she's anyone important. *Especially* when she arrives in London after disappearing without a trace from Hull."

The pit of Alexander's stomach twisted into a painful knot. She couldn't be a *proper* lady. Few *ton* families resided in Hull, and none had daughters of that age. Even if that were the case, how could she have made it to the docks disguised and undetected?

"It will be fine," Alexander said, trying to convince himself as much as Sam. "I'll find out who she is and make a plan."

"Very well." Sam stayed beside him. "Perhaps you should consider her sleeping arrangements. No matter who she is, it isn't right to let her sleep on the mess deck with the other sailors."

"Harvey's cabin is free." Though Alexander was reluctant to suggest it.

"Harvey's?" Sam's response held the appropriate level of hesitation, but what choice did they have?

"There's nowhere else. I'm not giving up my bed. You're welcome to give her yours."

"I'll have Harvey's cabin ready for tonight."

Alexander grinned.

"Perhaps we should tell the crew *Harry* is my cousin?" Sam suggested. "They're going to notice she's not a stray we found on the docks. Especially if we put her into Harvey's cabin."

"Are you happy with that? We don't know anything about her."

Sam shrugged. "She seems harmless enough. How much trouble could she get into? I think it's the least we can do until we get her back to England. You know how uncomfortable those hammocks can be when you're new at this."

"It all sounds good to me, Sam. You can inform Groves of your new relation, and perhaps suggest he assigns her a menial task to keep her busy. It would be best if she's out of the way until I figure out what to do with her."

"Of course." Sam left him and headed toward Groves.

Chapter Five

HARRIET HELD BACK the tears that threatened to betray her. She couldn't cry in front of all these sailors, and not in front of *him*. Being appraised was nothing new, but the way the captain's gaze lingered had heated her skin. Had he simply been reassuring himself that she looked enough like a boy to maintain her disguise? She glanced at her bound breasts, but the loose fitted shirt covered her well. He didn't need reassuring.

The ship glided around a bend in the river, and the breeze blew across the deck. She looked up as the busy town of Hull disappeared. What would happen to her now? She didn't know the first thing about sailing, or how to live on a ship, and he'd sent her off to work as though he truly believed she could pass for a sailor.

Crack.

Harriet jumped. The snap of timber hitting timber reverberated through the deck and into her feet. Her spine stiffened, and she searched for the source of the sound.

Crack.

Two sailors divided stacks of crates, dropping them in

front of the stairs. Her muscles relaxed, and she let out a sigh.

"Don't just stand there watching them. Go and help." The grumbled words of Mr. *Leatherface* Groves came from beside her. Despite being a great oaf of a man, he had a knack for sneaking up on her.

She started across the deck toward the two sailors. One descended the stairs, and she sized up the remaining sailor as she approached. He looked to be much younger than her, perhaps only fourteen or fifteen.

Reaching out for a crate, she asked, "May I assist you with that?"

He stiffened, arms outstretched.

She cursed out loud. If she was going to pass for a sailor, it was essential she change everything she'd learned about the English language and how to speak it. And lower her voice an octave.

The sailor laughed. Apparently, cursing was welcome. "First time sailing?"

"That obvious?" she asked in a deeper, more casual tone.

His smile was warm and friendly, and he held out his hand. She shook it, noticing how much larger and rougher it was against her own.

"Name's Jacob."

"Harry," she returned.

"Right. Well, we gotta get these down the galley." Jacob gestured to the stack of crates in front of them, then pointed behind Harriet.

She looked around. Was the staircase called the galley? Or was the galley a place below deck? She hadn't seen anything she would call a galley down there. These sailors had a language of their own, one she must learn quickly if she wanted to avoid making a fool of herself. She turned back to Jacob. An explanation did not seem forthcoming.

"The galley?" she queried.

"Oh, right." Jacob shook his head. "That's the ship's kitchen. Down them stairs, turn around, and keep walking. You'll see what I mean when you get there."

She bent to pick up a crate, but Jacob stopped her.

"Easier if I pass them down," he said.

She nodded and walked partway down the stairs, turning to face him. He lowered three crates with ease. A sweet scent wafted from the crates and tickled her nose. Jacob dropped the crates into her arms and stepped back. She wobbled under the weight. How had he held them so effortlessly? She checked her balance and made sure she had a firm hold on the crates, then continued as directed.

A few porthole windows, opened since they'd set sail, cast small circles of light onto the floor. The rich, dark timber was a stark contrast to the bright oak of the main deck. Once her eyes adjusted to the dim light, the galley was visible at the rear end of the ship. The second sailor from the main deck walked past, returning for another load. He dipped his brow and Harriet nodded.

Reaching the galley, she added her crates to a small stack and took a moment to look around. The air was cool, and the citrus-like tang from the crates overpowered the faint briny staleness. She turned back to the crates she'd carried and peered between the slats. One was full of ginger and teased at an earlier memory. Perhaps she hadn't imagined that scent on the captain. She swallowed hard and turned back toward the staircase, following the trail of porthole lights.

They completed relocating crates, and Harriet joined the others back on deck.

Jacob scrambled up a narrow rope ladder with a quick, "Crow's nest for me!" called over his shoulder. He scaled the rigging, each section smaller than the last, until he was at the top of the mast.

She shuddered. Avoiding that particular duty was paramount.

Mr. Groves appeared at her side again. She jumped and withdrew from his sudden presence. Seemingly ignorant of her skittishness, he pointed to a tangled pile of rope at the edge of the deck. "Fix tha' mess of dri'shee'," he grumbled.

Untangle rope? That she could do.

She crossed the deck. If they restricted her tasks to moving crates and untangling rope, she would surely manage. She bent and picked up an end, working to untangle and roll it into a neat coil on the deck. It wasn't long until she reached the other end and tucked it in. What would Mr. Groves have her do next?

"You there!"

The call came from behind her, and she straightened, the muscles in her back twitching. She recognized that voice without looking, alarmed that he was already so familiar. Turning around, she was mindful of any nearby sailors who might have been watching, but there were none.

Captain Alexander stood three feet away, towering over her with his arms crossed. His nostrils flared.

She sighed. What had she done now?

His brow lifted, but she ignored him and stood, taking advantage of her height. The top of her head almost reached his, and she leveled his stare. How had she not noticed the blue of his eyes earlier? The color matched the bright, glittering sea on the horizon. His brown hair was a little longer than the current styles men wore in London and swept away from his face. A few locks had escaped, and he raked them back into place with long fingers. She blinked and cleared her throat.

His frown deepened. Was he still angry? Her presence on his ship irritated him, but it wasn't her fault. She had merely been guilty of taking a walk unchaperoned. His fingers flexed and curled, digging into his arms where they were again crossed over his chest.

"You're on first watch tonight, *Harry*." The emphasis on Harry was not subtle.

"What?" The high pitch of her voice hid none of her shock. She couldn't do watch. She didn't know the first thing about what to do.

"All sailors attend watch duty every night. You cannot be exempt." Beneath his stern frown, his piercing blue eyes held her. "You can go to the orlop deck first. There is quite the mess of ropes down there." He glanced at the rope at her feet "Since you have so proficiently untangled this one, you can spend your afternoon tidying that."

She stared back at him, biting her tongue. If she spoke, it would not be with the control she needed. What was it about him that inspired such a response in her? She wanted to challenge him, though she couldn't figure out why. The first time she'd done so had ended with her being tied to a mast.

"When the bell rings four times, that signals your time to take rest. You will find hammocks on the mess deck. Be back for duty when the bell signals watch." Her confusion must have been plain on her face because the captain pointed to a large bell on the quarterdeck and said, "After sunset, that bell will ring eight times. Be here"—he jabbed a finger at the deck—"within two minutes."

Flames licked the inside of her belly, but she kept her

mouth closed, her teeth grinding together. She was glued to the spot, the inability to move born from a mix of indecision and anger.

"Was I not clear?" His clipped tone masked none of his annoyance.

"Perfectly, Captain Alexander," she ground out.

She stalked past him, headed for the stairs.

The final few steps into the orlop deck plunged Harriet into darkness once again. She lifted her hand at arm's length from her face and brought it closer until it was visible. A few inches at best. *Wonderful.* And he had sent her without a lamp. Returning to the main deck and asking for one was out of the question. It would be unwise to test the captain's patience further.

With small movements, she shuffled across the deck to the hull. Her hands ran blindly along the cold, thick timber, searching for any portholes, but she had little hope. As she'd suspected, this deck was below the waterline with no way of bringing light into the space.

She kneeled on the floor and sifted through the lengths of rope. The textures and thickness varied between each piece. She might spend the entire journey down here untangling this mess. That wouldn't be so bad. It was quiet and out of the captain's way, and the likelihood of making a costly mistake was low.

"Ah-ha!" By chance she'd grabbed one of the many ropes by its end. Was it possible she could see it in her hand? There might have been another few inches of visibility, but she couldn't tell if it was her imagination. She cleared a small space and coiled the rope beside her.

Untangling the rope kept her hands busy, but her thoughts soon drifted from the ship and back to her family. Her chest heaved with an ache that had nothing to do with her short, sharp gasps of air. She should have ignored the messenger and his threats and gone straight back to Uncle Frederick. Her family had always been gracious about her escapades, turning a blind eye on this, explaining a way out of that. This time she had gone too far. This would see the ruin of her sisters, and scandal for the entire Hazelby name. She tried not to think of Millie, whose marriage prospects would soon be nonexistent, all because of her recklessness.

"What have I done?" Harriet whispered into the darkness. She dropped the rope into her lap and covered her eyes as tears streamed down her cheeks.

It took time for her sobs to subside, and she returned to the task at hand. Her arms ached from twisting and pulling, and her fingers pained from sliding rope through them, the little fibers pricking her skin often. Her bottom was numb from sitting on the cold decking. There had been a few rings of the bell since she'd started, but only one or two at a time. *Four rings*, Captain Alexander had told her.

She waited for the one signaling that she could rest. Somewhere not too far away, she became aware of a soft, shallow panting. She stilled and listened. The sound moved closer.

"Wh—who's there?" She squinted toward the noise, and a blurry, gray mass hurtled toward her. Thick, soft fur muffled her squeal. She fell onto her back and crossed her arms over her face, wriggling to get away from the creature. It nestled itself on her chest, its short legs hanging over either side of her body. She pushed at the animal, trying to get a better look at it. It had the face of a wolf, but it was too small. Was it a dog? Even in the dim light, its black eyes glimmered. Now that it had stopped licking her cheeks, it smiled down at her, its tongue lolling out the side of its mouth.

"Hello there," she said cautiously.

The dog licked from her chin to her forehead.

She giggled, nudging it away. "Thank you, but I believe I've had enough kisses." She kept its head at arm's length from her face and scratched behind its ears. The whites of its eyes glowed, rolling upward, and it let out a content growl.

"Where did you come from?" she asked.

"He's mine." Captain Alexander's low rumble announced his presence.

Harriet flinched. "Oh, I am so sorry!" The words came fast, and she pushed the dog, but he wouldn't budge.

"Shadow, here."

Shadow was off her in an instant, running nimbly over the ropes to his master, who stood on the stairs. Captain Alexander held aloft a lamp and was illuminated in the soft, orange glow.

"Why are you here?" she asked.

He took a moment to answer, which sent her insides into wild turns. "I brought you something to eat." In his other hand was a bowl. He lifted it in her direction. "Stew. Unless you're not hungry?"

Her stomach clenched and gave a loud growl.

The captain chuckled. "Good timing on my part."

She didn't answer, didn't move.

"If you would prefer to lie there, hungry and alone, I'll take it back for myself."

Damn, she was still lying on the ground where Shadow had tackled her. In her haste to stand, the blood drained from her head, and she stumbled. Yards away, Captain Alexander stepped toward her.

She raised her hand and steadied herself. "I'm fine." The sensation passed as swiftly as it had come, and she walked toward him, lacking much of the finesse Shadow had demonstrated. After a few small stumbles, and a rather ungracious fall, she stood at the bottom of the stairs looking up at Captain Alexander.

His eyes remained fixed on her, but the corner of his lips twitched. "You're sure you are all right?"

"I am. Thank you for the stew." She held out her hand for the bowl, but the swaying she felt must have been more than her imagination. He pulled it back, out of reach. Grabbing the railing with one hand, she thrust the other at him, and he handed over the bowl.

"Thank you," she muttered.

He frowned, but the gesture wasn't threatening. "You hadn't expected to sit down here and starve, had you?"

She inspected the stew. Its appearance was rather appetizing, a few vegetables and chunks of meat in thick sauce. Cooked beef reached her nose and made her mouth water. In truth, she *had* wondered if he might forget about her or purposely leave her isolated. His intentions were still unclear.

"I see," he murmured. "I apologize that my actions today have been exceedingly discourteous."

Was he sincere? She needed to see his face before she could form her reply. Their gazes met, and her breathing stuttered. Her skin warmed against the cool air, and an involuntary shiver ran the length of her spine. She couldn't move, couldn't breathe. He blinked and twisted his face away, releasing her from his hold.

Captain Alexander coughed, but the sound seemed to come from a distance. "I'm sorry about Shadow. He gets carried away at times."

"What? Oh, Shadow"—she looked at the dog, having

forgotten him in his obedient silence—"not at all, he's a beautiful... he is a dog?"

Shadow gazed at his master with a proud smile.

Captain Alexander laughed, and bent down, his hand ruffled over the animal's head. "Yes, he's a dog."

"I've never seen one like him before."

"I'd be surprised if you had. He's a Keeshond," Captain Alexander said.

"A what?" she asked, as if the name of his breed was any means of clarification.

"Kays-hond." He slowed the word down, but his tone wasn't mocking. "It's Dutch. Some call them Wolfspitz."

"I can see why."

Shadow turned his wolfish grin on her. He was beautiful.

"They are bred to be companions on the barges in Holland. Incredibly affectionate and loyal animals. He rarely leaves my side, my Shadow." The gentle hum of his voice had a loving quality. This captain was different to the one she'd met that morning.

"Where did you get him?" she asked without thinking.

"Holland," they said in unison.

She let out a shaky laugh.

"I rescued him from a riverbank as a pup, and he's been with me ever since." Captain Alexander straightened, meeting her eyes once more, and again she lost herself in his gaze. "I must get back. I'll let you eat in peace." He turned to leave but paused with one foot hovering in the air, then swung back to face her again. "Have you been working in the dark all this time?"

Was he offended?

"Yes, but it hasn't been a problem." Until now. Now that he'd been down with a lamp, her eyes would need adjust again, but she didn't want to cause any issues, not after he'd been kind enough to bring her a meal.

"You should have asked for one. I didn't think." He held the lamp out. "Here, take mine."

She reached up and curled her fingers around the handle. He released the lamp, his hand brushing hers. His skin was a scant few degrees warmer than her own, but heat shot up her arm. He wheeled around and thumped up the stairs with Shadow in tow, leaving her alone on the orlop deck once again.

Harriet waited for the captain's footsteps to fade and sat on the stairs with her dinner, setting the lamp beside her. It cast a small circle of light and was a significant improvement on the situation, lighting up more than half of the deck. The mast she'd been tied to was in the middle, and off to the left was a wooden chest. Was that what he'd been doing when she ran into him?

The first bite of stew warmed her insides and tended the ache in her empty stomach. She wasted no time finishing it. Leaving the lamp and bowl on the bottom step, she made her way across to the chest. More rope twisted and curled on this side of the deck, but she crossed without any more stumbles.

She crouched in front of the chest, placing her hands on the lid. Holding her breath, she gave it a push. Locked. And none of her business. Whatever Captain Alexander was doing, she'd be better off not knowing the details. She sighed and leaned back against the chest.

Four rings of the bell sounded high above.

She walked back to the stairs, gathering the lamp and empty bowl on her way to the mess deck.

Chapter Six

THE SETTING SUN'S golden glow shone through a porthole window onto Harriet's face. She scrunched her eyes against the brightness that had woken her. That she had slept at all was surprising, but the gentle sway of the hammock rocking her to and fro had been soothing.

A deep, discordant rumbling echoed around the mess deck. Were the sailors so accustomed to the ship's order that they would sleep until the bell rang? She peeked at the hammocks swaying around her and stayed quiet, listening for the eight chimes of the bell. What would await her on watch? She would happily spend the time on the orlop deck if it kept her out of the way, but the space was cold. It would be almost unbearable after sunset, especially without a coat.

Sliding out of the hammock, her feet landed with a soft thud on the deck. She'd kept her boots on while she slept, hesitant to leave them lying around should a sailor notice they were a women's style. Half the crew was asleep, and the remainder worked throughout the ship, but this situation called for caution.

She climbed the stairs to the main deck, passing a sailor mopping the stairs. He hummed a rhythmic tune unlike any melody she'd heard before. Her foot slid sideways, and she gripped the rope railing, the surface rough on her tender palm. Once she set foot on the main deck, silence descended on her, and rich, scented oil filled her nostrils.

The view beyond the taffrail stole her breath.

Sunsets weren't like this at home. They could be beautiful, but nothing to rival this. Turquoise water shone with a golden glimmer, reflecting the sinking sun, and stretching as far as the eye could see. The sun dipped below the horizon, and the last rays of light streaked across the sky. It transformed to light purple, and the faint orange line of the horizon faded. A single star twinkled timidly in the evening sky. She ran her hand over the freshly oiled taffrail, the timber soft beneath her fingertips. Not even the swish of the sails above her head could bring her close enough to reality to deny the joy of the moment.

The bell rang twice from the quarterdeck, piercing the silence. She turned toward the undeniable reminder of her current situation. Captain Alexander stood alone beside the bell, his face awash with the glow of the lamp hanging above him. He swung the bell's rope twice more, sending a resounding ring through the cool air. Turning toward her, he met her eye, and a warm smile stretched across his lips. His hand stayed wrapped around the rope, and he swung it twice again. He beckoned her with a gesture of his free hand and then swiveled the sandglass beside him. Her stomach tightened. The seventh and eighth rings of the bell faded into silence, and he released the rope.

Heavy footsteps thumped on the deck behind her. The sailors hurried to take over from their comrades, and soon the deck was quiet again. She must move, but her feet were reluctant to comply. She lifted her eyes back to the captain where he stood, still watching her. At last, his pull was too strong to resist, and it spurred her forward. She walked to the stairs, her mind dazed.

Captain Alexander clambered down and closed the gap between them, an unexpected calmness washing over her as he drew nearer. How could he be responsible for both inciting and quelling disquiet within her?

"Impeccable timing, sailor." His smooth voice matched his smile, and the last knot of tension in her chest slipped away.

"I'm on watch with you?" The words spilled from her mouth, not at all how she would have liked them to sound.

He looked as though he couldn't decide whether to laugh or reprimand her. "Is there a problem?"

"No, of course not. I—I didn't expect you to be on watch," she said, biting her lip.

"I told you all sailors on my ship take their turn doing watch. What sort of man would I be if I didn't include myself?" He grinned, flashing perfect, straight white teeth. "Besides, occasionally there is a new sailor on board whom I would only trust myself to guide."

What kind of man was he indeed? His piercing blue eyes held her still, and she had to remind herself to blink. And breathe.

He continued, apparently as unaffected by her as any other man. "I put you on watch with me for the next few hours to teach you about the ship. I can't have anyone less than helpful sailing with my crew. I would have preferred to do it this afternoon, but I wanted to avoid drawing too much attention to you."

He glanced around the deck behind her, and she followed his gaze. The change of watch had passed, and the sailors who had been on the previous duty were gone. Those who remained worked quietly at their tasks; some tended to the mast while others scrubbed sections of the deck. None of them paid her or the captain any heed.

"They wouldn't think twice about it, but it's simpler to keep the truth about you concealed." His tone was smooth and reassuring. "This crew is loyal to me, and they respect the way I run my ship. If I told them I had brought a woman on board, they would accept it, however superstitious they may be. I pride myself in hiring sailors who uphold my values. Well, I did." He eyed her and raised a brow.

She heaved in a breath, readying to defend herself, but he interrupted her.

"Come this way," he said, leading her to the front of the ship. He stopped and pointed to something at his feet. "What is this?"

She looked down and frowned. Surely he didn't consider her *that* stupid.

"Rope?" she answered.

"Are you asking me or telling me?" His mocking tone sparked a fire within her, and the remaining calm and comfort disappeared.

"It's rope." She drew herself up to her full height. "I do hope your instruction extends beyond the ordinary objects found on board a ship or in any common stable yard. Do you think so little of my competence?"

A spark flashed in his eyes. "I do not even know your name, *Miss Harry*. Never mind how competent you believe yourself to be. What you are"—he regarded her with an intense stare—"is a little spitfire."

Spitfire? It was his fault she was stuck on this ship. *He* could have let her go. What did he care if someone killed her in Hull? She bit her tongue. It wouldn't do to prove him right.

He picked up the rope and held it out to her. "Now, I've seen you tie a reef knot, can you tie a bowline or any hitches?"

Keeping her eyes fixed on his, she took the rope from him, tied a bowline, and handed it back. She couldn't stop the slight rise of her brows, or the twitch at the corner of her mouth. That would show him to assume she was a halfwit.

He turned the knot over in his hands, inspecting it, and nodded approvingly. "I see," he murmured. Then he shrugged and said, "That's the most important one you need to know. If anyone asks you to tie a knot you're unfamiliar with, tie that. It will get you through."

"Yes, Captain Alexander." It was unlikely she'd be asked to tie an unfamiliar knot, but the range of her skills could remain a secret until she knew more about the captain.

"Now, a lesson in language." He untied the bowline and lifted the rope between them. "You're right, this is a rope, but on a ship they each have different names depending on their uses. Do you know what this one is called?"

This was the same rope Mr. Groves had directed her to untangle earlier, though now one end was tied to the length of timber supporting the sail. She *thought* she knew its name.

"A dripsheep?" she offered, lacking the conviction she'd have liked to possess.

Captain Alexander's barking laugh was enough to tell her that no, it was not called a *dripsheep*. Warmth flushed her cheeks, and the rosy color would be obvious to him, curse it.

"On a ship"—he paused, stifling another chuckle—

"ropes are called sheets. This one is the *jib sheet*." He emphasized the last words, his eyes alight. "It's attached to the forestay which supports the jib sail." He pointed to the sail and where the rope was tied to the length of timber beneath it.

"Do you usually spend your time with new sailors laughing at their lack of knowledge?" she snapped.

He crossed his arms and leaned against the taffrail. His eyes raked over her body. A heat that had nothing to do with irritation spread through her.

"A dripsheep?" he teased. "Can you honestly tell me you don't see the humor in that?"

She could—very, *very* deep down. Acknowledging it was beyond her.

The silence between them dragged on.

Captain Alexander cleared his throat. "There's a large hole in the mast net that will require more than two hands to fix. You know how to lash, I assume?"

She nodded.

"Of course you do." He sighed. "This way."

They repaired the hole quickly, albeit with an excessive amount of touching. It was to be expected for such a task, but Harriet's awareness of him spread further than her hands, moving through her body in waves of heat, and settling deep in her core. It hadn't helped that she'd been unable to keep her eyes off his long, tanned fingers while he twisted the rope. An involuntary shiver on more than one occasion hadn't gone unnoticed. Each time the sensation washed over her, he'd glanced in her direction and muttered an apology, holding her gaze long enough for her breath to catch.

She shivered again at the memory and wrapped her arms around herself. They were deep into what she'd called

A Ship's Introduction by Sarcasm, but silence had descended upon them. How long had it been since he spoke? She wouldn't give him the satisfaction of knowing his teachings were informative as well as mildly entertaining, so she stayed quiet, eyeing him cautiously.

They'd made it to the bow of the ship and were alone in the small space, hidden behind a low sail. Her attention dipped to his arms. His sleeves were rolled up to his elbows, exposing sun-tanned skin and strong rippling muscles. She dragged her gaze away and back to his face. He stared at her, his eyes twinkling. Had he asked her a question? She was certain he'd been explaining in great and unnecessary detail what the taffrail was. She chewed her bottom lip and waited.

"Your name isn't Harry." His statement was unexpected, but not surprising. "Will you tell me what it is?" he asked.

She shook her head. How would he react if he discovered her identity? Keeping it a secret was her safest option. It was the only way to protect her family, and all she could do now.

"Miss Harry it is, then."

She gnawed the inside of her lip, and her voice was a mere whisper. "Why didn't you let me go?"

"Mm?"

"Why did you keep me here on the *Seren*?"

"I already told you." His tone was grave. "That man would have killed you. I'm sorry if you cannot believe me, but I appreciate your lack of trust. I deserve that."

"Why would he have killed me?" she asked. "What did that message mean?"

Captain Alexander's face was unreadable. "It's hard to explain," he said. "I could have sent you back with a response, but even then, I couldn't guarantee your safety. If he hadn't already planned to dispose of you once you returned, but discovered you are a woman, he would have... Well, it doesn't do to dwell on the possibilities."

"For someone who is so put out by my presence on this ship, I cannot comprehend why you would care what happened to me. Why did you tie me up and condemn me to this journey?"

"How did you get out of those bonds?" he asked. "I checked the rope, and it wasn't cut. Clearly you untied yourself, but how did you do it?" His curiosity boosted her confidence. She liked that she had surprised him, and it quelled the fire within her slightly, but she wouldn't be deterred.

"I'm not answering your questions until you answer mine, Captain Alexander." She met his stare, but her conviction faltered. "I must know if you kept me here for your own," she had to force the word out, "pleasure." If what he stirred within her resulted from manipulation, she wanted to know.

He snorted. "If I have given the impression that your presence brings me pleasure, I must sincerely apologize. You are the last thing I would consider pleasurable."

She sighed, unable to ignore how his words stung. "What does that message mean? You were prepared to let me go until I gave it to you. Why didn't you leave me in Hull while you sailed on your merry way to wherever?" She paused. "I would consider it prudent to know where in the world I am now sailing against my will."

"Leaving you in Hull was not an option, but I may reconsider my decision not to throw you overboard if you continue." His voice was a low whisper, but it was loud in her ears. They had drifted closer together, and his face was inches from hers. The bright blue of his eyes might have pierced her earlier, but closer, in the lamplight, gold flecked the deep pools. Now they dazzled her.

The soft whoosh of air leaving her lungs made her lips tingle, so she touched the tip of her tongue to them. He lurched away, his mouth pulled into a tight line. She withdrew too, unaware of precisely what had happened.

He put his hand over his heart. "I cannot risk you inspiring a mutiny among my crew."

She rolled her eyes at his feigned distress.

"And where would you take my ship and my crew, Captain Miss Harry? Would you continue our journey to the Caribbean? Or might you be the kind to lead a crew into the life of piracy?" A wicked glint flashed in his blue eyes.

The Caribbean? Her heart plummeted. He'd told her it would be three weeks until she set foot on land again. A journey to the Caribbean would take months. If she set foot on land in three weeks, it wouldn't be English soil. She gulped for air, her breaths coming in short, sharp gasps.

"Miss Harry, I—"

He stepped toward her, eyes wide with false concern. He didn't care.

She waved him away and turned to look out over the taffrail, gripping it tightly. The water beyond was black under the moonless night.

Breathe, she told herself.

Months on a ship, and her family unaware of her whereabouts. Could she send a letter to them? The captain must keep parchment and ink somewhere on this godforsaken ship. But then, he would read the intended address and know her identity. She focused on the stars twinkling above, slowing her breaths. It wouldn't matter if her family knew, she might as well be dead for all the trouble this would cause them. Better that they not know the details.

A cool gust blew across the deck, and a few strands of hair danced wildly around her face. She shivered. How cold would the journey get before they approached the tropical islands?

"Do you have any warmer clothes, Miss Harry?" Behind her, Captain Alexander's deep voice turned gentle.

"I don't have any other clothes," she snapped, refusing to look at him. "Did you see a portmanteau when you tied me up?"

His soft footsteps retreated, and the waves lapping against the hull of the ship were the only sound. She peeked over her shoulder. He was gone. Leaning back against the taffrail, she worried her lip. What was she going to do?

Captain Alexander returned, dipping his head under the sail, and joined her at the bow. He held out a thick woolen coat by the collar. "The days will be warm while you work, but you will need more layers overnight. If you're still too cold, please tell me."

She frowned and considered him. His erratic changes were dizzying, but a fool she was not. Spinning around, she shrugged into the coat, embracing the warmth it offered. The weight of the thick material rested on her shoulders and calmed the turmoil inside her.

He adjusted the collar, his fingers grazing the back of her neck, and she was right back to that damn warm and tingling sensation. An intriguing blend of salt, sandalwood, and ginger filled her nose. Tilting her head toward the collar, she allowed her senses to be shrouded in the delicious smell. His fingers were still in place where he had fixed the collar, and her cheek brushed over them. She stepped away and turned back to face him, lifting her gaze to meet his. She opened her mouth to whisper a quick thank you, then closed it again, the words lost in her throat.

He turned away, his long strides taking him back to the sail barricade. She waited until his attention was elsewhere, and nestled further into his coat, burying herself in his scent.

"I need to check on our heading," he said.

Her gaze snapped to him, and she muffled a quiet groan. Had he seen her sniffing his coat?

"Are you coming?" he asked, his voice strained.

She hastened to follow him across the deck and up the stairs to the quarterdeck.

"Ship's wheel," Captain Alexander said, adding an unnecessary emphasized gesture to the giant wheel in front of him.

Harriet crossed her arms and pursed her lips. She did her best to glare at him, failing miserably.

Chapter Seven

ALEXANDER STOOD at the ship's wheel, directing his attention out to the dark ocean.

Again.

He'd left Miss Harry on the main deck, needing yet another momentary escape from her presence. Never in all his years of sailing had he frequented the quarterdeck so much on a single watch. The sails fluttered in the gentle breeze above his head. Their course wouldn't be altered if he stayed down on the main deck for extended periods as usual, but *he* might be. His will to treat Miss Harry with indifference and his growing desire to kiss her clashed with spectacular force. He would be punished in every way for bringing her with them.

He glanced to where she stood on the deck, wrapped snuggly in his warmest coat. Miss Harry lifted the collar to her nose and inhaled, her eyes fluttering closed. The shiver that traveled through her body was visible from the quarterdeck. Her lips parted, and she sighed.

Alexander groaned and curled his fingers tighter around the ship's wheel. He wanted to free her hair from that knot, and thread his fingers through the brown strands. To trace those lush pink lips with his tongue and explore the heat of her mouth. He wanted to make her moan, feel her sigh on his lips. *Lord*, could he stop imagining what it would be like to kiss her?

He moved the ship's wheel a touch right, and with his other hand made a quick adjustment to his breeches. Undone by a woman's sigh, and she wasn't within ten yards of him. Gripping the ship's wheel, he cursed the curiosity and gentlemanly instincts that had driven him to put them on watch together. Now he was stuck with her every duty for the entirety of their journey. That or explain to the crew why he'd made an uncharacteristic change to the duties.

Besides, the woman hated him, and she had every right to be angry. That fiery attitude had seen her through a day which might have been too much for another stowaway, particularly if Sam was right and she was a gentlewoman. Spitfire indeed, the determined little thing. She'd remained composed, followed orders, and done her best to be part of the crew. Alexander couldn't fault her at all.

A loud snore ripped from the ball of fur at his feet. Alexander rolled his eyes and glanced at Shadow. What an easy life that dog had, and his presence made Alexander's life lighter. Shadow had healed something in him over their past four years together. He kneeled and scratched behind the dog's ears.

"Is there anything else you would have me do, Captain?" Miss Harry's question broke through the silence on the quarterdeck, and Alexander recoiled.

He leaped to his feet and glared at her. "Don't sneak up on me!"

Her eyes twinkled, and one corner of her mouth

quirked. Her head cocked to the side. "I didn't sneak up on you," she said, her voice sweet as honey. Her hands swung at her sides and came together in a neat fold in front of her. She came a step closer, and one foot crossed in front of the other. Could she be more obviously feminine? He wouldn't believe for a second that she didn't know it. Her pose was as well-practiced as it was ignored. That's what he told himself.

"You did," he grumbled, turning to look out at the main deck.

"I didn't do it on purpose." The hint of innocence in her tone prompted him to turn back. Her eyes were wide, and she'd taken her bottom lip between her teeth.

"Very well," he said, priding himself on the fact he hadn't growled. "Would you come here?"

"Can I refuse an order from the captain?"

Why was she so hesitant? They'd spent many moments in much closer quarters over the past few hours. Was he behaving that much like an ass? He didn't ponder the answer.

"No," he said, watching her. "Though I doubt rules would stop you from doing as you wished. Besides, this is more of a request than an order." Thank the Lord no one else had heard him say that. When did he start giving his sailors requests? Since one of his sailors was a woman he'd kidnapped, forced to maintain a disguise, and ordered to work on his ship.

A moment later, she took a few steps forward and met him at the ship's wheel. He thanked her inquisitiveness, which outweighed her objections.

"Take the wheel." He gestured to it and stepped back.

She hesitated, her hands hovering inches away from the handles. "Are you sure?"

"Rarely am I unsure." The lie slipped easily through his teeth, but the weight of it settled in his chest. Hadn't he lied enough?

"Indeed." Her comment was so low, he couldn't be sure she intended for him to hear it.

Reaching for her hand, he placed it on the wheel where his had been moments before and dropped his hand to his side. He flexed his fingers, then curled them into a fist, but a prickling sensation lingered where their skin had briefly met.

"What now?" A small laugh followed her question.

He couldn't help but laugh with her, and they shared the same nervous quality. "We need to alter our heading slightly. Come a touch to port."

"Excuse me?" Her high pitch made him chuckle. She had been so keen to learn and had mastered many aspects of sailing, he forgot she might not know simple sailing terms.

"Port is to the left," he said. "Every sailor has a different way of remembering it. *Johnny left port, keep some port left over*. I simply like to think that the two words have four letters each." *Christ*, now he was rambling. He cleared his throat. "You want to move your left hand down."

The wheel moved a fraction of an inch under her hand.

"A little more," he said.

She peeked back at him, her brows creased. Did she doubt herself?

He smiled, hoping the gesture looked reassuring.

"It's so heavy," she said.

He kept his feet fixed in place and clasped his hands behind his back, intent on encouraging her with words alone. "You can do it."

All sailors on his ship had the skill to operate the ship's

wheel in case they were required to take control at any time. But teaching Miss Harry was different, and no matter how much he told himself it was normal, he wasn't convinced it was that simple.

With a not-so-subtle glance over her shoulder, she met his eye, locking him in her gaze as she'd done earlier on the orlop deck. The deep emeralds now twinkled with a mysterious quality. Or was it a reflection of the starry sky above them?

He blinked but couldn't force his gaze away. Her smile glowed with an inkling of pride, and he was only too happy to have been the one to put it there.

Her hushed whisper interrupted his reverie. "How do you know where to go?"

"What?" he asked, resisting the urge to shake his head.

She inclined her head to the bow of the ship.

He pointed at the sky and followed her gaze to the stars, then glanced back at her face. She stared unblinking, and the twinkle in her eyes intensified.

EIGHT RINGS of the bell signaled the end of their watch, and it hadn't come soon enough. Against his better judgment, Alexander had let Miss Harry do the honor. His hand had been on the bell's rope when she'd asked in a most splendidly seductive voice if she could ring the bell. He'd let go of the rope and stepped aside, any notion he had control of the situation slipping away. His hesitation transformed to deep fascination as he watched her swing the rope, her face a picture of joy. How could she be here with such apparent enthusiasm when just that morning she had been taken from her home? Here she was, making the best of the situation and putting her trust in him. He deserved to walk the plank and be keelhauled under the ship for what he'd done. Too bad they didn't have a plank or a long enough rope. He would have to settle for whatever punishment awaited him in London.

The final ring faded into the dark night. Alexander stood in stunned silence, and Miss Harry turned away. It would have been easy to let her go, to let her spend the night in a hammock and show her the cabin tomorrow. But she looked exhausted and would be better for it if she spent the night in a bed. He couldn't make her suffer any more than she already was.

He swiveled the sandglass, having neglected it in his moment of distraction, and took the stairs two at a time. "One more thing!" he called.

She stilled.

Jumping over the last four steps, he landed on the deck beside her. "Do you see that door?" He straightened and pointed to a door parallel to them under the quarterdeck, realizing a moment too late that it wasn't visible from where she stood.

She leaned toward him and peered in the direction he was pointing. Her intense focus looking for the door brought her close.

"No." The soft breathy response whispered across his face and stirred the ache in his groin.

Instinct pulled him away and he closed his eyes. On a deep inhale, he silently cursed the beginnings of a cock-stand forming in his breeches. It was a sigh, dammit.

"This way," he ground out. Gesturing toward the door, he took long strides away from her. There was a moment of silence, and he glanced over his shoulder. Her footsteps quickened behind him, light on the timber deck.

"This is my cabin," he said, stopping in front of the door. "Should you require anything, night or day, and I'm not on the quarterdeck, you will find me in here." He wasn't sure if he'd been expecting an answer, but none was offered. "There's also the issue of your sleeping arrangements."

"Excuse me?" Her eyes widened.

"I won't be giving you my cabin. Nor asking you to share it with me." He ignored the parts of his body that might have enjoyed that prospect. "I can't let you sleep on the mess deck either. I doubt the crew will pay you much heed, but they can be a rowdy bunch. Come this way, and I'll show you your cabin."

"My what?"

"Cabin." He confirmed with a quick nod.

"I'm fine in the hammock, Captain. I rather enjoyed the swaying."

"Swinging from the deck head isn't so bad, but if you're too slow getting in you could end up sleeping on the floor." He allowed a moment for her to consider. "That is irrelevant. I won't permit you to stay on the mess deck with the other sailors. This is an order from your captain, and it is not negotiable," he added when she opened her mouth. "Your cabin's this way, Miss Harry."

He made his way down the stairs to the mess deck and led her along the dim passageway. She matched him stride for stride. Stopping in front of the two officers' doors, Alexander pointed to the one on the left.

"That's Sam's cabin. He's second in command of this ship. I'd prefer you to come to me, but he will do, should you require anything. Though he is on the opposite watch to us, so he won't be in there when you're here."

"He knows, then?" she asked. "About me."

"Yes." He kept the answer simple and found the handle to her cabin. He twisted it and swung the door open, keeping his eyes on her face.

Her gasp made his heart race. What now? She turned her mask of distaste on him, with wide eyes and her mouth agape.

He sighed. What could be *that* bad? It took all his effort to turn and look into Harvey's cabin. A single low lamp on the wall lit the space, casting a dim, orange glow around the cabin. The red satin sheets soaked up the light, turning the small space into a dark den of depravity. His gaze tracked up the wall where an intimately detailed painting of a woman hung above the bed. Or perhaps she was a contortionist?

Alexander cursed before he could stop himself and pushed a hand over his eyes. How he wished he could disappear at that moment. "Sorry," he murmured. "I shouldn't have said that. Harvey has a flair for extravagance..." He trailed off. That would never be explanation enough. "Harvey's our, ah, and he's, er..." Words failed him again and he struggled to compose his thoughts. What could he say?

"Yes?" Her soft prompt dragged him back to the problem at hand.

"He's... ashore." The answer was simple and unconvincing. He owed her so much more of an explanation. "I do apologize for this, sincerely." He waved his hand into the cabin. "It is not ideal, I know. But it is still preferable to the mess deck."

She peered into the cabin, her mouth curved downward. "I don't think it is."

"Humor me." The dark tone was not what he'd intended. It was necessary he extract himself from the situation before she made any assumptions. As if her opinion of him could fall any lower.

Miss Harry strode into the cabin and twirled back to face him. The image of her in that space, bathed in the golden glow of the lamp from behind, was the last thing he needed to see.

"Happy, Captain?" The smile on her face was a test, and it wiped his mind clear once again.

"I, er..." He fumbled with his thoughts.

"Yes?"

"Sleep well." He snapped the door shut and walked away.

This day refused to end.

He was beyond tired and sure his bed was calling him, but he bypassed his own cabin. Sam was the person he needed to speak to now, and he found him on the quarter-deck, having taken over control of the ship's wheel in Alexander's absence.

"Satin sheets, Sam?" Alexander groaned. "*Red* satin sheets?"

"I know. I'm sorry, but I couldn't find anything else."

"Take the linen off my bed in future, or yours." Alexander scowled at Sam. "And what about that painting? Surely you could have taken it off the wall?"

Sam crossed his arms. "Harvey's glued it to the wall, the scoundrel. I assume to not have it fall on his face in rough seas. Or stolen."

"I'm going to pry that thing off the wall and hit him with it next time I see him." Alexander's words were curt. "That will serve him right for hanging a painting of a naked woman in his cabin. And with such *detail*." He could scarcely believe it and perhaps wouldn't have if he'd not seen it with his own eyes. "I'd hate to see how he decorates his own ship if he thinks it's appropriate to deface mine in that manner."

"I know," Sam replied. "When I'm back on my ship, the first thing I'll do is check his cabin."

"Not that I ever expect to be in such a bizarre situation again, but might you consider a forewarning next time? The look on her face as she took it all in..." Alexander covered his eyes with a hand. "She looked worried I would ravish her then and there." Worse, she looked as though she would rather hurl herself overboard than be near him. The events of the day had not painted him in a favorable light.

"Of course. How did she go on watch?" Sam asked.

Alexander sensed a deeper meaning to his friend's question, but if Sam was insinuating anything about his behavior, he could ask outright.

"Surprisingly well," Alexander said, keeping his tone light and staring out at the dark sea. "She has an interesting knowledge base for a young woman. I don't know where she learned it all. Oh, and I should probably tell you she believes we're sailing to the Caribbean."

"Why on earth would she think that?"

Alexander glanced at Sam. "Because I thought that might prepare her for however long this journey takes. I can't promise she'll be home in a matter of weeks."

Sam brushed his hand across his chin and shook his head.

Alexander didn't know what to make of the gesture, and he was too tired to make sense of it. "What is it, Sam? And if you dare say *it's something about you that I can't work out*, I'll send you down to the orlop deck with her tomorrow to untangle rope for the day." Perhaps he would have better luck finding out her name.

Sam leaned against the taffrail and crossed his arms.

"Nothing like that at all." He chewed his lip, the corners of his mouth tugging at a grin.

Alexander groaned. What was the matter with him?

"What is it?" Alexander snapped.

"You remember asking me to talk to Groves this afternoon?"

"Yes," Alexander answered through gritted teeth.

Sam frowned, but the gesture was far from concerned. "Well, when I told him Harry is my cousin and will be sleeping in Harvey's cabin, and that he'd never sailed before..."

Alexander scowled. "Spit it out, Sam." He was tired and didn't care what Groves had said.

"Well, he suggested we make Harry your cabin boy instead of Jacob, and I couldn't convince him otherwise." Sam avoided his glare.

"You could think of absolutely no reason for her not to be my cabin boy?"

"He believes *Harry* is much younger than Miss Harry really is. I assume she's eighteen or nineteen, but he's under the impression Harry is only fourteen or so. He said he's got duties that would suit Jacob, and Harry's coming aboard was perfect timing. It has worked out well in that regard. In some ways, it might be better. She is now under your direction instead of Groves's."

Alexander could think of many reasons it was *not* better. He'd now lost any assistance he'd had from Jacob. And he would not be allowing Miss Harry anywhere near his cabin, let alone inside it.

"She can stay in Harvey's cabin," Alexander said. "I don't want her near mine."

"Don't you think it would be better to keep her nearby? You'll be able to watch over her, and she can come to you if she has any issues. I know she's in the cabin next to mine, but that's not helpful on opposite duties, is it? You should have put her on my watch."

Alexander clamped his teeth together. He was aware of the multitude of mistakes he had made regarding Miss Harry, and he'd known the woman for less than a day.

"If there are any issues, it will be *because* of her, not anything else," Alexander said. It was logical to make her his cabin boy, and for her to sleep in the small cabin next to his. That didn't mean he liked the idea. "I'll sleep on it and see how I feel in the morning. I'm not going back to her cabin now in any case, she'd likely faint if I knocked on the door."

Sam beamed. A provocation.

"What now, Sam?"

"You've become so used to getting your way, Alexander, it's fascinating to see you challenged."

"I do not always get my way. I have faced plenty of adversaries." Though he doubted Miss Harry could best him. It was keeping himself away from her that posed such a challenge.

"You're four-and-twenty and the captain of your own ship," Sam offered.

"So are you."

Sam shrugged. "You'll have to forgive me for being entertained by the situation you've gotten yourself into. I'm interested to see what you make of it."

Alexander would not make anything of the situation. It was going to take everything he had just to make it through the next few weeks.

"Come on, Shadow," Alexander said.

Shadow woke at the mention of his name, and stood, shaking out his fur in one fluid motion.

Alexander walked back to his cabin with Shadow strutting at his side.

"What do you think of it all, boy?"

Shadow's head cocked to the side, his tongue lolling out the side of his mouth.

Alexander collapsed onto his bed with a hollow chuckle. "I don't know what to make of her either."

Chapter Eight

Soil, damp from recent rain, mingled with heated spices the street vendors cooked, and infiltrated Alexander's senses. He inhaled the familiar scent deep into his lungs, savoring the memory of a Singapore summer evening. A sudden, delicious mix of gardenias and mint overwhelmed him.

Lying side by side, her soft hands, unaffected by the manual work of sailing, rested in his calloused ones. Even softer lips found his, and he surrendered to the kiss. Her lips parted, allowing his tongue to explore the heat of her mouth. He twisted his fingers through her hair and pulled her closer, wanting her body on every inch of his. Her fingertips danced across his shoulders, and he shivered.

Alexander moaned, longing for more. For all of her. With each movement that brought him closer to her, and his release, burning desire surged within him. He slid his hands down her back, cupping her perfect backside, and rolled her atop him. She straddled him, her knees resting on either side of his waist. The slow rock of her body, grinding on his erection, was almost too much, but he matched her movements and dug his fingers into her hips. He sat up and buried his hands in her hair. His shirt came over his head, and he wriggled free of it, letting her take control.

Shadow's booming bark reverberated around the cabin, and Alexander startled awake. He squeezed his eyes closed and rammed his face into the pillow with a groan. Releasing fistfuls of linen, he stretched out his aching fingers.

Another bark echoed across the cabin.

Alexander lifted his head and glanced around. Pale light from the quarterdeck lamps filtered through the stern windows running the length of his cabin. Beyond that, the night and the sea disappeared into darkness.

Shadow stood with his nose at the door, his ears pointed upward. Whatever it was could wait, though Alexander doubted anything was amiss. Shadow had a low threshold for any perceived danger. Besides, the door was unlocked. If it were important, Sam would let himself in.

Alexander rolled onto his back, trying to dispel the images of Miss Harry from his mind. As annoying as Shadow's barking could be, he was relieved to escape the torment of that dream. A lamp burned low in the corner of his cabin, and Alexander stared at the beams on the ceiling, following the familiar patterns and creating new shapes from them.

Eighteen hours Miss Harry had been in his life. Eighteen hours to completely disrupt his existence. What had she done to him? He ought to have left her in Hull, but he couldn't change that now, and he never would have done it. All he could do was endure the journey and hope it was a short one.

The bell rang out above, the muted sound alerting him

and the crew to the change of duty. He rose, thankful for a reason to move and for falling asleep fully clothed.

Alexander stepped out of his cabin, Shadow half a step behind, and the crisp predawn air hit him. His frustration dissipated with each step toward the quarterdeck and each lungful of fresh air, and his plan solidified.

Sam waited at the ship's wheel, his haggard expression reflecting Alexander's exhaustion.

"Long watch?" Alexander asked.

A weary nod was Sam's reply, and he stepped away from the helm.

"Before you go…" Alexander's tone would be enough to alert his friend.

Curiosity sparked in Sam's eyes. "What is it?"

"That girl." Alexander sighed. "I don't want anything to do with her. I don't want to see her. I don't want to hear a word about her. Is that clear?"

A frown creased Sam's brow. "Alexander?"

"I don't care what you do with her. If I hear so much as a whisper, I'll…" What? What would he do? Throw her overboard? No, he knew the threat to be as empty as she must. What he would do would be far worse. At least, the consequences would be. Wanting her was out of the question.

Years ago, when he'd discovered the truth of his father's temper and the way his mother suffered, Alexander swore he would never act in a way that emulated the man. He'd sworn it to his mother's memory at her grave. Whatever he felt, or *thought* he felt for Miss Harry, didn't signify. He'd kidnapped her, crossing a line that could not be uncrossed. Kissing her would be unforgivable.

"What could she have possibly done to you in the past few hours?" Sam asked.

Alexander fixed him with a severe stare.

"I'll find a way to keep her busy." Sam bade him good-night and hurried away.

HARRIET AROSE FROM HER HAMMOCK, having spent the night on the mess deck among the crew. Sneaking back there once Captain Alexander left had been easy, and there were more than enough empty hammocks to accommodate her. No lie, argument, or threat could convince her to spend another minute in that dreadful cabin.

The illusion she had risen early evaporated as she emerged onto the main deck, the morning sun already high in the sky. Sailors worked about the deck, and those nearest to the stairs frowned at her. She ignored their stares, the sudden eagerness to find the captain surprising her.

The man standing at the ship's wheel was not Captain Alexander, however. It must have been his second in command. Would he treat her the same way the captain had?

She stepped onto the quarterdeck, holding her head high.

"Good morning, Miss," the man said, smiling. His warm brown eyes regarded her with a knowing look.

"Good morning, sir," she replied, inclining her head.

"You missed your duty this morning." That explained the looks from the crew. He continued, his voice smooth. "The captain asked that you not be woken, but so you are aware, when you finish watch at midnight you are expected to return at four o'clock. Watch duty alternates each night. So tonight, you will be on duty from midnight until four. It will continue to alternate that way, and you will soon fall into the routine."

"Yes, sir."

"You may call me Sam," he said. "The rest of the crew does."

Harriet listened to Sam explain the various watch duties and changing times. Dog watch was split into two shorter duties to account for the crew alternating shifts each night. The bell rang in thirty minute intervals, marked by the turning of a sandglass beside it. The routine bells had sounded since the ship had sailed, but she hadn't noticed the pattern. It seemed obvious now.

"Right, Harry." Sam eyed her and raised a brow. "You're to spend the day back on the orlop deck. There's more than enough to keep you busy down there. Try your best to keep out of the captain's way for the remainder of the day."

"Yes, Sam. Thank you." She didn't waste time wondering what she'd done overnight to offend the captain, happy to return to untangling rope without fuss.

"Oh, and I must inform you that the crew is under the impression you're my cousin. I personally don't see the resemblance," Sam said with a playful wink. "It makes a few things easier to explain. That is all, Miss."

She smiled and took her leave, eager for the isolation of the orlop deck.

The day stretched on, and Harriet worked through the ropes at an excruciating pace. A sailor would bring her food right around the time her hunger would hit, either Mr. Groves, Jacob, or a third man who had negated introductions. They lingered long enough to ask how she fared before disappearing back up the stairs. The beef stew was on repeat, but she couldn't complain. It filled her stomach and warmed her for a good half hour. In the moments her fingers ached too much to continue, she took pause. Though the lack of movement meant that not even her borrowed coat was warm enough to fight off the chill of sitting below sea level.

At last, the end of first dog watch arrived. She made her way back up to find a hammock to settle into until her next watch. Her plan, when she woke, was to return to the orlop deck. It didn't appear she would be given another task, and she was eager to follow Sam's advice.

"Right, lad?" Mr. Groves appeared beside her on the mess deck and clapped a hand onto her shoulder. "'Tis hard work down there on your own. See Sam before you rest up."

Harriet heaved a sigh. She had made it all day without setting foot back on the main deck. Surely Sam didn't need to speak with her again. And what would happen if she ran into Captain Alexander?

"Off you go now." Mr. Groves said, his gruff voice taking on a fatherly quality.

She set off for the quarterdeck, hoping she could avoid the captain. But if it was change of duty, wouldn't he be with Sam at the helm? Stepping out on the main deck, the sunset blinded her, the brightness stinging her eyes after hours below deck. Shielding her face with one hand, she trudged along the deck. She detoured the long way to the stairs, passing Captain Alexander's cabin beneath the quarterdeck.

A long, desperate howl came from behind the door. Shadow. Was he in pain? She hesitated at the door. If she ran into the captain anywhere on the ship, outside his cabin would be the worst. Shadow's howls continued, becoming more distressed by the second.

She stepped closer to the door and pressed her ear to it, grabbing the handle. Was Captain Alexander in there, listening and doing nothing? His affection for the dog was obvious in the short time she'd spent in their company. He wouldn't let Shadow suffer.

She knocked on the door, loud enough to alert anyone inside of her intention. The noise inside changed from a howl to a booming bark and grew louder until the dog slammed against the door. Her instincts forced her back, despite the solid barricade between them. The barking intensified. Now she'd done it.

"Hush, Shadow," she called, scrambling back to the door, but he didn't stop.

Grasping the door handle, she twisted it slowly, not sure if she wanted it to be locked or unlocked. It slid open, and she dashed inside. She fended off Shadow's keen attentions and looked about. No sign of the captain in his cabin.

His cabin. She was inside the captain's cabin.

Shadow leaped up with such enthusiasm, he pushed her back against the door. For a small dog, it took a solid effort to force him back onto all four paws. She kneeled in front of him, keeping a firm hold on his shoulders. He responded with a big, wet lick up the side of her face.

"Thanks," she muttered, wiping her cheek on her shoulder.

His big, brown eyes sparkled, and his mouth broke into a lopsided grin, his tongue lolling out the side. She grinned back. He was fine. The little devil just wanted attention. Shadow ran away from her and dug under the bed, his nails scraping the timber floor.

She followed him, and he dragged out a knotted piece of fabric, dropping it at her feet. She stooped and grabbed it, holding it by one tattered end. A toy?

A low, threatening rumble came from behind her. "What the hell is going on?" The captain's calm manner instilled more fear than if he'd yelled.

She drew a sharp breath and spun around, coming face to face with Captain Alexander. His eyes were narrowed to slits, and his lips pressed into a thin line. The hairs on the back of her neck stood on end.

"I'm so sorry," she said, wishing she could find the words to explain herself.

"Get out," he said in the same flat tone.

She opened her mouth to apologize again for the invasion of his privacy, but nothing came out.

"Get out of my cabin." The muscles in his jaw worked, and his hands curled into fists at his sides. "Now."

She gestured to Shadow, the dog having already made his way to his master. Captain Alexander glanced down at him with a half-raised brow, then returned his hardened stare to her. Uneasiness spread through her bones. She fiddled with her collar, a meaningless gesture to protect herself from the way his glare exposed her. His nostrils flared, and jaw clenched, his top lip curling.

"I'm sorry," she whispered, and rushed past him out the door. In her haste, her arm brushed his, and she could have sworn he growled. How could she have been so reckless? Sam had warned her to stay away from the captain. Was she so set on testing the man that she couldn't help herself?

And why had the rush of fear caused by Captain Alexander's voice sizzled into another sensation? One that made her skin prickle and heat. An awareness she'd never experienced before sparked again. It had happened each time he'd entered her thoughts, something she'd been trying hard to avoid for most of the day. But she was drawn to him in a way she couldn't explain. Sam, the crew, even Captain Alexander himself had made it clear she should avoid him. Why was it so hard?

She kept running until she reached the stairs and

descended into the ship. Sam and his instructions could wait. She was likely banished to the orlop deck for the rest of the journey.

"Join us for a game, 'Arry?" Jacob's question came from behind her.

"What?" she asked, forgetting to adopt her masculine disguise. She blinked and turned toward Jacob.

He leaned against the mess deck opening, a simple rectangular hole in place of a door. "Cards." He gestured behind him to where the hammocks usually hung, revealing a few scattered tables.

Harvey's cabin was steps away and where she ought to be should the captain come looking for her. But how much trouble could she get in for a game of cards? Surely not much more than she already was for entering his cabin without permission. The opportunity to escape her reality for a moment was too difficult to pass up.

She beamed at Jacob, determined to make the gesture genuine. "What are we playing?"

He grinned, and she followed him into the mess, glancing at the fellow sailors congregated around the tables. Judging by their hands of seven cards, this wasn't a game she'd played before.

Harriet squeezed herself between Jacob and another sailor whose name she didn't know. Six of them crowded around one small, scarred wooden table in the fading light. The hammocks, usually strung across the deck, now bunched to one side, swaying with the ship's rhythm. More sailors grouped around the other tables, entertaining themselves with cards and dice, all games she didn't recognize. The rowdy din couldn't be classified as positive or negative, but no one seemed to argue in earnest. Sea air and the mingled tang of food and sweat were becoming familiar.

The sailor across from her began dealing. "All right, we're playing five queens. Everyone knows the rules?" His gaze scanned around the table, waiting for each of them to acknowledge with a nod or grunt. He paused on her.

"I'll make sure he catches on," Jacob piped up, giving her a swift elbow to the ribs.

The jab sent a shock through her ribcage, and she nodded, although she'd never heard of five queens. Curling a hand around her waist, she rubbed the place of Jacob's impact.

The deal finished, and the other sailors picked up their cards. Instead of taking the cards dealt in front of them, they picked up the pile to their right. Each sailor placed a card face down in the middle and drew another. Harriet followed their lead. Then they threw small coins onto the table.

"Jacob," she whispered. "I haven't any money."

"Oh, right," he said in a hushed tone. "Well, I'll give you a few to start, but you owe me." He dug in his pockets, elbowing her repeatedly in the arm and ribs, and then dropped a couple of coins into her hand.

She added one, a shilling, to the pile. Another round of cards went down on the table, and they all drew again.

"What do you make of the cap'n putting him down on the orlop deck?" the man sitting beside her asked.

Harriet glanced up from her cards.

"Dunno what tha's about," Mr. Groves replied, his eyes narrowing. "'Tis not like him to do that to a young lad. What have you heard, Knapp?"

"Nothing." Mr. Knapp's shoulder lifted against Harriet's arm in a shrug. "No idea what he's up to."

They returned to their cards, but Mr. Groves was still watching her.

The game ended in Harriet's favor, as did another four rounds. She still didn't have the faintest idea of how to play five queens, even after two hours at the game. How she had walked away with two shillings more than she'd started, she had no clue. It was beginner's luck, they'd all agreed, and she couldn't argue. She paid Jacob back but kept her winnings. When no one was looking, she tucked the coins into her corset.

"Right then." Mr. Groves stood and stretched as he spoke. "Back to it, lads." They extracted themselves from the table with groans of displeasure. She wasn't sure what she'd expected of sailors, but she rather liked this crew.

Harriet placed her hands flat on the table and made to stand.

"Not you, boy," Mr. Groves said, fixing his stare on Harriet.

Her body stiffened, and she met his eyes, trying to stop her own from widening. How much more could she handle in one day?

"If the cap'n is giving you too much trouble, come and see me, all right?" He reached over and slapped her on the shoulder. "He's barely more than a lad himself, but a good man and a good cap'n. But if he's not treating one of us right, I wanna know about it."

Well, she didn't know what to make of that.

Chapter Nine

ALEXANDER STAYED in bed longer than usual, lying on his back and tracing the grain of timber above him with his eyes. A dreamless, uninterrupted sleep had put him in a better mood, though the events of the previous two days gnawed at him. Particularly how he'd reacted to Miss Harry appearing in his cabin last night. He'd had multiple watch duties alone to reflect on his actions and wasn't at all pleased with himself. No mortal sin or egregious offense had been committed on Miss Harry's part, nothing to deserve the manner with which he had regarded her. But seeing her in his cabin after that dream had been more than he could handle.

He shook the image from his mind for what must have been the hundredth time and vowed that today would be better, or *he* would be. The least he could do was treat her with a little more kindness. It wasn't fair that she suffered because of his own insistent desires. His body could be controlled or ignored.

Alexander rolled out of bed and whistled to Shadow.

The dog jumped up from his own bed and made his way across the cabin.

"What am I going to do, boy?" Alexander asked.

Shadow answered with a lazy grin.

Alexander reached down and scratched behind the dog's fluffy, black ears. "I know *you* like her, but that doesn't help me." He sighed and walked to the dresser. His glowering reflection was distorted thanks to the crack running from the top right to the bottom left corner of the mirror. His hair was getting longer again, and it was in a right state. He raked his fingers through it, taming it away from his face into a less wild style. He forced a smile onto his face but landed on a strange, twisted grimace that made him laugh. Surely he could be civil to the woman without being pleasant. That would have to do.

He glanced down at the clothing he had neglected to change since returning from his errand in Hull. Had that only been two days ago? The neckcloth had been tossed unceremoniously into the corner of his cabin the instant he'd walked onto the ship, and the rest joined it now. He pulled on a loose linen shirt from his dresser and a pair of long trousers. His oldest, most scuffed, and comfortable Hessian boots completed the ensemble.

Alexander left the cabin with Shadow trailing behind, and they made their way toward the quarterdeck.

"Quite the beginner's luck he had last night."

The unusual phrase was enough to capture Alexander's attention, and he slowed his pace. Eavesdropping was well below him, but the beginner must be Miss Harry, and it was prudent to stay informed about her actions on the ship.

"I ain't never seen anyone pick up a game that quick." Jacob's excited voice chimed in. As Alexander's next to newest recruit, Jacob was still learning to sail and shouldn't know the first thing about gambling at a mere fifteen years old. The boy had gone from a scrawny pickpocket to a flourishing and skillful young sailor within months of honest hard work. Groves and the others should know better, but Alexander couldn't protect him forever.

Alexander strained his ear and tugged at a fraying rope tied around a beam, reluctant to move on until he'd heard enough to confirm his suspicions.

"That lad has played before. No way was that the first time he'd picked up cards."

Who was that? Had they all stayed up gambling last night instead of sleeping? It wouldn't be the first time.

"Dunno how he would. 'Tis his first trip. And I never heard of that game before I sailed with you."

Well, Knapp's words all but confirmed it. Miss Harry had joined the crew's entertainment between watches. Why couldn't she stay in her cabin? All Alexander wanted was for her to keep to herself, yet she seemed intent on defying him. Gambling wasn't too bad in the larger scheme, but his men sparred at times. What would she do then?

He snapped back to standing and hastened along the deck. Above him, Sam rang the bell. Alexander turned up the stairs to the quarterdeck, catching movement out of the corner of his eye.

Miss Harry.

She must have been right behind him when he'd walked out of his cabin. Her wide eyes and grimace indicated she had also overheard the conversation. Alexander pursed his lips and stared at her, raising his eyebrows. She remained frozen in place until he broke the connection and headed up the stairs.

A slow grin spread across Sam's face as Alexander stepped onto the quarterdeck.

"What now?" Alexander asked, shaking his head.

"Nothing," Sam replied.

He didn't have the patience for Sam and whatever vague theory he had conjured up today. He suspected it would hit too close to the mark.

"We should make port before tomorrow morning," Sam said.

"Excellent. Do you think we'll have any luck in Holland?" He had little hope.

"No, Harvey wouldn't have stayed where we left him. He's not that stupid. But we have to start somewhere."

Alexander glanced at Shadow, the dog staying at his heel. "He'll have to stay with you while I go ashore." He looked back at Sam, who seemed hesitant. "You know I can't take him with me."

"I know, but, my word, he is a pain when you're not here."

Alexander laughed. "Thank you, Sam. I'll put him in my cabin when I go. You'll only need to check on him and keep him away from the gangplank."

"Of course." Sam narrowed his eyes at Shadow as he replied. "You had better behave yourself."

Alexander couldn't give that reassurance on Shadow's behalf, so he stayed quiet.

"How did my cousin go last night?" Sam asked. "Is she still being sent to the orlop deck each duty or have you accepted her role as cabin boy?" Sam's question was innocent enough, but Alexander could sense the meaning behind it. Sam wasn't happy about her punishment either.

"It hasn't done any good," Alexander admitted. He still hadn't told Sam about finding her in his cabin. "Apparently, she joined Groves and the other sailors for a bout of gambling between watches."

"Did she?" Sam exclaimed, his mouth curving into a wide grin.

"Try not to sound too impressed. She'll land herself in even more trouble before she knows it. Although it sounds as though she won."

"Were they playing five queens?"

"I'd say so. Do they play much else?" Alexander asked.

"She must be good." Surprise colored Sam's voice. "I haven't won a hand in months. I swear they change the rules on me every time I play."

"The game has no rules, as far as I can tell."

"So, you don't win either?"

"No," Alexander grumbled.

The knowledge that he, too, couldn't win the impossible game evidently buoyed Sam.

"Bet it annoys you to no end that *she* has the knack for it."

"What annoys me," Alexander said in a low timbre, "is now I need to keep an even closer eye on her."

"What will you say to her?"

"About what?"

They both whirled around at her question.

"I swear," Alexander growled. "If you don't stop doing that, I *will* throw you overboard. Have I made myself clear?"

"Doing what?" she asked.

"Sneaking up on me." The volume of his voice rose beyond his control. "You're like a damned cat."

Her bemused smile changed into a serious frown. "Sorry, Captain. Mr. Groves sent me."

He sighed. He'd done it again, lost his temper in a flash. What was it about her that made his self-control slip away? And why did it make him feel so wretched?

"Infuriating," Alexander murmured. He turned back to

Sam, who was watching him through narrowed eyes. He'd gone too far. Again. Alexander squeezed his eyes closed and pinched the bridge of his nose. He had to do it, but that wouldn't make it easy. "Miss Harry," he said using his gentlest tone. He turned back to face her.

Cabin boy?

Harriet didn't have long to ponder her new task.

Captain Alexander continued his lecture. "Jacob has been my cabin boy since he joined the crew. However, it has become apparent that I need to keep a much closer eye on you. Clearly, you are determined to put yourself in precarious situations without any consideration for the consequences."

This was about the conversation he'd overheard between Mr. Groves and the other sailors. She shouldn't have done it, but it hadn't been such an exceptional event. From what the men had said, all they cared about was that she had won. They hadn't discovered she was a woman or questioned the circumstances that had brought her on board. And why should it matter? Sam had already given the excuse of her being his cousin.

Captain Alexander continued speaking. Apparently, her input was not required.

"Jacob needs to develop his skills under Groves's guidance. You, on the other hand, have no need to learn any more than the basics to get you home safely."

She scoffed. His eyebrows raised at the sound, but the rest of his face remained set in a scowl. She pursed her lips, keeping her thoughts to herself.

"You will remain at my side for the remainder of this

voyage, ready to attend to any task I assign to you. Is that clear?"

She tried to muster her confidence, but she found it failing in that moment. At his side? For the remainder of the voyage? He could not be serious.

"Is that clear?" Captain Alexander asked again.

"Yes," she choked out.

"As for your sleeping arrangements, there is a small cabin next to mine where you will sleep from now on." His eyes narrowed. "You will not sneak onto the mess deck to sleep again."

She couldn't hide her surprise. "How do you know I did that?"

Captain Alexander folded his arms across his chest. "It is my responsibility to know everything that happens on my ship. Though I can't lay the blame entirely with you for leaving Harvey's cabin, I can assure you this one is suitable. Do I have your assurance on the matter?" His tone indicated there would indeed be consequences if she disobeyed this direct order.

It took all her effort to suppress her groan. "Yes, Captain," she conceded.

The rest of her afternoon passed at an excruciating pace. She spent most of it standing behind Captain Alexander at the ship's wheel. At times, he sent her to various destinations across the *Seren* with no task or purpose. How had he made this worse than rope duty? There was no question he was punishing her now, but no matter how frustrated she was, she resisted the urge to speak her mind. The fear he might send her to the crow's nest to be rid of her was very real. She had pushed him far enough even for her comfort.

Despite the lack of conversation, her knowledge was

expanding through keen observation. In those few slow hours, she learned and memorized the bell signals and the names of almost half the crew. She had a new appreciation for how each sailor performed his individual task, and how they all flowed together to ensure smooth sailing. And she had well and truly fallen in love with the sea.

The waves glittered and winked at her from every direction, as though they withheld great secrets beneath their depths. Captain Alexander's eyes had a similar quality, though she was much less curious about his secrets. That's what she kept telling herself.

"Miss Harry." He directed his words over his shoulder and kept his back to her.

What now?

She begrudged him an answer, keeping it short to avoid releasing the torrent of insults she wanted to hurl at him. "Yes, Captain?" She fought to keep her tone neutral.

"We will sail into port this evening, and I need to leave the ship. I expect you to behave appropriately while I am gone." His dry, disapproving tone did not make it easy to remain polite.

She reserved her response for herself and fixed her gaze over the taffrail.

He spoke again, this time much closer. "I expect an acknowledgment when I give an order."

She willed herself to stay calm and slowly spun around. "Define *appropriately*."

He glared at her with a rigid stare that flowed into his posture. A hint of something flashed across his face, but he maintained his composure. "No gambling." He held out his hand and tapped his fingers as he listed his expectations. "No sneaking down to the mess deck to sleep. No leaving the ship. And do not enter my cabin again. Shadow will whine until I return. You can leave him."

The prospect of being caught in his cabin a second time, even without him expressly forbidding it, had no appeal. The rest of his rules would be easy enough to follow. She had no idea where they were arriving, except that it wasn't England, and it would be dark. She had no desire to leave the ship whether he forbade it or not. And despite not doing anything of note through the day, she was exhausted enough to fall into a deep sleep as soon as her body was horizontal.

"I can do that," she said.

"Good. It's the end of your duty now. Go and get some rest. I expect we'll arrive before you wake." He gazed at the horizon to the port side, squinting at something Harriet couldn't see. She turned in the opposite direction and looked out the starboard side. The sun set with a final golden burst across the sky. The sight captivated her, and she gasped. The sky transformed from a bright glow to a more subdued orange.

"It's beautiful, isn't it?" His voice was a murmur behind her.

"Yes," she whispered, realizing that its beauty had rendered her breathless. She'd never experienced anything like it.

Without another word, she headed for her new cabin.

"YOU'VE HAD A BUSY DAY, young Harry." Groves had taken her aside when she came out of her cabin for watch duty. The cabin boy's cabin was the same size as Harvey's, with a small porthole window that opened. The sea breeze flowing into the cabin was blissful. She'd been right about her exhaustion. Sleep had claimed her the moment her head touched that surprisingly fluffy pillow. Shadow's bark had woken her, and the night had enveloped them by the time she emerged from the cabin.

"He's being hard on you," Groves said. "Are you all right?"

Harriet glanced down at the man who had displayed undue kindness to the newest addition to the crew. His blue-gray eyes were bright. A soft soul existed beneath the battered exterior. "I'm fine," she choked out, the words coming out in a throaty grumble.

"Come down to the mess."

"Isn't it time for watch?" she asked.

Groves shook his head, smiling. "Not when we're in port."

She followed his gaze around the deck, and her eyes landed on the twinkling vista beyond the taffrail. Lamps blazed in the dark night, lighting the way along the dock and into the small town.

"When we're in port, only one or two lads is needed for watch. The rest of us have a break or go ashore. The cap'n is likely to be back before long, so we'll stay put."

She considered that. This wouldn't be disobeying Captain Alexander's precise orders, but there would be trouble if he caught her. He'd told her not to sneak to the mess deck to sleep, which she wasn't, and she would not gamble or leave the ship. But spending time with the sailors had been an implied restriction. Disregarding her reservations, she followed Groves to the mess deck. What the captain didn't know wouldn't hurt him.

"Ah, 'Arry!" Jacob's beaming face was the first to greet her.

Knapp handed them each a mug as they entered. She peered into it, then sipped the amber liquid. The sweet liquid burned her throat, and she stifled a cough. A hot sensation traveled down into her stomach, warming her insides.

"Go easy on him, lads. Cap'n has been giving him a hard time," Groves said, clapping her on the back and making her cough on another sip of rum.

"You're getting soft in your old age, Groves," another sailor replied.

"Bollocks," Groves said. He left her in Jacob's company and joined a group of older sailors playing cards.

As usual, Jacob was there to fill her in on the proceedings. "We often have a tot or two when cap'n goes ashore. Not so much to do when the ship ain't sailing, and there's no cargo to move either."

Harriet nodded, already aware of the effect the small taste of rum had on her. She took another sip. How bad could it be? She'd had nips of port and sherry before.

"Let's play cards," Jacob suggested. At her hesitation, he added, "Not for money this time. You can teach me how to win five queens."

"I'm afraid I won't be much help. It was beginner's luck," she insisted.

"I don't believe tha' for a second." Groves spoke from behind her. "Never seen anyone win five games at once."

"Settle it with a friendly game?" Knapp suggested.

She couldn't argue with that. Then they might believe she didn't know how she'd won so many times. Following Jacob's lead, she took another pull from her mug.

Nothing.

She peered into the mug, and a small drop rolled around the bottom. A moment later, an unknown hand reached out for it. The man filled it to the top and thrust it back into her hand.

"We'll play teams," Jacob said. "Me and 'Arry and you old pair."

"Careful, you," Groves warned, one side of his mouth tilting upward.

Even sober, Harriet had no idea what the game was about or how to win it. She had no hope of teaching Jacob anything useful in her current state, which was declining with each mouthful of her drink. Harriet had grown accustomed to the burning sensation now, and the liquid slid down her throat. She had come to appreciate its sweetness.

The tingling started in her fingertips. It had gradually progressed up her arms until it made her whole body warm and heavy. She wanted to strip out of her layers, but her coat would need to stay in place in such close quarters with the other sailors. Needing cool air on her skin, she excused herself in the same fashion the other sailors had done throughout the evening. Mumbling about the bowsprit, she headed out the door. Hopefully, she'd recover her composure with a few cleansing breaths of fresh air.

Stumbling out of the mess, she grasped at every little nook she could find on the walls to keep herself upright. The ship seemed to sway much more than when she had entered the mess deck. Had they sailed already?

She tripped over her feet, and all-too-familiar hands wrapped around her waist.

Chapter Ten

ALEXANDER COULD NOT BELIEVE what she had done. Miss Harry wasn't some feisty, headstrong woman. No, she was a challenge sent to him by the gods.

"You're drunk," he said, pulling her to one side of the mess deck corridor and out of sight of the crew.

Her shoulder hit the wall, and her head tilted to the side. "No-mm-not," she slurred.

Alexander groaned, not bothering to hide his irritation. One slip and the rest of the crew would become aware of her. He'd had a hard enough time explaining his actions to Sam. If the crew found out she was a woman, they'd know he had lied.

"Do you have any idea how irresponsible you are?" he asked. "You can't drink this much. If you keep up with them, you'll kill yourself." He was trying to chastise her, but she was oblivious.

She beamed, her mouth lopsided, and he rolled his eyes. Talking to her now was pointless, she wouldn't remember a word he said. It would have to wait until tomorrow. Right now, he had to get her to her cabin, *fast*. He'd never helped a drunk sailor to bed before, and it wouldn't do for anyone to witness this.

Alexander steered her along the deck but made the mistake of loosening his grip around her arms. She went sideways and almost collapsed. Grasping her tighter, he shadowed her steps, holding her upright as she dragged her feet along the mess deck.

It was of no use.

He glanced around for any onlookers, hurled her into his arms, and carried her along the deck.

"Can I not leave you alone for a few hours?" he muttered.

She blinked, the motion slow and lazy. "Are you going to tie me up again, Alexander?"

He almost choked. The use of his first name in isolation caught him off guard. So too did the extent to which he liked it coming from her lips. He watched her face out of the corner of his eye. She batted her eyelashes, and her head bobbed with each step.

"I ought to if this is what you do when I'm not with you," he said. "You're not going to be farther than ten yards from me from now on."

"Lucky me," she murmured.

Alexander grumbled a curse under his breath. She was inebriated, had no idea what she was talking about, and she reeked of rum. That didn't stop his throat from tightening. He glanced down at her, and she did a long blink. It was the rum. Lots of rum. Nothing sparked between them, not on her part at least.

At the top of the stairs, he put her on her feet, keeping his hands on her hips while she regained her balance. She staggered forward, and he caught her again. A giddy grin lit her face as she looked at him. She covered her mouth with one hand, muffling a giggle.

He shook his head, sweeping her into his arms once more. "You're impossible."

She would have a hell of a bottle ache tomorrow. Served her right, too. What did she think she was doing, drinking with sailors? His men drank like fish. It had cost him a small fortune to resupply in Hull. Lucky he'd found her when he had, and no one else was out now except Sam.

Alexander stared pointedly ahead of him and avoided any temptation to glance up at the quarterdeck. He opened the door to her cabin with a relieved sigh and deposited her on her feet, pushing her inside. With his shoulder against the doorframe, he watched her stumble into the cabin. She looked around the space in a daze. He smirked, unable to stop himself from enjoying her inebriation just a little.

"Goodnight, Miss Harry." He stepped back, closing the door, but she wedged her foot in the way. She was agile when she wanted to be, even in this state.

"Thank you for rescuing me." The sweet accompanying smile seemed more like her than the rum.

"I would hardly call that a rescue," he said, letting the door swing open. "Although I doubt you would have made it all the way back without me. So, you're welcome."

She held his gaze, and her fingers glided up his arm, over his shoulder, reaching his collar. His muscles tensed, and he steadied himself.

"You're beautiful, you know," she whispered.

Alexander could have laughed if it weren't for the burning gleam in her eye. He knew that well, it was mirrored within him. That desire had not left him since she'd first fallen into his arms on the orlop deck, but he would never take advantage of a woman in this condition. Inebriated and kidnapped. His feelings for this woman were wrong. And her desire didn't mirror his in earnest. She was drunk.

Her fingertips trailed down his chest, over his shirt. He caught her hand before she reached his navel. Had she gone any further, he would have been powerless to stop her. His cock was already hard and aching. If she glanced down, he had no hope of hiding it. In her current state, he wasn't sure what she might do if she noticed. He stirred again at the thought and resented that his breeches exhibited more restraint than he did.

He moved his hands to her shoulders, keeping her at arm's length, and forced her back into the cabin. He kicked the door closed with his heel. "You need to rest. I'll wake you in the morning. Hopefully, that's enough time to sleep *this* off."

She took a step back, out of his grasp, and her coat dropped to the floor. Then she tugged her shirt from her breeches. "Can you help me with this?"

"Absolutely not." It took everything he had to refuse her request. He could not help her undress, of that he was emphatically certain. "Why do you need to take that off? You're the only woman on a ship full of sailors. Doesn't that mean anything to you?"

"I'm not planning to take a walk across the deck in my corset alone. It's so hot!"

No, he wouldn't do it. Admirable as his control had been thus far, it would not withstand such temptation. A man could only handle so much.

She stared at him with wide, innocent eyes. A mask of determination crossed her face.

He didn't budge.

"Fine," she grumbled, and she threw herself onto the bed. Her breathing fell into a soft rhythm.

He stared at her motionless figure. She was already asleep. That had been easier than he'd expected. He reached behind him for the door handle and took a step out of her cabin, keeping his eyes on her. The door closed with a soft click, and he spun around, lurching back against the timber.

"Christ!" he hissed.

Sam, less than two feet away, frowned. "You *are* quite skittish, aren't you?" His face broke into a grin, and his eyebrows waggled. "She's got you in a right spin. What were you doing in there, anyway? It can't have been much fun if it only took a minute."

"Don't you dare..." Alexander threatened.

"Oh?" Sam replied. The dark line of his eyebrows lifted further until they were almost hidden in his hair.

Alexander walked past him and opened the door to his cabin. "Get in here," he ordered, pushing Sam in by the shoulder. He slammed the door. "She's drunk."

"Really?" Sam's surprised expression was genuine. All the playfulness had disappeared from his face and voice.

"Judging by the state of her, she's done her best to keep up with them." He gave Shadow a quick pat, placating the dog from his excitement.

Sam looked thoughtful before he spoke. "You think she won't be up for duty tomorrow?"

"I don't think she'll be alive tomorrow. If she does manage to pull through, she'll be in no state to work. Can we leave her be?"

Sam shrugged. "We don't usually let anyone off for this sort of thing, but being the newest and youngest of the crew could be reason enough for compassion. They have obviously taken to her if they invited her for drinks."

"I thought the same," Alexander said, pacing the length of his cabin. "We'll stay in port for the night and cover for her tomorrow. One of us should make sure Jacob hasn't got himself into a similar state."

"I'll do that," Sam said. "How did you go? Any leads?"

Alexander stopped pacing and faced his friend. "Yes."

Sam crossed his arms over his chest. "I didn't think Rotterdam would prove a useful stop."

"Neither did I, but I'd say we're not far behind him."

"Harvey was still here recently?" Sam asked.

"He was, and if the weather stays good, we should catch up to him."

Sam's face was grim as he replied. "I don't like our chances. I think we'll hit a storm in the next few days."

Alexander groaned. "You know, Sam, I wish you wouldn't do that. Every time you make a prediction, it always follows through. I don't know if you're good at guessing, or if you make it happen by speaking it."

"We'll see," Sam replied with a shrug.

Harriet woke with a start. Yelled orders carried through the small half-open porthole. She rubbed her hand over her eyes and stared at the low beam that ran across the ceiling. What happened last night? Her last memory was leaving the mess deck and then...

No. She hadn't.

A wave of nausea rolled over her, and she jumped out of bed. With one hand clasped to her stomach and the other over her mouth, she dashed to the porthole. It wasn't large enough for her to poke her head through, but the fresh air was calming. She heaved in deep breaths, and the roiling sensation subsided.

Half of the dock was visible through the porthole, and she focused on what was happening down there. Alexander had returned last night, if her fragmented memory could be trusted. Why were they still in port? As if that thought had produced him from thin air, she spotted him striding along the dock toward the ship. She pulled back, waiting until he passed out of sight, and climbed back into bed.

A quiet knock sounded at her door, which sent Shadow into a frenzy in the captain's cabin next to hers. She ignored the sound, not ready to face anyone, but whoever it was seemed too impatient to wait for her response. The door opened a crack.

"I have some things for you, Miss Harry. Would you mind if I came in?" Alexander asked.

She stared at the door, unable to speak. Of course she minded. Living on a ship had not robbed her of a sense of propriety.

The door opened further, and Alexander edged into the cabin, closing the door behind him. He had a small parcel tucked under his arm.

She sat upright and shuffled to the edge of the bed, swinging her legs over the side. The action was too quick for her sluggish head to handle. She grabbed onto the bed sheets to keep from swaying.

Alexander took the bundle into his hands, and a grin stretched across his face for the briefest moment until his gaze landed on her. His eyes widened, and his jaw slackened.

She touched her fingers to her hair, then her face. Both seemed to be in place. Her hands dropped to the front of her shirt except her fingertips went straight to the fine material of her corset. She glanced down. Where the hell was her shirt? The sheets rustled as she scrambled to bring them across her chest. She spied her shirt on the floor, out of reach. She clutched the sheets closer and grappled for an explanation.

"I—"

"These are for you." His quick words cut her off, saving her from whatever excuse she'd been about to pluck out of thin air. He held the parcel out, his eyes raised to the ceiling. "I thought you might like clean clothes. There is more of a need for them than I first imagined." He chuckled, the sound nervous.

Harriet made to stand and reached for the bundle, but her stomach convulsed. She collapsed back onto the bed and buried her face in the sheets with a groan.

"You're not well," Alexander said. It wasn't a question, but she shook her head regardless. "You drank with the sailors last night."

"Too much," she admitted, her words muffled.

"Yes," he said. "We won't be sailing for a few more hours. It should be enough time for you to recover for duty."

She moaned. "I don't know if it will, Alexander."

His steps sounded across the floor, drawing nearer, and his fingertips stroked her bare shoulder. The pressure was so light against her skin, but the burning seeped into her bones. She leaned into his touch, and he didn't withdraw.

"You will be fine," he said, his voice close beside her. "Though I daresay you won't be drinking rum again any time soon?"

"Ugh." She swallowed. The thought of the sweet, spiced

liquid set her stomach off once more. "Don't say that word again. I can't bear to think of it."

"Good, that's the most reasonable thing I've heard you say since we met. Now, would a glass of raw egg help?" Mischief resonated in his tone.

She suppressed a shudder and buried her face in the pillow.

"No? Well, make sure to eat something this morning, or you will feel worse tonight. You're expected for duty as normal."

"That's it?" She raised her head. He was kneeling beside the bed, his face level with hers and much closer than she'd expected. She pulled back, and his hand fell away from her shoulder. It rested on the bed between them. She eyed it, but he didn't move. She met his gaze once more. "I'm not in trouble?"

"No. We've all been there." His eyes narrowed, and a smirk tugged at his lips. "Do you want to be in trouble?"

She gasped. "No!"

"I think you've learned your lesson. I'd be surprised if I heard about you drinking again. Besides, the crew only drink when we're in port, so you won't get another chance for a few days." He stood and fixed her with a pained expression on his face. "I will see you on the quarterdeck this afternoon." His voice had lost its cheerful tone and turned back into the stern captain she was beginning to know too well. "Do ensure you're dressed appropriately."

She scowled at his back as he left.

~

ALEXANDER SNAPPED the cabin door shut behind him. Of all

the possible situations he could have walked into, that was the least desirable.

Liar.

It was undoubtedly the last thing he had expected, but he couldn't deny the desirability. He closed his eyes and took a deep breath, leaning back against the wall. What was it about her that had him so undone? He hadn't even learned her name, not that he had made a sincere effort. Might she be more agreeable to his attempts to keep her safe if he treated her more like the woman she was, rather than a stowaway sailor?

He opened his eyes and pushed away from the wall. The ship was quiet as it sat waiting to sail. Most of the crew were still below deck, likely recovering from their own bottle aches. He shook his head. Trust them to go hard as soon as they arrived in port. Tradition or not, it had only been four days since they left Hull.

Jacob appeared from the stairs, a jug in hand. The boy might be young, but he had been one of the most valuable assets to this crew. And he was discreet.

Alexander dashed inside his cabin and grabbed the small bathing tub. He returned to Miss Harry's cabin and opened the door. A soft snore greeted him. Pushing the tub inside, the metal grated across the timber, but she didn't stir.

He greeted Jacob in hushed tones. "Put the water in the tub, and wake Harry when it's full. A kick to his foot should do it."

Jacob nodded and emptied the jug into the bath, steam rising from the water.

Alexander left him to his task and headed to the quarterdeck.

"Are we ready to sail, Captain?" Sam asked, standing at the helm.

"Yes, I think we will have a clear run through to Saint-Malo."

"Saint-Malo?" Sam asked, surprise obvious in his voice.

Alexander glanced at his friend. "Didn't I tell you last night?"

Sam rolled his eyes. "No," he huffed. "I detest Saint-Malo. It's full of pirates."

"What better place to find one?" Alexander grinned as Sam rolled his eyes again. "It will be fine."

"If you say so."

THEY HAD BEEN SAILING for a few hours before Miss Harry appeared. She seemed much improved and wore her new clothes.

Sam left the quarterdeck, mumbling about the galley. He'd likely witnessed enough of Alexander's overreactions when it came to Miss Harry and wanted to avoid this one. Alexander hadn't seen fit to tell Sam he'd try being kinder.

"How are you?" Alexander asked.

"I'm fine, Captain," Miss Harry replied without meeting his gaze.

"Not Alexander?" He rather liked that she had dropped the formalities earlier.

"Oh, I didn't mean..." she trailed off.

He frowned. No quick remark or fiery retort? It appeared her night had humbled her.

"Not at all," he said. "You call Sam by his first name. It is natural for you to do the same with me." Though the rest of the crew didn't.

"Thank you, Alexander." She fiddled with the collar of her shirt as she spoke, sliding a finger along the neckline.

He silently listed every curse word in his vocabulary and clenched his jaw. This wasn't going to be easy.

Her eyes were wide, and she chewed on her bottom lip, her finger still stroking the soft skin of her neck. "Is there anything you want me to do?" she asked.

Hell, there were a great many things he wanted her to do, and that he wanted to do to her. Taking her back to his cabin and removing that abomination of an outfit ranked highly on that list. He had been right about the fit of her clothes, much to his detriment. Whatever she'd been wearing before was perhaps a size too big. He'd somehow bought a shirt that clung to her figure, hugging all the right —or wrong—places. The trousers weren't much better. And he'd believed her last pair tight. He had been *very* wrong. How could his entire crew be so oblivious to there being a woman on board?

"Just..." He waved his hand at the taffrail behind him. It took an exceptional amount of effort to concentrate and form a coherent sentence. All he could think about was unbuttoning those too-tight-trousers, sliding them over her hips, and down her thighs. "Stand over there," he choked out. "I don't need anything right now."

"You want me to stand here?"

"Yes, please," he said through gritted teeth. "And be quiet for a moment." If the image of her naked body stayed in his head any longer, he might explode. And to make matters worse, her soft voice had filled his head with wicked thoughts. Though she stood some distance from him, he could imagine her lips at his ear, moaning and sighing her pleasure. He had to keep her behind him, where she wouldn't see the reaction his body had to her.

This treating her kindly was off to a dashing start.

Chapter Eleven

"Coming for another game tonight, 'Arry?" Jacob asked.

Harriet flinched. She'd stood so still, for so long, that when Alexander gave her leave to eat, her legs had been reluctant to move. She had walked to the mess deck in a daze and couldn't blame Jacob for sneaking up on her.

A third night socializing with the sailors was out of the question. But how could she get out of it?

"Harry still has work to do tonight, Jacob," Alexander said.

Her back stiffened, and she closed her eyes.

"Aye, Cap'n," Jacob replied. He returned to the other sailors.

"I'm curious," Alexander said, a playful hint in his tone. "Were you considering joining them again in earnest?"

She spun around. "I'd have said no, I can assure you."

Alexander leaned his shoulder against the wall, crossing one foot over the other. "Clever girl."

"What do you want?" she snapped.

"Ah, back to yourself, I see." He stared at her. "Do you remember much of last night?"

She groaned. "What did I do?" Her memories of the night before were vague at best, and she was having trouble identifying the point at which they had turned to dreams. Such delicious dreams.

Alexander laughed and strode across the deck, closing the space between them. "It wasn't so bad. Now, let's get some supper." He placed a hand on the small of her back.

She should have resisted his touch, pulled away or pushed him off her. Instead, she leaned into his warmth and let him steer her to the galley, her heartbeat fluttering.

The small space overflowed with sailors and a hush descended as they approached. Alexander's hand dropped from her back, and he vacated the space behind her. He stepped around her and filled his plate, unperturbed by the presence of his crew.

The sailors paid her little heed, returning to their conversations. She picked at the food, taking a small serving of meat and potatoes. They seemed least likely to inspire a stomach upset. She followed Alexander out of the galley and to the main deck. After such a long day, she was eager for the peace of her own cabin. Her hand was on the door handle, seconds away from reprieve when Alexander's voice pierced the air.

"Where do you think you're going?"

"My cabin," she replied, shooting him a quizzical glance.

He opened the door to his own cabin. "In here."

She balked, but the reaction wasn't borne from offense.

"Oh, please"—he rolled his eyes—"all we're going to do is play cards."

"Cards?" she asked, trying to ignore the way her chest deflated.

She chastised herself. He wasn't interested. Not in the

same way her body seemed to be interested in him. She shouldn't be surprised. Desirable and Harriet were not synonyms.

"Yes, cards," he said.

"Why?"

"Can you do as I ask without arguing?" He glanced around as he spoke, but they were alone on the deck. His bright eyes regarded her before he spoke again, more kindly this time. "I want to see for myself if you're as good as they say, or if it was beginner's luck."

"You truly want to play cards?"

"It is the social thing to do when off duty. Even the captain needs a way to pass the time. And though my crew respects me, they enjoy taking my money a little too much."

"Very well," she agreed, taking a few hesitant steps toward him. "Are we playing five queens?" She wouldn't stand a chance at beating the captain at his own ship's game.

"Ah, no." He frowned. "We'll play brag. Are you familiar with that one?"

"Well enough," she replied, unable to keep the excitement from her voice. Making a swift recovery from her disappointment, curiosity filled her. Would he want to place bets?

He regarded her through narrowed eyes but remained silent.

She stepped past him and into his cabin. Shadow launched himself at her, his paws landing on her thighs, almost knocking the plate from her hands. Alexander snagged the plate, and she wrangled Shadow to the floor. The dog tried to lick her cheek, and she turned her head out of his reach. She caught sight of Alexander's unimpressed face as he walked to the table and set the plates down.

"Shadow!" She laughed. "Stop it."

"Shadow, down," Alexander's voice was firm. He lounged in a chair with his feet resting on the table, ankles crossed. He threw a piece of meat to the floor, drawing Shadow's attention.

"He's so sweet," she said, joining Alexander at the table.

"Mm-hmm," he agreed, his gaze still on Shadow. "And apparently more loyal to you." He gestured to the food without looking at her. "Eat."

Harriet took a small nibble, testing the agreeableness of the food. Her stomach rumbled. She shouldn't have been so conservative with her portions.

Alexander's plate scraped across the table, and she glanced up. He watched her, his gaze intense.

"Take what you want," he said. "I'd wager I've eaten more than you have today." He smiled and brought his feet back down to the floor. "Eat. I want to see your card skills in action."

She finished both plates, and Alexander dealt the cards.

Minutes later, Harriet threw down her hand and grinned.

Alexander cursed. "Where did you learn to play like that?"

She shrugged. The gesture was meant to be nonchalant, but she couldn't keep the smug smirk from her face. "Picked things up here and there. It's not important." From her sister, Millie, and Alexander didn't need to know that.

"That's debatable," he grumbled. "Now, it's your deal. It will take more than one round to prove you're better than beginner's luck."

She took the deck of cards from his outstretched palm, and he leaned back in his chair. They'd reached a mutual camaraderie since they'd started playing, and she enjoyed seeing him relax. It was a new side to the captain he hadn't shown before. His gaze didn't leave her as she shuffled the cards, and a slight frown creased his brow.

"What?" she asked.

He shrugged. "It's nothing."

She slapped the cards down on the table and kept her hand over them. "What is it?"

"I can't work out who you are, Miss Harry." His frown deepened, and he tilted his head to the side. She fought hard to return his intense stare and resist the way it fizzled to her toes.

"Nothing is too much for you," he said. "You have dealt with a great deal since you walked onto this ship. More than you expected, but you just get on with it. I'm trying to figure out what kind of woman can do that." He'd moved closer as he spoke, leaning over the table, and his chest hovered above her hand. "There's a fire inside you to be sure, and that helped you get through. You've done better than I'd expect of any greenhand." He shook his head and leaned away.

Her breath came in shaky gasps, and she pulled back too. Those were the first encouraging words he'd said since she'd boarded the *Seren*, and she hadn't the faintest idea how to take the compliment.

"Now." He chuckled, eyeing the deck of cards beneath her palm. "Back to the game."

She finished the deal and picked up her cards, peeking at Alexander over the top of them. He lifted the corner of his cards, looking first at them, and then back to her.

"Shall we raise the stakes this round?" he asked.

"You know I don't have any money." She would not acknowledge the two miserable shillings she had to her name, still hidden in the folds of her corset.

"Not money," he said with a shake of his head.

Her heartbeat soared to an uncomfortable rate. What would he ask of her?

"If I win"—he regarded her with a gleam in his eye—"you tell me your name."

So that was his game?

She looked back at her cards, fighting the disappointment that settled in her chest. He wouldn't ask for something as brash as a kiss. And why should he? She studied her cards. She could win this round without bluffing her way through it.

"And if I win?" she asked.

"You can name your terms."

She considered him for a moment. What did she want from this man? If she was being honest, she wanted him to kiss her. Her return to England now, if she made it home, would be marred by rumor and gossip. Her marriage prospects, nonexistent. Alexander might be her one chance to experience a kiss, but she wasn't that bold. And his inevitable rejection would sting.

Instead, she said, "I want you to teach me more about sailing."

His brows furrowed. "Why?"

Her answer had surprised him, and she liked that. "I find it fascinating, and I want to learn more while I'm here. Not that untangling rope or standing beside you in silence hasn't been riveting."

"All right," he agreed, picking up his cards. "Next watch I'll teach you more about sailing. *If* you win."

She beamed.

Discarding one card was all she needed, and she had the winning hand. Harriet met Alexander's eye with a sweet smile, and his frown deepened. She laid her cards between them. He grumbled something that resembled another curse and glared at the cards, but then his face broke into a wide grin, and he laid his cards on the table.

"Damn!" she hissed.

He rubbed his hands together, his eyes shining. "I think this is the part where you tell me your name."

"Why are you so desperate to know?"

"That's not part of the bargain, but since you asked so nicely"—he raised an eyebrow when she opened her mouth to speak—"I'd prefer to stop calling you Harry."

She cursed the warm sensation flooding her cheeks. "My name is Harriet."

"Harriet who?"

"I can't tell you," she said, staring at the cards between them. She couldn't risk her family's reputation or their safety.

"We had a bet!"

"Yes, you wanted to know my name, and I gave it to you. It was you who failed to stipulate the terms."

This time, his grumble was more coherent, but she ignored his cursing. She was sure she would be punished for that little maneuver, but she waited for him to break the silence.

At last, he spoke, his words subdued. "It's almost time for watch. Take some time in your cabin before duty."

THE MOON GLOWED as Alexander took up watch. Harriet arrived on the quarterdeck soon after, illuminated by silver radiance. Everything that had the potential to tighten at the sight of her, did, from his throat, all the way to the tips of his toes.

"Harriet," he said, his voice a quiet murmur in the wind.

"Captain Alexander," she responded with a dip of her head in his direction.

"Back to the formalities again?" he asked.

"I—"

"If I am to call you by your given name, you may continue to call me Alexander, if you wish." His tone sounded pleasant enough to him. Hopefully, she thought the same.

"You're not angry with me?"

"I'm not particularly happy, but I'm sure I'll survive. Next time I wager against you, you can be sure I will stipulate the terms."

Her lips twitched.

"I do believe knowing your family would make things easier when I return you to England."

"And when might that be?" she asked.

Alexander wished he could give her an answer. All he had was the truth. "I don't know."

"I can handle myself on our return."

She believed that and that was the problem. Whatever she had been running from in Hull would be waiting upon her return. Not to mention they would arrive hundreds of miles away. If he were to trust his sense of foreboding, which had been reliable thus far, his challenges would not end when they sailed up the Thames.

The incessant flapping of the sail drew his eyes upward, and a dark, starless patch of sky in the distance caught his attention. He frowned. Curse Sam and his predictions. They would be in the middle of a storm by daybreak, if not sooner.

Alexander yanked the halyard and tied it off, securing the sail. He couldn't take his eyes from Harriet. The way her gaze held him unsettled him to his core. She closed the space between them, a tender smile on her face. He followed her gaze down to his hands where a tangle of rope sat stupidly, nothing close to the knot he thought he'd tied.

She crouched beside him, taking the rope from his hands. "There you go." She met his eye, and her voice faltered. "That is what you wanted, isn't it?"

"What?" He shook his head and glanced at the knot without seeing it. "Oh, yes. Thank you."

She watched him through her eyelashes, still smiling. It was a genuine expression, no hint of teasing behind it, and his clumsy and incoherent self had put it there. To see her smile that way every day would be a true delight. That snapped him back to reality in a heartbeat.

He jumped to his feet and backed away, holding up his hands. "Don't do that!"

"Do what?" she asked, coming to her feet.

"Look at me that way."

Her brow creased. "I didn't look at you in any way."

He grabbed her elbow, keeping his grip as loose as he could manage. "I swear, I'll—"

"You'll what?" she snapped. "Throw me overboard?" One eyebrow lifted, and she scoffed. "Do you know how many times you've threatened me with that?" Her chin tilted upward, and those deep green eyes darkened, reflecting the stars above. "Go on then, do it. Rid yourself of me and all the problems I have supposedly burdened you with."

Her head twisted toward the main deck. Did she expect a witness to their encounter? The few sailors on duty were scarce and focused enough not to care what the captain was doing at the helm. Besides, her voice wouldn't travel over the wind in the sails.

Alexander steered her back to face him. "No," he said, his tone dark and measured. "I won't throw you overboard. I'll kiss you."

Her lips pursed, and her frown deepened. "You wouldn't."

His eyes narrowed. "Are you testing me?" He couldn't be alone in feeling the sparks between them. The air practically quivered whenever she was near.

"N-no. I simply don't see why you would want to kiss me?"

She could not be so daft.

He drew a deep breath. Keeping the truth from her would not serve either of them any longer. "I have wanted nothing else since I first laid eyes on you," he said. "While it was your beauty that first drew me, you are the most remarkable woman I have ever met. You are skillful and courageous, and it is irresistible."

She blinked, speechless for once.

He loosened his grasp on her elbow and dropped his hand to his side, giving her a chance to escape and opening himself to further torment. "When I kept you here, I swore I would do everything in my power to protect you and see you home safely. You are already here against your will, and for that I truly am sorry. I cannot deny it has been torture at times, keeping myself away from you."

She stepped closer, her shoulders squared. "You're lying."

"I swear to you, that is the truth. My behavior since I found you on the orlop deck leaves much to be desired." He kept his eyes locked on hers. "I cannot earn your trust with such questionable foundations and unsatisfactory treatment of you."

"I trust you, Alexander. Do not ask me to explain, but I do."

"Then why don't you believe that I want to kiss you?"

She looked at him as though he'd asked her to describe the color of an orange. "You could not wish to kiss me," she whispered. "A man like you would not ordinarily see a woman like me and want to kiss her, I can assure you."

Had a man looked at Harriet and not wanted to kiss her? The possibility was beyond reckoning. One look at Harriet had him wanting to—well, he wanted to do more than kiss her.

"I don't know what delusions you have about yourself or how they came to be," he said. "They are wrong. Do you recall, last night, you asked for my assistance to undress?" It was difficult to ignore the flush of color that crept up her neck. Had it spread over her breasts as well? He cleared his throat. "I am a gentleman. You were drunk, and that made it easy to leave, but there is a limit to what I can handle. I have reached that limit. I cannot tolerate to be near you when I desire you so."

She glanced down at the space between them and back at him. Thick lashes partially obscured her dark green eyes. Her bottom lip was pinched between her teeth. Alexander wanted to draw that lip into his mouth and taste her.

"You still don't believe me, do you?"

She shook her head.

"Fine." He grabbed her arms and swung her about, so her back was against the mast. The three feet of timber provided enough protection from any eyes that might glance up at the quarterdeck in the next few moments.

He lifted his hand to her temple and caressed the side of her face with his fingertips. Her eyes closed and she sighed, her breath whispering over his lips. He traced down the soft curve of her neck and along the edge of her collarbone exposed through her shirt. His lips brushed over hers, and she sucked in a breath.

"Do you believe me now?" he murmured.

~

HARRIET SHOULD HAVE STOPPED HIM, but she couldn't deny how much she wanted this. His body pinned her against the mast, his hard against her soft, each touch awakening something deep inside her, and she ached for more. She lifted her chin, allowing him access to her neck. His fingertips left a burning line that he traced with his lips and tongue. She wrapped her hands around his arms, and his muscles, warm and strong beneath the linen shirt, tensed beneath her fingertips.

He pushed her harder against the mast, and the heat of his body ran along hers. His hands were strong on her hips, fingertips digging into her flesh. She pressed herself against him, leaning into the place where her desire met his. His lips brushed over hers, and another sigh escaped her, but he pulled away. She opened her eyes, searching his.

"Tell me to stop," he said, his voice husky. "Otherwise, I can't."

"Please," she whispered. His head tilted to the side, and she fought against his impossible strength to pull him close again. "Don't stop—" Her words were cut off by his mouth hard on hers. Her hands flew to the back of his neck, and she wove her fingers into his hair. His tongue rolled along her bottom lip, and she opened her mouth to him. He tasted of ginger, and the spice tickled her tongue. She matched his kiss with a passion she hadn't known she possessed.

He tugged her shirt out of her breeches, and his hands slid up the corset still wrapped around her waist. She wished she could have done away with it when she bathed. He cupped her breasts with a light squeeze, and her back arched away from the mast. Each response to his touch was involuntary. Instinctive. She needed it, *needed him*.

He reached under the edge of her loosened corset and caught her nipple between his thumb and forefinger, rolling it gently. The exquisite sensation swirled through her body, and her thighs quivered. She moaned into his mouth, and any remaining objections slipped away.

He jerked away. "I'm so sorry, Miss—"

"Hazelby," she breathed. She clapped one hand over her mouth a moment too late.

"Hazelby," he whispered. His brows furrowed, and his head cocked to the side. "Hazelby?" A wall of cold air slid between them as he dropped his arms and stumbled backward. "No," he whispered, shaking his head. "No. No."

Before he could speak again, she ran down the stairs.

Chapter Twelve

ALEXANDER STARED at the mast where Harriet's face had been, not paying attention to the grain of the timber or the rope twisting around it. Seconds ticked by, slipping away into minutes, but he couldn't move. She wasn't the daughter of Lord Hazelby. She couldn't be. There was no reasonable explanation for such a woman to be on the docks in Hull, disguised as a boy. And the earl's country residence was in Selby, not Hull.

Alexander combed through every detail and interaction. Harriet was good at sailing, confident, and had a worldly quality about her. Daughters of earls did not come like that. And the likelihood of her being sent onto his ship and running into *him*... What were the chances of that happening? Improbable, if not impossible.

No matter how hard he tried to deny it, it must be the truth. She didn't know who he was but had kept her name fiercely concealed. If anything, her reaction to the slip had only reinforced the fact. Miss Harry, the insubordinate, vexatious, and confounding stowaway, *was* Harriet Hazelby.

He tore his eyes from the mast and paced around the helm, his boots thundering on the timber deck.

Harriet Hazelby...

He groaned.

He had kissed her! *Oh*, he had done worse than that. He'd kidnapped her. A gentlewoman, the daughter of an earl, the youngest sister of a duchess, kidnapped and taken hostage on a voyage to find a known pirate. Finding Harvey dropped several points down Alexander's priorities list, his own wellbeing be damned. He needed to get Harriet home, soon, and in one healthy piece. But if they returned without Harvey, she would be in an even more precarious situation. He couldn't help her when he was hanged for murder. There wouldn't be an opportunity for explanations or excuses.

Alexander kicked the platform of the ship's wheel.

Of all the people in all the world, why did it have to be her?

"What have you done to the poor girl this time?" Sam's voice came from the stairs behind him. "Did you send her off to work on the orlop deck again?"

Alexander turned. "No, she ran off. And there is nothing *poor* about that woman." His anger flared, and he did nothing to hide it. Though it had little to do with the fact that he'd kissed her, and more to do with Sam calling her a girl. Harriet Hazelby was not a girl. She was a woman. A *very* desirable woman, and an innocent one.

"What happened?" Sam asked.

"I kissed her," he said, his blood turning to ice and sending a chill through his body. He'd kissed her and *enjoyed* it. He should never have touched her.

Sam beamed, mischief glinting in his eyes. "Well, that *is* interesting."

"That's not even the half of it."

"How hard did you kiss her?" Sam's tone was curious, if not a little concerned.

Alexander groaned at the suggestive image that sprung into his mind, but he pushed it away. He could not think of Harriet that way. Not her hair tangled around his fingers, not the taste of her tongue, or her moans of pleasure when he buried himself in her. Not the sweet minty freshness of her soap that still lingered despite her bath.

He froze. That damned soap. No wonder the scent was familiar. His cursed brother made the stuff for the three Hazelby sisters using plants Alexander had brought from Singapore.

He cleared his throat. "I kissed her hard enough to stun her into telling me her name."

Sam raised his eyebrows, smirking. "Well, who is she?"

"She would be one Harriet Hazelby."

Sam's eyes widened, the smile wiped from his face in an instant. "One of Lord Hazelby's daughters? The *Earl of Selby*, Hazelby?"

"I believe so," Alexander said. "His youngest daughter, if memory serves me correctly."

Sam frowned and then burst into an outrageous fit of laughter.

"This isn't funny," Alexander snapped.

"The earl is going to kill you." Sam forced the words out between his laughs, which stopped with a gasp.

"What?"

"Her sister is Eliza Malstern. The Duchess of Eldon."

Alexander was already aware of the implications. This wasn't news.

"Your brother is going to kill you!" Sam's laughter resumed at full force.

Alexander's breath rushed through his clenched teeth. "And I am going to kill *you* if you don't stop it."

Sam merely looked at him. His laughter died away, but his eyes were still dancing. He tilted his head, and his brows drew together. "Do you hear that?"

Alexander strained his ears. Except for the wind, and the occasional sailor calling across the deck, there was nothing. "I don't hear anything amiss."

"No," Sam drawled, "I can definitely hear something." The smirk had not left his face, and Alexander was close to wiping it off.

"What are you about, Sam?" Alexander grumbled, knowing that he didn't want to hear the answer.

"That's it!" Sam said, slapping a hand to his forehead. "Wedding bells!"

Alexander's face dropped, and his stomach seemed to think his boots were a more appropriate location to reside. "What?" he breathed.

"Well, I suppose congratulations are in order, now that you'll be marrying her on our return." Sam clapped him on the back. "And, yes, I'll be your groomsman." His grin widened, delight clear on his face. "It's a good thing you're in love with her."

"I," Alexander started, but he hadn't a clue which point to argue first. That was a hell of a lot of information for a man to receive in as many sentences. He fixed his gaze on Sam and tried to organize his thoughts. "I'm not in love with her?"

Sam's eyebrows crept upward. "Then why did you say that like it was a question?"

"She's the most irritating woman I have ever met." Not to mention that he'd sworn to protect her and had failed miserably. He'd known the woman for less than a week and hadn't been able to keep her safe in that short time. Besides, he couldn't offer Harriet the life she deserved.

"And yet, you kissed her," Sam said.

"That doesn't mean I'm in love with her," Alexander protested. Love didn't exist in this world. Or if it did, it only led to pain. His thoughts turned to his mother, and then to the unfortunate situation Harriet's older sister experienced in her marriage. Did Harriet know about that? Is that why she had run away? To escape such a future for herself? Alexander couldn't blame her. He'd been running since he was fourteen.

"What are you then, Alexander?"

"I..." he started. What did he feel? Lust? Undeniably. And he was intrigued, definitely. But it wasn't love. Was it? "Not that!" he protested. Although if love was pain, perhaps the sentiment had merit.

"We'll see," Sam muttered.

Alexander ignored him. There were more important matters at hand. "We need to take her off all duties. A woman like her should not be on a ship, and I'll be a dead man if anyone finds out I made her work or, heaven forbid, she hurts herself."

Sam's expression sobered. "We'll work it out."

Alexander sighed, the weight of the situation settling on him. "I don't know what I'm going to do, but I'll get her home safely and deal with the rest once this mess with Harvey is cleared up. I hope he's in Saint-Malo. The sooner we get home, the better. I don't fancy chasing him halfway around the world with her in tow."

"No," Sam murmured, "that would be less than ideal."

"What if we can't find him?" Desperation leeched into his voice.

"We will," Sam reassured him solemnly.

Alexander looked back at his friend, and all he could do was hope Sam was right.

"Doesn't anything worry you?"

Sam's shoulders lifted. "Not really."

Alexander huffed. "Why are you up here? You're not on duty for another few hours."

"I can never sleep the first night after a stop at port. I should know better than to spend a full night in bed, but the temptation is too strong. I'll stay for this watch."

"There is no need," Alexander said, his words curt.

"I'll be up anyway," Sam insisted. "I'm not tired."

"Well, if you're going to be here annoying me, I might find a better use for my time elsewhere."

Sam's smirk returned. "Perhaps take care not to get caught kissing the cabin boy, eh?"

Alexander shook his head and mumbled a profanity.

"Care to say that to my face?" Sam asked.

"You heard me," Alexander called as he walked away, unsure where he was headed.

ALEXANDER RAISED his hand to Harriet's cabin door again, and his knuckles hovered in mid-air. He'd walked the length of the *Seren* twelve times and still wasn't resolved on his course of action. He summoned a steadying breath through his nose and knocked. The immediate answer was Shadow's loud bark and then the scraping of his nails on the door. It shouldn't have surprised him, but if she wanted to hide herself away, it had been a mistake to take Shadow. The barking subsided, but the door remained closed.

Alexander reached for the handle. "Harriet," he said in a low murmur, "I know you're in there. Open the door." He jiggled the handle to no avail, sending Shadow into another round of barking. A spare key was in his cabin, but forcing his way in would not help his case, especially if he wanted her to comply with his next orders. That awareness did not stop the frustration from prickling under his skin. He couldn't stand here much longer without drawing attention to himself. He was almost ready to abandon his attempt to speak with her, and return later, but the lock clicked.

The door opened a crack, and a sliver of her face appeared.

"Is there something you need me to do, sir?" Her eyes were cast downward, her tone polite and reserved. He didn't like it one bit.

"You may allow me into your cabin," he said. "And stop calling me sir." It was impossible to gauge her reaction to his gruff order through the narrow opening of the door.

"No, Alexander." She lacked the conviction she had previously displayed.

"I need to speak with you for a moment." He glanced behind him at the few sailors on duty. "In private."

She looked past him out to the deck, sighed, and stepped back. The door swung open. He side-stepped between her and the door and was greeted by an enthusiastic Shadow. He reached down and patted the dog. The door closed behind him, shutting out the sounds from outside.

"What is it?" Harriet asked.

He straightened and faced her, taking in her proud figure with her arms crossed over her chest. A lamp in the corner cast a golden glow over the room and her. He raked his gaze down her body, lingering on the places he had been flush with her.

Shadow's nails clipped across the timber floor as he trotted toward her bed.

Alexander cleared his throat, forcing his gaze back to her face. "You cannot work on the ship any longer."

"Excuse me?" Her reply was indignant, expected, and more like Harriet than those last few subdued sentences.

"Do you expect me to allow Lord Hazelby's youngest daughter to be a ship hand?"

Her brow creased. "Why do you care what I do whilst I'm here?"

Alexander coaxed a slow, deep breath into his lungs. He settled on the closest version of the truth. "I'm not sure it has occurred to you, but you have put me in a difficult position for our return. I'd like to make sure you arrive home unharmed."

"The position I have put *you* in?" She bristled, and her wide eyes demanded an explanation. "I didn't ask to be here, or to be placed under the near-constant guard you keep over me."

"That has proven to be very well-advised," he said.

She continued as if he hadn't spoken. "I suppose you believe tying me to the mast was prudent as well?"

He stepped closer. What he wouldn't give to have been able to escort her home that morning on the dock instead of keeping her here.

His angry tone matched hers in ferocity, but he was only irritated with himself. "Tying you to the mast was a desperate attempt to keep you safe."

Her eyes rolled. "Well, which is it, Alexander? Was I in danger in Hull or am I in danger now? I cannot be both."

He groaned. She could be both. Just as she could be vexing and desirable, whilst holding every ounce of his rapt attention.

"And how do you know I'm his youngest daughter?" she asked.

The abrupt change of subject pivoted his anger to confusion. "What?"

"You said the youngest daughter of Lord Hazelby couldn't work on a ship. A man of your *wit*"—he did not care for the emphasis she put on the word—"could deduce I am one of his daughters, but you so astutely noted that I am the youngest. I'm sure he is not so popular to be known outside of London, especially not the details of his daughter, who has yet to come out in society. Do you know my father?"

"No," he answered with the truth. "I do not know your father." He hadn't met the earl, but he knew of him, and more about her family than he could say. Now was not the time to expose those connections.

The look with which she pierced him was severe, but so contrary to her features, he had the most unusual urge to laugh. Her face twisted into a scowl, and he realized too late that he hadn't muffled the sound.

She huffed. "Never in my life have I met someone so, so..." Her gaze darted around the cabin, as though she expected to find the perfect word hidden in the timber's grain. "So supremely irritating."

He laughed, a deep, throaty sound. "Supremely irritating? I'm certain I have never been described as such."

"Well, that is a surprise," she said, her voice thick with sarcasm.

"Would you like me to tell you what delightful adjectives come to mind when I think of you?" he asked. Remarkable, clever, stunning. The list went on.

"I suspect you would say something similar," she said.

"You have not concealed your contempt for my being here despite only having yourself to blame."

"Indeed, you have been the pinnacle of irritation and without doubt the most insubordinate person ever to set foot on my ship. You have lied—"

"I didn't—"

"I have not finished," he said, lifting an eyebrow. It was so much easier to ignore his feelings when she argued. What was difficult to ignore was the flush of pink that peeked out from between her breasts and crept up her neck. He tore his eyes away and met her gaze once more.

Her lips pressed into a thin line.

He continued with his list, feeling like a fool the more he spoke. "You did not tell me your name when I asked, nor did you explain what you were doing on my ship dressed as a boy. You didn't give me a good enough reason to get you home while I still had the chance. And since your stubborn appearance in front of the crew, forcing my hand to put you to work, you have challenged me at every opportunity. It is infuriating, and I'll tell you what else is infuriating." He looked her straight in the eye, and his stomach knotted. "I wanted nothing more than to keep protecting you. Stopping you from returning to that man on the dock seemed so simple at the time." He fixed her with a desperate stare. "But now I know who you are, and I know I have failed spectacularly, albeit in ways I could never have anticipated."

"I don't understand," she said, frowning.

He sighed. "The one thing I can't protect you from is myself. I tried to stay away from you, to keep my distance, but I cannot. I am drawn to you in a manner I can't begin to comprehend or attempt to explain." His voice dropped to a whisper, and he stepped closer. "Every single thing about you intrigues me, and I want to know more. What you think, what you feel, *how* you feel. I want to touch you, your face, your body. I *want* you." He finished his declaration in a low growl. He had no right to feel this way. Not for Harriet Hazelby. Sam was right. His brother would kill him. And Alexander deserved everything coming his way.

An unreadable expression crossed her face, and she lunged at him. He wrapped his arms around her and stumbled backward but couldn't stop them from crashing to the floor. The impact knocked the air from his lungs, and he landed with Harriet lying on his chest. Whether she had intended to hit him that hard or simply underestimated the force with which she attacked him, he wasn't sure. He squeezed his eyes closed as he caught his breath and braced for the moment her fists made contact. But it wasn't her fist that collided with his mouth. He recognized the soft fullness of her lips the instant they pressed against his. With his back flat on the floor, he could not maneuver away, not that he would have made an earnest attempt.

Her fingers slid around his jaw and massaged the back of his neck as she kissed him. With his free hand, he copied her movements, twisting his fingers into her hair. The weight of her upper body pressed onto his chest, keeping him still and at the mercy of her movements. Their breathing synchronized in short, sharp gasps. He parted her lips with his tongue, but before he could explore her further, her tongue invaded his mouth. He groaned and pulled her against him.

The heat of their first kiss was a mere echo of the fire that engulfed him now. He moved his hands under her shirt and slid them up her back, over the ribbons of her corset. Soon, he would not possess the ability to stop this, but he had already relinquished control.

She withdrew and placed the softest of kisses along his jaw and down his neck.

"Harriet," he moaned. He was hers in that moment, and for many more moments to come. To hell with his promises.

Her lips left his skin, and he could feel her watching him. He opened his eyes and stared into the glittering emeralds set above her shy smile. Groaning, he clenched his teeth.

"Sorry," she said, breathless.

He let his head thud to the floor. "Never apologize for kissing me."

"Sorry."

With every ounce of control he possessed, and with his hands on her hips, he pushed her off him and far enough away so he could sit up. He brought his knees to his chest and wrapped his arms loosely around them.

"I must go," he said, "but I, er, need a moment."

"Can I help with anything?"

He fixed her with a stern glare, but she could have no idea what her question implied. Her mind wouldn't have gone to his breeches and what she could do inside them. It was hard to reconcile this innocent woman with the stubborn stowaway he'd found on the orlop deck. He shook his head and chuckled.

"What?" she asked, indignation coloring her voice.

His laugh had annoyed her, he hadn't meant for it to. "It's nothing," he said, "but you can't kiss a man like that and expect him to get on with his day posthaste." He stood. "I don't want to see you out for duty again."

"Please," she begged.

He leaned against the small table and regarded her. "Is that why you kissed me?"

"No," she said. Her cheeks colored. She was a terrible liar.

"I thought you were going to hit me."

She studied him, and his skin heated under her gaze. "I hadn't decided until I was on top of you." Her cheeks flushed a delightful shade of pink, and he would have done anything to keep it there.

"Very well," he agreed. "But no more night watch. No one will notice you missing, and you can get a proper night's sleep. I will see you in the morning."

Damn, she could have him eating out of her hand if she wished.

Chapter Thirteen

A VIOLENT LURCH of her stomach jolted Harriet awake, and she pressed her hand to her mouth. A bead of sweat rolled down her temple, and her abdomen clenched. The sensation passed as quickly as it had come, and she opened her eyes. Dim gray morning light filtered into the cabin and raindrops splattered across the porthole, obscuring her view of the horizon. A sheen of sweat covered her body.

She frowned. Something was wrong, but she couldn't pinpoint it. She squinted past the raindrops as the horizon came back into view at the bottom of the porthole. It kept rising until it passed out of sight again, and she was staring straight down at the churning gray sea. Her stomach flipped, and she squeezed her eyes closed. The wind and waves roared.

Lying still for several minutes, she waited for the moment the ship overturned and sent them deep into the ocean, but it didn't happen. Instead, the bow of the ship tilted upward, and they floated on the crest of a wave accompanied by a peaceful pause in motion. Then, the bow lurched forward and rode the wave at speed. She held her breath, but they darted back up and the cycle began again.

If she focused on the movements and kept her gaze away from the horizon, she could tolerate the corresponding upset in her belly. Whether she could move was another question. The effect of the motion wouldn't be half as bad if she could make it out the door into the fresh air. A rail lined a section of the deck within ten paces of her cabin. If she could make it there, she could ride the waves outside and put an end to the stomach cramps and nausea. But what if she missed? She'd be thrown into the sea.

Deciding on the best moment to leave her cabin proved difficult. Those few seconds when the ship reached the crest of a wave were the calmest, but the steep plunge that followed was not a desirable time to be moving about the open deck.

The ship rode another seven waves before her determination to move was strong enough to act. She sat on the edge of the bed, porthole behind her, and waited. Handfuls of bed sheets crinkled beneath her stiff knuckles. She coaxed a deep breath through her nose and released it through clenched teeth. The instant the bow reached the crest, she dashed across the cabin and grasped the door handle, holding on tight as the ship descended again. The bow darted upward, and she threw open the door, rushing out onto the deck. Her hands twisted around the rail as the ship tipped forward. Rain sprinkled on her face, but she didn't care. She'd made it.

There was a moment of calm, and she watched the next wave approach the bow. In the chaos of the storm, an eerie stillness settled over the ship. Anything loose had been tied down or removed from the main deck. The ship, its cargo, and the crew moved as one piece through the tumultuous waves of a wild sea.

Five sailors lined the port side, hugging the taffrail. Another four leaned out over the starboard side. She mustn't be the only one unable to tolerate the motion, but it hadn't occurred to her that sailors would get seasick.

For the first time since she'd made her brave dash onto the deck, Harriet glanced at the helm. Alexander stood tall at the ship's wheel with his hands wrapped around the handles. His sleeves were rolled up, and he worked to keep the ship true to course. A deep frown set his brow and his jaw was tight.

Sam stood not far behind Alexander, his face bearing no hint of the same concern or concentration. The waves crashing around them and the wind whipping in her ears made it impossible to hear what Sam said, but Alexander twisted his head back and joined in with Sam's laughter.

ALEXANDER RETURNED his attention to the bow, glimpsing Harriet. The laughter left him, replaced with an all-encompassing terror. Harriet stared back at him, her face matching his dread with a disagreeable grayness to her complexion. She grasped the rail as though her life depended on it. Why had she left her cabin?

They'd sailed into rough seas earlier that morning, a combination of leaving the English Channel and meeting the storm Sam had predicted. It had been enough to wake Alexander, but it wasn't too serious. He'd joined Sam half an hour ago, and they had been enjoying the challenge of navigating the waves. He hadn't expected to see Harriet until it settled.

Alexander recalled the first time he had sailed into a storm in his inexperienced youth. He'd feared they would capsize. Most ships gave that impression in rough seas. It must feel much worse to her than it was. Still, he didn't want her out on the deck.

Go back to your cabin, he mouthed.

She stared back, her expression blank.

Sam reached across the ship's wheel and shoved him out of the way, taking control.

Alexander rushed to Harriet, the sway of the ship rocking him from side to side as he ran down the stairs and across the deck. He could appreciate why so many of the crew had succumbed to seasickness this time. He might have too if he wasn't so accustomed to it.

Alexander reached her, taking hold of the rail she clung to. He had to yell over the noise of the sea and gale. "Get back to your cabin. It's too rough out here!"

Her eyes widened. "Please don't make me go back in there."

"Harriet, you can't stay out here. If we hit a wave the wrong way or you lose your grip... there's nothing I can do to get you back. Please go inside." He tried to pry her fingers from the rail. Perhaps she was strong enough to hold on despite everything the ship did to cast her off, but he couldn't risk it. "Harriet, let go!"

"No!" she cried.

"Why not?"

"I can't stand it. The movement. The confined space. It's suffocating and churning my stomach. I need air." She was seasick, too, but not as severely as the others. He could help with that.

"Fine. Go below, to the orlop deck, and lie down in the middle of the ship," he said.

She didn't move.

"Do I need to carry you there?"

Her body convulsed.

"Then get yourself down there now." He pried her hands off the rail and kept a tight hold on her, waiting for the right moment to let go. The ship reached its brief pause, and he pushed her toward the stairs. She disappeared down them. The wait for the next pause seemed to last minutes rather than seconds, but it came, and he dashed down the stairs behind her.

A quiet groan greeted him on the orlop deck.

"Harriet, where are you?"

"Over here." Her response came from a place to his left, and he squinted into the darkness. In his haste to follow her, he hadn't lit a lamp.

"I'm not moving," she said.

He chuckled, relief washing over him. "In that case, I'll need a light. I'll be right back." He raced back up the stairs and returned to the orlop deck, fixing a lamp into a dusty bracket.

Harriet lay motionless not far from where he stood. The orange flame cast his shadow onto the wall, and he made his way to her. The deck was much easier to navigate now. She had untangled most of the ropes and had them coiled in neat circles.

"How do you feel?" he asked.

"As though I might be dying." Her voice cracked, emphasizing her statement.

Alexander pressed his lips together, fighting back a laugh. "I don't think that's the case."

"You don't know that."

"I'm fairly certain. Do you feel better down here?" She should. The lowest deck in the middle of the ship was the least affected by motion. His own stomach had settled significantly since descending the stairs.

"Marginally," she grumbled.

"Have you suffered seasickness before?" he asked.

Even in the dim light, the strain in her jaw when she clenched her teeth was obvious.

"Oh, yes, every time I sail."

"In fact," he kept his voice smooth despite wanting to laugh, "this is your first voyage, and you appear to be seasick. One might argue you *have* been seasick every time you sail." He grinned, but she'd covered her face with her arms. So, she was well enough to emanate sarcasm, but not in the mood to take it. Perfectly Harriet. He changed tack. "Do you get sick with any other motion?"

"Not like this," she replied. "At times I'm ill in a carriage, but it's bearable."

"It has been rather smooth since we left Hull. We came around the tip of France this morning and are in more open waters now. There's a storm encroaching on us that's making it a little worse."

Harriet sighed.

"Sailing takes some getting used to, but even the most seasoned sailors can still be affected on a day like today. You have done well to get this far and keep the contents of your stomach where they belong."

"Charming. If you came down here to impress the sickness out of me, that's not going to do it."

"Actually, I thought you might benefit from advice from a well-traveled sailor who also suffers with such sickness." He kneeled beside her.

She lowered her arms, enough to open one eye and peek at him. "*You* get sick?"

He nodded. If it weren't for the lump of ginger he'd been chewing, he'd be hurling over the taffrail as well.

"Why on earth did you become captain of a ship?"

"That's a fair question, but most of us get seasick at some point. You would be surprised how rare it is to find a sailor who doesn't. It's part of this life, and we all do what we can to get on with it."

"You're not sick now, though."

"Hence the advice," he said. "Now, would you like my help?" Knowing she would be too stubborn to answer, he didn't wait for a response. He took her wrists in his hands. Her skin was soft under his fingertips, and he found the point where he needed to apply pressure.

She jerked her arms away. "What are you doing?"

"Helping you. Well, trying to." He reached for her wrists again but waited for her permission this time. "Did you know the captain of a ship is required to have knowledge about illnesses, to manage his crew while sailing? I learned about this on a trip to China, though it's not particularly useful when one needs to get work done."

"You've been to China?" Awe brightened her tone. Her arms relaxed into his grasp, but her eyes stayed closed.

"Many times." He turned her wrists over and used his fingertips to find the right point. He watched her face as he applied pressure to the inner side of her wrists.

"What did you do in China?" Her voice was soft.

"Nothing important," he said. Everything important, he'd once believed. His perspective regarding his priorities had shifted dramatically in the past week. One didn't need to look far to find the reason why. He didn't expect her to be satisfied with his answer. Few people sailed from England to China more than once for *nothing important,* but she didn't press the matter.

The silence broke with her weak groan. "It's not working, Alexander!"

He chuckled, releasing her hand and pulled the ginger from his pocket. Placing it in her palm, he took hold of her wrist again. "Take a bite and keep chewing on it." He moved with her as she brought the ginger to her mouth and took a small bite. "Bigger than that. It needs to last you a while."

Her nose wrinkled, but she obliged. After a few moments, she opened her eyes. She blinked a few times, then her gaze focused on him.

"Better?" he asked.

"A little." She chewed on the ginger. "How does it work?"

"Not the foggiest of ideas, I'm afraid, but it does, so I don't question it."

She smiled, then the expression turned into a frown. "Why didn't you give me this when I was sick yesterday?"

"Well..." He hesitated. "It's not a very good cure for a rum headache. And I was caught off guard at the time. You were dressed in your corset if you recall." He shifted his eyes away from her face.

"I do," she whispered. "I need to talk to you about that."

His gaze shot back to her face. "What about it?" Was she going to demand that he marry her on their return to London? Women had been compromised in far less questionable circumstances and secured a proposal. It was the least she deserved, but he couldn't make such a promise yet. He would do the right thing by her, even if that meant breaking the vows to his mother's memory. Sam's words sprung into his mind. If he was right, and Alexander was falling in love with Harriet, would that make marrying her all right?

"Well..." Her gaze darted to every possible object on the orlop deck except his face.

"What?" he asked, not keen for any conversation that involved the topic of her corset.

"It's so tight."

"Loosen it," he said with an abruptness he hadn't expected.

"It's already as loose as I can make it. I need it off so I can breathe properly."

His jaw slackened. This was brilliant.

"Ouch!" she exclaimed, pulling her hands away. "You're hurting me."

He forced his fingers to relax. She was asking him to take off her corset. This was his punishment for allowing things to get so far out of hand. He *had* kissed her shamelessly twice now. He deserved far worse.

Her wrists twisted until they were free of his grasp. "I can manage for a moment while you untie it." She shuffled into a seated position facing away from him. "It's tied off at the bottom."

"I know how a corset is tied," he grumbled. Even from behind, he saw the blush coloring her cheeks. Of all the times he had dreamed of this moment, not once did he imagine it would be in the chill of the orlop deck to assist with her seasickness.

She raised her arms and lifted the shirt over her head, and he was left staring at—he wasn't sure what. Whoever had tied Harriet's corset must have intended to keep her in it for a month. The discomfort of wearing a corset was well known, but he'd never met a woman so averse that she had to be restrained into it. No wonder she had made it out of his bonds. They were nothing compared to this.

"Alexander?" she prompted.

It had been a time since he last spoke, but what could he say?

"Ah." The sound was more of a sigh than a word. It was all he could manage. He frowned at the ribbons and knots, unsure where to start, but neither a corset nor a maid would outwit him. Short of taking a knife to the wretched thing, he wasn't sure how to get her out of it. "This will take a while."

A knot was tied in every second crisscross of the ribbons. The maid who had restrained Harriet in the corset had taken the same approach he had with her bonds. Though these knots weren't there for the purpose of keeping it tight, that much was obvious. This was a well-practiced pattern that allowed for Harriet's desire to loosen it whilst securing her in it. Once he understood what was happening with the knots, the process was completed with relative speed.

He held the ribbons together at the last loop and cleared his throat. "Do you want to…"

"Yes." She pulled her shirt back over her head.

He let go of the ribbons and withdrew his hand.

She wriggled out of the corset, and it fell into her lap. "Thank you."

He averted his gaze as she turned around. "How do you feel now?"

"Much better. Is this suitable?" she asked, waving a hand in front of her chest.

He had tried so hard not to look at her breasts, and now she was asking him to do exactly that? This was punishment in its truest form. He flicked his gaze over her figure and back to the hull of the ship.

"You look fine."

"You can't see anything through the shirt?" she asked with wide eyes. She glanced down.

He forced his eyes to her breasts, and his thoughts back into line. "No, I can't see anything." But he could visualize what was there. Her perfect breasts that would fit in his hands. Soft pink nipples that would harden with the most subtle squeeze between his thumb and forefinger. He swallowed. "I'll leave you here until you are well enough to return to the main deck."

"I'm all right now."

"No," the word rushed from his mouth. "There's no need. Stay here until the storm has passed. I suspect it will get worse before it gets better, and I don't need to worry about you being up there." He was distracted enough as it was. "Stay. Please."

Her brows furrowed, but she agreed, and he left.

At what inconvenient point would she present back on deck this time?

Chapter Fourteen

HARRIET STIRRED, her body stiff from falling asleep on the cold, hard deck. The air was still, and the lamp Alexander had left had burned out.

A mighty shout came down the stairs, reaching her loud and clear on the orlop deck.

"All hands on deck!"

The crew raced to answer the call. Heavy boots thundered up the stairs. She didn't have a hope of learning what was going on from this far below deck, and she was a sailor, too—*all hands* would mean her presence was required as well.

She rushed to the stairs. Her heart hammered in her chest as she joined the last of the sailors. Some of them appeared as though the call had woken them, and they all wore concerned expressions. What did an *all hands* call signify?

Stepping onto the main deck, rain pelted her, drenching her in seconds. It ran into her eyes, and her attempts to blink it away were in vain. It took another few moments to comprehend the scene.

The crew lined the port-side taffrail, and they pointed at something in the water. Their shouts merged into an indecipherable commotion. What were they looking at?

She bolted across the deck and squeezed between two sailors, her heart plummeting when she spotted him. Enormous swells dragged Jacob up to the crest of the wave and then down into the deep trough. The helpless way his arms flailed barely kept his head above the water.

Groves cast a rope over the taffrail, but the end was swept out of Jacob's reach. Another sailor did the same, and then another. None of the ropes stayed close enough for Jacob to grab. How long had he been overboard? His movements had slowed and were becoming less purposeful in the few moments she'd been watching.

"He's going to drown!" she yelled, but no one paid her any heed.

Groves and the other sailors pulled their ropes from the water and prepared to throw them again. They would never get him this way.

She returned her desperate gaze to Jacob, and her plan solidified. She wheeled around and sprinted toward the stairs. A stack of coiled ropes would be at the base on the orlop deck where she had put it. She had no need for a lamp. All the time down there had committed the space to her memory.

The light on the mess deck was poor, and she was in complete darkness before she was halfway down the stairs onto the orlop deck. She grabbed the closest rope and thanked herself for having had the good sense to order them by length. This rope was the longest. It *had* to be enough.

She raced back to the main deck and secured one end of

the rope to the taffrail. With the other end, she tied a bowline around her waist. Groves was the nearest to her and had reeled in his rope. She snatched it from his hands and tied a small loop in the end. The moment their eyes met, his bulged into an alarmed expression she didn't pause to consider. Before he or anyone else could stop her, she slipped her arm through the loop and vaulted over the taffrail.

The fall lasted seconds as Harriet plummeted toward the water, wind whipping her skin. She plunged deep beneath the surface, the force expelling the air from her lungs. Salt water flooded her nose and turned her throat to fire. She had severely underestimated both the distance between the ship and the water, and the impact that hitting such strong waves would have. If she'd had any sense, she would have waited for the crest to be beside the boat. Too late now. She opened her eyes, but the water was too turbulent and dark under the storm. Without any sense of direction, she was helpless.

The rope around her waist pulled taut and dragged her backward through the water. She leaned into it and kicked with all her might until she broke through the surface. The raindrops hit her face like tiny shards of ice, but she'd never been more relieved. Water gushed from her mouth and nose, and she took a desperate breath. Pure air sliced at her raw throat as she dragged breaths through her teeth. The small black spots obscuring her vision soon disappeared, and she focused on her task. Hopefully, Jacob was still fighting.

She searched the water for his face as the sailors yelled from the ship behind her. A gigantic wave lifted her up and she reached the crest. Jacob's frightened face was right down in the trough. He seemed close to defeat, and his efforts to keep his head above the water were less determined than they had been moments ago.

The rope around her waist loosened, as did the loop on her arm. She worked with the waves and swam. At last, she reached him, and she gripped his shirt with both hands.

He mouthed her name, but no sound came out. "'Arry," he mouthed again. His eyes rolled backward.

"Don't give up, Jacob!" She tried to yell, but her voice sounded like gravel, tearing the inside of her throat. "Open your eyes, dammit!"

Their heads bobbed in and out of the water, and she kicked with all her strength. Sheer determination was all that kept them both afloat. She took the rope from her arm, reached around his waist and tied a bowline. Tight enough to stop him from slipping through should he cease his efforts before they made it back. She returned her attention to the *Seren*. Concerned faces lined the taffrail, all eyes fixed upon Jacob and her. Alexander at the helm drew her gaze, but she couldn't bear the intensity of his glare. She tore her attention from his face and focused on Groves instead.

With all the strength she could muster, she called, "Heave!"

The crew hauled her and Jacob toward the ship while she did her best to stop them from going under. Her muscles ached from the effort despite spending mere minutes in the water.

"Take Jacob!" she hollered once they were close enough.

The tension on the rope around her waist did not falter when she reached the hull. They lifted Jacob straight out of the water. Every fiber in her body fought against it, but she pushed away from the ship and waited. Her head dipped under the water as she drained her energy, barely keeping afloat. They hauled Jacob up and pulled him through an opening on the mess deck.

The rope around her waist tugged, and she swam closer to the ship. With one hand on the rope, she used the other to keep in contact with the hull and stop from swinging into it. The crew heaved her up much faster than Jacob. She reached the opening, and many hands grabbed hold of her, dragging her in. She crawled a few paces and collapsed onto the deck. Someone covered her in a heavy woolen blanket. Groves and others tended to Jacob just feet away.

"Is he all right?" She choked out the words, her voice a hoarse whisper.

A hand rested on her shoulder, and she glanced up. Sam watched her with a cautious expression. "He's exhausted, but I'd say he'll be fine. What about you?"

"Tired," she said.

"You're lucky the pair of you didn't drown. Alexander isn't happy."

"I know," she admitted. She'd had time to consider the way he had glowered at her from the helm and dreaded his reproach. Was she lucky not to have drowned?

Sam sat quietly beside her as the sailors moved around them. One approached her, but Sam waved them away. Jacob was the one who needed the attention, and she was grateful Sam seemed to think the same.

"You take his legs, and I'll take his arms." Groves gave directions to another sailor, and the two of them lifted Jacob and carried him out with ease.

She stirred. No one needed to carry her back to her cabin.

Sam's hand was still on her shoulder, and he whispered, "Stay here for a moment."

She obliged and let her eyes close, no longer fighting to keep herself awake.

A voice thundered from beyond the doorway. "Where is she?"

Harriet withdrew behind Sam.

Alexander stomped across the deck, stopping in front of Sam. She avoided looking at him. She deserved everything he had to say and more, but she didn't have the energy to listen now.

"Harriet, you get over here now." The demand hissed through his gritted teeth.

"Alexander!" Sam chastised. "She's barely conscious."

"Oh, barely conscious, is she? She's lucky to be alive."

"Yes, she is, and so is Jacob, thanks to her. He was going to die. We could all see it. He is fifteen years old, and whether they'd admit it or not, the crew care for the boy. It would have killed them if he'd drowned, and you know it."

Harriet's chest swelled. She had acted without consideration for herself, but she couldn't have let Jacob drown. It was the right decision, and the crew would defend her.

Sam continued. "It would be wise for you to consider what you mean to say. The crew might consider tossing *you* overboard if you aren't careful."

Alexander's pacing stopped, and his breathing filled the momentary silence. The tension between the two men was palpable, and it was all her fault.

"Damn you, Sam. Must you be right about everything?"

Sam made a shuffle against her back that she presumed was a shrug.

"Harriet?" Alexander's tone was much quieter when he addressed her.

Sam answered before she could. "I think she's asleep. She hasn't moved for a few minutes."

She tried to tell them she was awake, but no sound left her mouth.

Alexander was beside her in an instant. He lifted the blanket, his burning touch roaming over her body. An involuntary shiver rippled through her.

"She's all right, isn't she?" He tucked the blanket back around her, his gentle touch lingering on her face and neck. "She'll be all right?" His voice broke on the last word.

Harriet lay motionless, unable to muster the energy to open her eyes, but her chest squeezed.

"She was more worried about Jacob when we pulled her through, didn't seem hurt at all. You would be asleep too if you ever did anything that expended that much energy," Sam said.

The smile was evident in Sam's jibe, and the corners of her lips twitched.

Alexander's hands moved to her shoulders, and a few moments passed in silence. "I thought she was gone, Sam. I was going to watch the woman I"—he choked on his words—"I was about to witness her drown and could do nothing about it."

Did he—was he crying?

"I know," Sam mumbled. "But she's here."

She was here, and she wanted to reach out to Alexander and give him the reassurance he needed.

He sniffed and cleared his throat. "I'll take her to the cabin now."

His arms slid beneath her, and she groaned a protest.

"Do you need help?" Sam asked.

"No, I've got her. Just fetch another blanket, she's almost dry."

She was not short or slight, and at that moment, was as much of a dead weight as she could be, but his arms wrapped around her back and under her knees, showing no sign of struggle. He lifted her off the deck and curled her body against his. Her face pressed into his chest, and she inhaled his sweet ginger and woody scent. He didn't falter as they returned to her cabin.

BRIGHT GOLDEN SUNLIGHT streamed into the cabin and onto Harriet's face. Had they sailed through the storm already? She scrunched her eyes closed and turned onto her stomach, pulling the thick blanket over her head. Her muscles resisted the movement. They were as stiff as her dry, salty clothes. Now that she was awake, she was painfully aware of each breath as it sliced through her chest.

How long had she been asleep? And how had she made it back to her cabin? Much of what occurred after she had been hauled back onto the ship seemed like a dream. Though the memory of Alexander's anger remained with a distinct and uncomfortable clarity. Had it not been for Sam, there would have been no escaping his onslaught. But she recalled another faint memory, something Alexander had said or done that made her wonder. Her head hurt trying to remember.

Beyond the closed door, a cacophony of men bustled about the deck. Joining them was most unappealing, not that she considered it in earnest. Alexander and his reprimand could wait. She had no desire to seek out *that* conversation. Besides, yesterday he'd asked her to stay in her cabin. If she belatedly followed his orders, he couldn't be angry with her for it.

She rolled onto her back and stretched her arms gingerly overhead. Keeping herself afloat in the ocean had taken an incredible toll on her body, and every muscle ached. How long would that last? She peered at the ceiling, past her outstretched hands, and frowned. Her heart lunged into her throat, and her mind scrambled. She sat up, ignoring the painful defiance of her muscles.

This was not her cabin.

She rubbed her eyes, hoping that when she opened them again, she would be back in her own familiar surroundings. Light streamed into the cabin through wide windows that stretched along the rear of the ship.

Alexander's cabin.

She was in his cabin. She was in his *bed*.

A warm bundle at her feet responded to her movement. Shadow rose and shook himself out. He climbed over her legs and sniffed her shoulder. She scratched behind his ear, and a soft rumble sounded in his belly.

"Morning." The deep, measured greeting came from the darkest corner of the cabin, and she snapped her head in Alexander's direction.

A barely audible croak was all she could manage.

Alexander was beside her in an instant, a mug held aloft. He towered over her, but instead of intimidation, a calming reassurance accompanied his presence.

"What are you doing?" she asked. The burn of the salt water had caused a severe hoarseness to her voice.

Alexander's face twisted. "Drink this first, before you shred your throat any further."

She took the mug from his outstretched hand and peered inside. The cup warmed her hand, and steam rose from the contents. She tipped it to her lips. The warm liquid tasted of honey and a mix of spices. It soothed her throat as soon as it made contact, and once it reached her stomach, her hunger flared. She drained the cup, and Alexander refilled it from a large jug.

The soothing effect of the drink made speech more tolerable. "Why are you here?" she asked. Although asking why she was in his bed might have been more pertinent. She gazed into his eyes. They were dark and creased.

"You have been asleep for sixteen hours. I was"—he cleared his throat—"it has been a long night. I was beginning to worry you might not wake up at all."

"I slept for sixteen hours?" she asked. It wasn't sunset that had woken her. It was sunrise. "And you have been here the entire time?"

"Except for when Sam forced me down to the mess to eat."

She waited for him to elaborate.

He didn't.

"Why?" she asked.

He pointed at her feet. "May I?"

She hugged her knees to her chest, ignoring the aches that accompanied the movement, but they had already eased.

He sat down, moving his hands from his knees to his neck, then crossed and uncrossed his arms. What was he doing? He rested one hand on his knee and patted her foot with the other. His gaze darted to Shadow, the dog jumping off the bed, and then back to her face, a slight hint of indignation in his eyes. Shadow had been spending more time in her company in recent days. She waited for Alexander to speak. This was not the unleashing of anger she had anticipated, and now she didn't know what to expect.

"We arrived in port early this morning." He held her gaze with an intensity she could not fathom, nor could she look away. "I had hoped you would wake earlier. There are important... I need to tell you..." He sighed and glanced at the ceiling. His long fingers raked through his mussed hair. "We must discuss..."

What on earth was he trying to say? He hadn't been this incoherent in the time she'd known him.

He closed his eyes and sighed again. One of his hands moved to hers and curved around her fingers. The other covered his face. "All this time I was worried about your return to England. I thought the earl would kill me for kidnapping you, which may be what I deserve. But as I stood at the helm, fighting to keep the ship close enough to give Jacob a fighting chance, I watched you throw yourself overboard."

She bit her bottom lip. Causing him distress had not been her intention. "It was my decision to dive in after Jacob, and none of this would have happened if I hadn't been on the docks that day. You're not responsible for me." But what if he was? What if he wanted to be? More than a captain responsible for an accidental stowaway.

Alexander shook his head and his hand dropped to his lap. "I am, and if you hadn't made it back, I—" He drew in a breath and met her gaze with a look somehow more intense than the last. "You wanted to know why I stayed with you last night? Well, once I had you in my arms, I could not bear to let you go. If you hadn't been beyond consciousness, I would have stayed here beside you. Sitting across the cabin was as far as I could force myself to go until I could be assured you were well."

"It wasn't your fault," she reassured him, though her mind lingered on the idea of them together in his bed. She wished he had lain with her, that she had woken up in the strength and security of his arms.

"It was not guilt that kept me here, though I *am* responsible for everything that has happened since you walked onto this ship. It was—it is—" He stopped again.

He had never been so inarticulate, and she desperately wanted to understand what he was talking about, if his thoughts were in line with hers.

"I need to go into port soon, and I will find a doctor in town to come and examine you."

The change of topic did nothing to help her comprehension, so she did her best to keep up. "I'm perfectly all right," she said, but the rasp made the statement rather unconvincing.

Alexander raised a brow. "I'll let the doctor determine that. He will need to see Jacob, too. You might as well let him in to examine you."

Her thoughts were redirected again. "How is Jacob?" she asked.

"Much the same as you. He woke an hour or two ago and came straight up to check on you. Along with Groves and a few others. They're impressed with you, and I suspect worried about what I might do to you for punishment." The corner of his mouth lifted into a small smirk. It did not relieve him of the serious expression. "They're rather protective of you."

"Do they know?"

"Oh, yes. As it turns out, they've suspected you're a woman since soon after you boarded. It wasn't I who gave away your secret yesterday, but it did inspire an interesting conversation. Apparently, they weren't aware I knew, nor were they prepared to expose you. Given my already less than fair treatment of you, they took it upon themselves to protect you." He rolled his eyes. "As if I wouldn't know. It turns out if I set one more toe out of line, there will be a mutiny."

"For me?" she exclaimed. "That's absurd."

"Is it? I've never known a person to take to sailing as fast as you did. No one else considered diving in after Jacob. He's much like a son or a younger brother to many of them, but the thought wouldn't have crossed their minds. It was reckless, but also extremely courageous. You showed strength they could never have anticipated, and they are indebted to you. All of us are."

"It's nothing." Her cheeks warmed under his gaze. She wasn't accustomed to such praise. Usually, she would have been reprimanded for whatever improper thing she had done.

Alexander's cool fingertips moved from her hand and rested on her cheek. "It's not nothing. You are very special, Harriet."

Before she could respond, he leaned over and kissed her. This kiss didn't match the intensity of the previous two. It was slower, softer, and made her insides ache with yearning. As the kiss built, so did her desire.

Chapter Fifteen

RATIONAL THOUGHT WAS QUICKLY ABANDONING Alexander. Stopping this should have been his priority. Instead, he made a gentle move to pull Harriet into his arms, but she didn't need guidance. She slid atop him, settling onto his lap as though she was made for him. He tugged her shirt loose from her breeches, keenly aware she was still without a corset. Sliding a hand beneath her shirt and up her back elicited a shiver and stirred the pool of desire that waited in his groin.

Her fingers interlaced at his nape, and she pulled his face closer, deepening the kiss. Each touch of her lips, her hands, her body against his, burned, leaving a tingling awareness in her wake.

Trailing his fingers across the back of her neck evoked another shiver, and he twisted them into her hair. He lingered there, not wanting to turn this into a frenzied exchange, but he couldn't remain still for long. He took in every curve of her body, committing them to memory. Her soft breasts filled his calloused hands, and she shuddered at the intimate touch. He reminded himself that this was all new to her, and that he had to do it right.

The past sixteen hours had given him plenty of time to think, and he was committed to his decision. Her near-death experience had made him understand. What had grown between them wasn't simply lust or desire, though both were undeniable. He planned to marry Harriet and would do whatever it took to show her what she meant to him. Showing her how much of a hold she had over him was a start.

Alexander massaged her breasts first, then teased her nipples between his thumb and forefinger. Her back arched, pressing her breasts into his palms. He moved his hands over her ribs, skimming the soft skin beneath her breasts, and she moaned.

Soft pink peaks pressed against the linen of her shirt. He placed his mouth over one, her sweet taste mixing with the salt that coated her clothes. Her hips swayed back and forth across his lap, and her fingers entwined in his hair, keeping his mouth in place. Her breaths were ragged gasps, and her back arched, her head dropping back. He caught a handful of thick brown hair as it tumbled down her back and held her steady with an arm around her waist. Her hips ground against his erection, driving him wild. She must know how much he wanted her. How could she ignore it? She tugged his shirt from his breeches, and her deft hands moved to their fastenings.

He withdrew his attention from her breasts and sought her gaze.

"I want you," she said. "But I don't know what to do."

He growled, the sound deep and possessive. Whatever happened on their return to London, he would ensure she was taken care of. He would go to the ends of the earth for this woman.

"Aren't you sore?" he asked. She'd resisted movement when she'd first woken, and swimming against such a strong current would still cause her pain. He didn't want to hurt her more.

She shook her head. "It eased once I moved. And when you started kissing me, I forgot about it." Blush crept up her neck.

He had been ready since the first touch between them, but he was uncertain of what she would expect. Releasing himself from his breeches, he searched her face. Her mouth had formed a silent *oh*, and her eyes, already so big and innocent, widened.

"It's all right," he reassured her, touching a fingertip to her cheek. He would make this right for her, be sure not to rush or do anything she wasn't ready for. Did she know what happened between a man and a woman?

"I know it might hurt," she said, surprising him. "I've been... informed. Somewhat."

"Then what is it?"

That delightful blush colored her cheeks, and she bit her lip. "It's nothing."

"You must tell me what you're thinking," he insisted, hanging on her every word.

She nibbled on her lip until he thought he might explode. "Now I understand..." She hesitated.

"Understand what?"

"What this ache deep inside me yearns for." She met his gaze, and he lost himself in her dark green eyes. "It's for you."

He swept her mouth into another kiss, working to

unfasten her breeches. Pushing the material over her hips, she lifted enough for him to slide them off her legs. He traced up the inside of her thigh, reaching her flushed, wet heat. He slid a finger inside her, and she moaned.

"Are you sure this is what you want?" he asked.

She kissed the base of his neck, trailing up to his ear. "Yes," she whispered, the heat of her breath making his skin tingle.

He positioned himself at her entrance and kept his movements controlled. Holding her hips, he guided her down inch by glorious inch. Her nails bit into his shoulders, and she let out a small gasp. There was a flash in her green eyes, and then she squeezed them shut. He paused. A moment later, she opened her eyes, and her stare bore into the depths of his soul. He laid it bare for her. He tried to rally his thoughts back into order, but she thrust her hips against him, burying him deep. A sound escaped his lips that he'd never heard before.

She felt *good*.

So good that he had no hope of making this last. He would need to make it up to her later. Quickening his pace, she met him thrust for thrust.

Alexander withdrew not a moment too soon, spilling his seed between them. Her arms wrapped around his neck, and she buried her face in his collar.

A loud knock on the cabin door sent a sleeping Shadow into a fit of barks.

Alexander pulled away, groaning deep in his throat. Whoever was at the door, probably Sam, could go to hell. Instead, they knocked again.

"I know!" Alexander called, setting Harriet on the bed without taking his eyes from hers. "I must go, I'm sorry.

We've been in port too long already. There's more we need to discuss this afternoon. It's hard enough for me to leave you as it is, but I won't be long. Can you promise to stay here and not to do anything without prior consideration of my nerves while I am gone?"

She looked content and on the verge of sleep, her eyelids drooping. She didn't answer.

"Promise me," he said again, standing and fastening his breeches. "I can't leave unless I know you're safe here until I return."

"I'll be here," she said. Her brow knitted into a frown. "What do we need to discuss? Will you tell me what you do on these visits in port?"

"Perhaps," he said. He wanted to tell her everything now, but he needed to go. "Once I've found what I am looking for and we return to England, I will tell you what I can about that. But there is more." He had to give her his assurance that he would marry her. He didn't want her wondering whether he would leave her ruined, but he hadn't planned to propose at his bedside after a hasty tumble. None of this had happened as he'd intended, but he couldn't bring himself to be sorry about it.

"Alexander." Sam's voice was muffled through the cabin door. "Hurry up!"

Alexander smiled at Harriet. "Please allow the doctor to examine you. It would be very reassuring." He would ask for her hand later, perhaps tonight, under the stars. He could explain everything. Then she would know his offer of marriage wasn't a reaction to what they'd just shared.

"I will," she said, taking his hand and kissing his knuckles. He wanted to melt under that tender touch.

"The bath is over there," he said. "I'll send someone up

with warm water, and I've put a set of clean clothes on the table for you." He'd have preferred to stay and spend time taking care of her, but they didn't have the luxury of time while they were docked in Saint-Malo.

"Thank you," she whispered.

He bent and brushed the top of her head with his lips, then tore himself away. "I'll see you soon." Not soon enough.

Alexander almost ran into Sam on the main deck, and they spent much of their walk into town in silence.

"Do you want to talk about it?" Sam asked.

"Talk about what?" Did Sam suspect what he'd done with Harriet? Worse, had he overheard?

"I haven't seen you since yesterday, and you weren't in a good state then. You didn't look much improved when you came out of your cabin." Sam elbowed his arm as they walked along the street.

Alexander tried to hide his smirk. He had been much improved this morning, but he certainly wasn't going to admit that. As if Sam needed any more ammunition.

"I'm fine," Alexander said, raking his fingers through his tangled hair. He hadn't slept in over twenty-four hours and must look a sight. "Harriet was insistent she is well, but could you please find a suitable doctor? We don't have much time, and besides, your French is better than mine."

"Of course," Sam said.

"Have him examine Harriet as soon as he can. I want to know that she is well before we sail again. And Jacob too," he added, very much as an afterthought.

"Are you sure you want to go on your own?" Sam asked. "You do recall the last time we were in Saint-Malo."

Alexander suppressed the shudder that ran through his body. The last time they'd been here, he'd been locked in a dungeon for a week and had made a narrow escape with his life. Both the courtesy of Harvey and the thugs that ran with him in his pirating days.

"I'll be fine," Alexander said, hoping that adrenaline would override his exhaustion should he come across anyone unsavory. "I doubt there's any need for concern. I didn't see Harvey's ship docked, so he's probably not here. If I can't find out anything about him within the hour, I'll return to the ship."

If they hadn't seen or heard anything helpful in that time, they were unlikely to at all, even if they spent the entire day in Saint-Malo, and that *wasn't* an option. The sooner they sailed away from this godforsaken place, the better.

Alexander inhaled. He had to tell Sam the truth. He stopped walking and tugged his friend's arm.

"Sam, if we don't find Harvey, we need to take Harriet home. I know we can't risk going to an English port, but I need to take her back."

Sam raised a brow. "Why do I feel as though you're about to tell me something I don't want to know?"

Alexander chewed the inside of his lip. "It's nothing you haven't already assumed will happen. I'm going to take her to Scotland and marry her. I'll set her up in a cottage or hire a coach to take her back to her parents, whichever she prefers. Then we'll resume our search for Harvey."

Sam nodded. "Keep your head down, Alexander."

"I will," Alexander said, grateful that Sam didn't need more of an explanation.

Silent, Sam held his gaze for a moment, the meaning clear.

Alexander replied with a curt nod, turning away from his friend. He wouldn't risk not getting back to Harriet now.

Alexander had been alone for a few minutes when he noticed them. He continued through the streets, pretending he hadn't seen the two dark figures keeping a steady pace behind him. Better to let them assume he was unaware of their presence. They could herd him if they wished. It would get him answers faster. Was it too much to hope that one was Harvey? One way to find out.

Glancing down a few of the alleyways, Alexander searched for one that would serve his purpose. Each led away from the busy main street, crisscrossing with other smaller streets, but none were deserted enough for a confrontation. He'd have to get them farther away from the docks. He buried his hands in his pockets and turned into the next alleyway on his left.

The men followed.

Alexander marched between the buildings, his boots clipping on the cold stone, much louder than his pursuers. Only someone well-practiced in stealth could make their footfalls so quiet, especially men of such size. A sense of foreboding settled over him, constricting around his ribcage. This alley was less busy than the others he'd passed, despite the hour and countless ships docked. The men stayed close behind him. He slowed, and they slowed. He could quicken his pace, but for what purpose? They would catch up with him.

Alexander rounded another corner. A brick wall loomed over him at the opposite end of the alleyway, blocking out the morning sun. Not ideal, but he had extricated himself from tighter squeezes. Hopefully, the isolation would be enough to loosen their tongues. Before he reached the end and they had him good and cornered, he spun around. There were three men now. How annoying that he hadn't noticed. What else had he missed?

The man in the middle was the new addition. He was taller, and the hood over his head kept his face well-concealed. The three of them mumbled in French quietly enough for Alexander to miss the words, not that he'd comprehend them at that speed. Sam and Harvey were always the linguists. The men leered at him as they spoke, and a shiver crept up his spine.

Alexander backed toward the wall, his feet scuffling on the stone. The men matched his slow steps, closing in. The two burly men on either side of him seemed far more formidable. His odds of escaping this one unscathed were getting slimmer by the second. Alexander darted a glance up at the high walls on either side of him. The lowest window was ten feet off the ground. His heart hammered in his chest.

One man spoke in a familiar gravelly tone. "Well, hello, Captain."

Alexander forced his eyes back to the men, and a solid fist collided with his jaw. It sent him stumbling to his right, and his shoulder hit the wall with a crack. Blood filled his mouth, and he spat it onto the ground. He glared at the man who had punched him, the one in the middle. His assailant's hood had fallen back from his face, revealing familiar dark, heavy eyes, skin naturally a few shades darker than his own, and a crooked nose. The look on the man's face was one of warning, but Alexander couldn't help the sense of relief that washed over him.

Harvey.

Alexander opened his mouth, but Harvey gave the slightest shake of his head, and his words stopped in his throat. Blood pooled in his mouth again, and he spat it out without taking his eyes from Harvey's face. What had Harvey got himself into?

Alexander couldn't ponder that any longer. One of the other men took him by the collar and thrust him backward. His head slammed against the wall, and his vision darkened.

A hand rummaged through his pockets.

Then everything went black.

Chapter Sixteen

RUSTLING. Scratching. Pounding.

Alexander couldn't differentiate between the sounds inside his head and those outside. He paid closer attention to the pounding. Definitely in time with his heartbeat. *Inside.* Scratch, pause, scratch. He swallowed. *Rats.* At least they weren't upon his person. Yet. And the rustling? He tried to isolate the sound. He sighed, the sound punctuated by his chattering teeth. That would be his clothes rustling from his incessant shivering. They must have moved him below the water level.

He opened his eyes, though he might as well have kept them shut for all the good it did. The space he'd been moved to was pitch black, the stone wall hard and cold against his back. He tried to sit up, but pain shot through his right shoulder. He shuffled away from the wall and used his left hand to push himself upright. Cradling his right arm, he moved it gingerly, testing its range. *Christ*, it hurt, but it would hurt more if it were broken.

The scrape of metal against wood pierced the air, sending the rats scurrying.

Alexander turned toward the sharp *click* of a key turning in the lock. The door swung open, and light flooded into the small room.

Two men stood in the doorway, but Alexander couldn't discern more than their silhouettes in the blinding lamplight. How long had he been down here in the dark? How long had he been unconscious?

"Captain Alexander Ordell," a deep voice drawled. "Welcome."

Alexander squinted at the men, trying to make out their faces, but bright specks of light filled his vision. He squeezed his eyes closed against the light that had only increased the pounding in his head.

"And where precisely in this hellhole am I being welcomed?" Alexander asked through gritted teeth.

"I thought you'd recognize this place," the man said again, the familiarity returning. And damn it, Alexander did recognize the room he was in. The same place he'd spent a week during his last visit to Saint-Malo. Where he'd vowed never to return to the godforsaken port town. Five years had not been enough time to distance himself from the memory of the rancid dungeon. Only, last time he was here, he'd been sharing a cell with Harvey, not imprisoned by him.

"Leave us," Harvey said.

The second man's footsteps drew away from the room, and Alexander opened his eyes.

The door slammed behind Harvey, the resulting gust causing the lamp in his hand to flicker. It cast a wild glow over an even wilder man. Harvey's bright white teeth shone through a wide grin bordered by a wiry black beard. His black hair reached past his shoulders and hung in the same unkempt manner. The man's clothes alone reflected his financial prowess and that he had retained some semblance of self-respect.

Harvey placed the lamp on a stool and crossed the room. He held out a hand.

Alexander glared at his friend's hand. "The other one. I can't use my right arm. I think someone broke my shoulder." He turned his glare on Harvey.

"It's not broken," Harvey said, withdrawing his right hand and holding out the left.

Alexander gripped Harvey's forearm and hauled himself to his feet, careful not to jostle his right arm. "How would you know?"

Harvey rolled his eyes, exposing far too much white. "Because I checked. You're not the only one with the skill required to set bones. It was much easier to assess while you were unconscious. Lord knows how much you would have complained if I tried to touch your shoulder now. I doubt you'd let me set a bone while you were awake." His grin turned into a smirk. "You never quite recovered from the effects of your birth, did you?"

Alexander punched his friend's arm as best he could with his left hand. "Being born a gentleman was not my error, and it didn't make me soft. Now, are you going to explain yourself?"

"Explain myself?" Indignation colored Harvey's voice, and his eyes narrowed. "Why don't you tell me why you thought it would be a good idea to come to Saint-Malo? Have you forgotten what happened last time?"

A shudder passed through Alexander's body. "I haven't. We need you back in London."

Harvey barked out a laugh. "To be hanged for murder?" He pierced Alexander with his black gaze. "No."

"We don't have a choice," Alexander said. "Lord

Edington and the rest think it was you who was killed. They're after me and Sam now. If you don't return to London, they'll hang us both."

Harvey shrugged. "So don't return to London."

Alexander averted his gaze.

"What did you do?" Harvey asked, sounding like a parent scolding a small child for taking a treat.

"Why does everyone assume I've done something?"

"Fine." Harvey huffed. "Why must we return to London?"

Alexander still couldn't meet Harvey's eye. "My brother lives there. They could ask questions of him if we were away for a prolonged time. And they're unlikely to forget we're wanted for murder in the next decade. I'd like to return home before then."

"Your brother can look after himself," Harvey said. "His rank alone is enough to protect him."

True, but it was beside the point.

"There's another reason we have to go back," Alexander said.

"Yes, I'm not a fool," Harvey retorted. "Would you hurry up and tell me so we can sort this out?"

"I have a woman on board the *Seren*."

Harvey blinked, and the smirk disappeared from his face. "Who?"

"Harriet Hazelby," Alexander mumbled.

"Did you say Hazelby?" Harvey's smirk returned. "What the hell did you do that for?"

"*I* didn't," Alexander insisted. "*She* did. And I must get her home."

His friend sighed. "Do you know what I had to do to get myself out of this cell this time?"

Alexander studied Harvey's face, unsure if he wanted to

know. "Well, it is you we're discussing. Did you kill a man? Three?"

Harvey raised an eyebrow and folded his arms over his chest. Unimpressed was an understatement. "I'm not in a position to confirm or deny that."

"Whatever it was, can you undo it?" Alexander asked. "Today?"

Harvey's eyes bulged.

"I wouldn't ask if I wasn't desperate," Alexander said, and he was beyond desperation. "We need to get back to London as a matter of urgency."

Harvey frowned, his gaze roaming over Alexander's face. "You're serious?"

"Absolutely," Alexander said.

"What is she to you?"

Alexander swallowed. "I don't know yet." Hopefully everything, if she would have him. "It depends on our return to London." Either way, he'd ensure she had the protection of his name before he was hanged.

"All right, but I don't think I can get you back to the *Seren* undetected."

Alexander's heart sank.

"How opposed are you to sailing the *Black Witch*?"

"Vehemently," Alexander said, his tone flat and dark. That ship was in Saint-Malo? He hadn't seen it in the harbor.

Harvey shrugged. "I can get you out of here fine, but you'll need to lie low until tonight. The crew on my ship are good men, and I trust them. They kept the ship in good order while I was away. It's hidden in a little cove. I'll stop there on my way to the *Seren* and tell them they'll have a new captain tonight."

Christ, the man was serious. *Brilliant.* So, Alexander was

going to sail a notorious pirate ship through the channel, up the Thames, and into London. What could go wrong?

"And what are you going to do?" Alexander asked.

"I'll sail on the *Seren* within an hour of leaving here. We'll be gone before they realize I've left. They have eyes on my ship, and when they see it's still there, they won't think too much of it."

Alexander frowned. "Who are *they*, exactly?"

"Best if you don't know."

Alexander groaned. Time was of the essence, and he didn't have any better ideas. He might not have minded Harvey's suggestion any other time. His concern was for Harriet. Getting her back to London and joining her there with his name cleared was his highest priority.

"Fine," Alexander bit out. "When can we leave?"

"Now. They won't question what I plan to do with you."

"I need to know that you'll keep her safe," Alexander said. He had absolute faith that Harvey could get them both out of Saint-Malo undetected, but he didn't relish abandoning Harriet.

Harvey waved a hand dismissively. "She'll be fine."

Rage filled Alexander, burning through his limbs. He fisted Harvey's collar in both hands, bringing the man's face within inches of his own and ignoring the pain that seared through his shoulder.

"I swear on my mother's grave," Alexander hissed, "I will kill you if anything happens to her. Do you understand? I will cleave your head from your body. Drown you. Tie you to a pyre and set you alight."

Harvey's hands rose on either side of his shoulders, and his eyes grew wide. "Do you think you could refrain from acting so rashly for the next hour? You need to keep a level head while I get us out of here."

Alexander didn't move. He needed Harvey to understand the importance of Harriet's safety.

"I won't let any harm come to the woman," Harvey said. "Good to know you've considered all the ways you can end me if necessary."

"They're not all the ways," Alexander growled.

"That's enough!" Harvey snapped, pushing Alexander's chest. "I can get her back to London without her getting hurt."

Alexander might have been compelled to believe Harvey if he hadn't spent a week on a ship with Harriet.

"She's determined to get herself in trouble," Alexander said. How else could he explain her?

"I'll keep her safe, Alexander. I promise."

Alexander uncurled his fingers and patted the front of Harvey's shirt. "Good. I've hunted you down once, I can do it again."

Harvey's eyes narrowed. "You are insane. Or..." His eyebrows waggled. "In love?"

Alexander didn't dignify that with a response.

"She'll be waiting for you in one whole, unharmed piece on your return to London," Harvey said.

All Alexander could do was trust his friend.

HARRIET AWOKE TO A DARKENED CABIN, alone except for Shadow sleeping at her feet. She'd never slept this much in her life. The bath was probably to blame. Sinking into that warm water without having to worry about keeping her corset dry had been heavenly and helped to relax her tense muscles. Or perhaps it had been what passed between her and Alexander that morning. A warm shiver swept up her spine. What did this mean for their journey and return to London?

Harriet tried to still her racing thoughts and recall if Alexander had been back during the afternoon. Sometime after she'd bathed, Knapp had brought up a meal with Jacob trailing in behind him. He'd muttered his thanks and apologies from the moment he stepped inside Alexander's cabin until Knapp dragged him out by his sleeve. She was glad he was well, having grown fond of the crew who'd supported her. She recalled little else after the doctor visited.

Warm bread, earthy and sweet, reached her nostrils, and she smiled. The food on port days was decidedly better than what they ate at sea, and despite eating enough for two sailors only hours ago, she was ravenous again.

She rose and crossed the cabin, leaving Shadow asleep on the bed. The same ache from earlier remained in her muscles, but it was manageable. One plate sat on the table, filled with meat, bright green vegetables she didn't recognize, and golden potatoes. Butter melted into a slice of bread, and wisps of steam rose from the food. Alexander must have brought it in, and she suspected that had woken her. He would have returned to the ship by now. Why hadn't he stayed? It would be a relief to reassure him that the doctor had examined her, and nothing was out of place. Aside from a slight question regarding her sanity, which she intended to ignore.

She sat at the table and ate quickly. The meal satisfied her immediate hunger, but it wasn't enough to fill her. She waited for Alexander to return and soon noticed an unmistakable motion in the ship. Walking to the wide windows, she peered into the darkness. There were no lights, or any visible shapes or shadows on the horizon. They had sailed.

That explained why Alexander wasn't here. He would be at the helm. Where would they be sailing next?

Rather than waiting alone in the cabin, she resolved to find Alexander. Whatever he'd wanted to tell her earlier seemed important, and now that her hunger was sated, her curiosity piqued. She sought his comfort, but there was more, too. She hadn't acknowledged it before, but now that she had, the void left behind in his absence was obvious. He'd mentioned he was a gentleman, and he knew of her father. Was there a possibility that they could marry on their return to London? She didn't hold any expectations after what they had done, but what if he wanted her?

She walked out onto the main deck, closing the door behind her. The motion of the ship was gentle compared to the last time she'd been out here. That should have settled her stomach, but the butterflies that fluttered inside her had nothing to do with seasickness. Doubt crept into her mind. What if he didn't want to marry her?

Reaching the quarterdeck, she stopped short. The man standing at the helm wasn't Alexander, or anyone she recognized. This man was tall and menacing. His long black hair fell below his shoulders, and his deep-set eyes were as dark as the sky behind him. A wild black beard covered his square jaw. He didn't look dangerous. He *was* dangerous.

"Who are you?" she asked.

The man glared at her as though she were nothing more than the dirt on his shoes. "Who am I?" he spat. "I should like to ask you the same question." His tone was as terrifying as his expression.

"Where is Captain Alexander?" Her voice wavered.

"*Captain* Alexander? I am the captain of this ship." He sneered, his glare too intense to meet.

Panic bubbled to the surface. "Where is he?" she asked.

"Alexander isn't here." His reply was smug, and she hated him for it.

Trusting the word of this man went against every fiber of her existence, but the truth settled deep within her. The *Seren* had sailed, and Alexander wasn't on board.

Sam approached her from behind and brushed her shoulder as he passed.

"Sam!" she exclaimed. "Where is Alexander?"

Sam shook his head and stood beside the evil man.

The *captain* spoke again. "You are relieved of your duties until we return to London. You may spend your time however you see fit but keep out of my way. Is that clear?"

"I demand you tell me where Alexander is." She marched as close to him as she dared, but the urge to beat her hands against his arm or chest disappeared as she drew nearer.

"Harriet," Sam muttered. His hand found her wrist and gave it a gentle squeeze. "This is Harvey. He'll be sailing the *Seren* to London."

Harvey fixed her with a wicked grin, baring surprisingly white teeth. Her mind went back to the night Alexander had shown her to Harvey's cabin. He was exactly the type of man she'd imagined.

"You will stay in the captain's cabin with Shadow, now that you've tainted it," Harvey said. "And when I say stay, I mean it. I don't want to see you outside that cabin. I don't want to think about there being a woman on this ship."

She could neither tolerate nor disobey his venom-laced voice. It was a threat, and she wasn't willing to push him. He was nothing like Alexander.

Chapter Seventeen

Six days. Harriet had been restricted to Alexander's cabin for six days, and they had dragged on. Her limited contact with the crew had been when a sailor brought her a meal three times a day, and that was done in silence. It was never Groves, or Jacob, or anyone else she knew. Harvey—she could not think of him as captain of Alexander's ship—had been clear and intentional in his spite. Though what she might gain from seeing a familiar face, she wasn't sure. Happiness? Reassurance? Was he so evil she couldn't be allowed that? She hadn't even been able to exploit the bowsprit for an excuse to get outside. Alexander's cabin had its own privy.

Entertaining herself within the confines of the cabin had proved difficult. Playing with Shadow occupied some of her time, but he slept for most of the day. He was curled in her lap where she sat on the bed, her back against the wall. She ran her fingers through his soft fur and stared across the cabin at Alexander's empty desk. A small bookshelf hung above it illuminated by a single lamp. He kept a collection of heavy tomes, contained on the shelf by crisscrossed strands of twine. She hadn't pulled any down in days. They were about sailing, which hadn't held her interest for long. The remainder of her time she'd spent thinking about Alexander. Where might he be? Was he all right? Would she see him again? The thoughts buzzed in her mind, an ever-present hive of bees. They stung the same way, too.

A sharp rap on the door drew her attention away from the bookshelf. Sam, again. His daily visits during evening watch, once Harvey had retired, had brought her little comfort. She wouldn't decline the walk, though it would again be spent in silence. Sam had taken Harvey's side with this and refused to answer any questions. He didn't seem concerned about Alexander's whereabouts. She ought to find that reassuring.

Another knock sounded on the door.

Shadow answered with a lazy bark, not bothering to lift his head. She chuckled and scooped him off her lap, laying him back on the bed. Rising slowly, she pulled her coat on and opened the door. Sam stood in the doorway, his face an inscrutable mask.

"Have you come to accompany me on my evening walk?" she asked, fixing her gaze at a point over his shoulder.

"Yes," he replied.

Her gaze flew to his face. His first word to her in five days. What did this mean?

"Walk with me," he said. "I need to return to the helm."

She turned to call Shadow over, but he was already panting at her side. They left the cabin together, following Sam to the quarterdeck. The prospect of a conversation filled her with hope. Would he tell her what had happened to Alexander? A tingling sensation rushed down her arms and into her hands.

"Are you speaking to me now?" she asked. Her voice rose considerably in her excitement.

"Not to tell you what you wish to know." Sam's response deflated her, but hope persisted, however small.

"Then to tell me what?" she hissed, her patience dissipating in the cool breeze.

Sam was quiet as he took up his stance at the ship's wheel.

"Come on, Shadow," she said. She didn't need to tolerate this.

Sam sighed. "Wait."

She crossed her arms and glared at him.

"We will arrive in London tomorrow," he said. "I thought you might like some time to prepare."

She frowned, struggling to contain the burst of relief that started in her chest and rushed to her toes. Tears welled in the corners of her eyes. She'd be home tomorrow?

"Is that all you wish to tell me?" she asked.

"If there's anything that will make your arrival home smoother, tell me tonight. I know this isn't what Alexander had in mind, so I'd like to be as much help as I can in his absence."

The mention of Alexander's name sent another thrill through her. "What did Alexander have planned? He wanted to speak to me when he got back on the ship. Did it have something to do with our return to London?" *Lord*, she was a fool. What did she expect Alexander to do? He hadn't declared his love for her with plans to whisk her away to the church to be married. No, were he here, he would have dropped her home and sailed away, relieved she was no longer his problem. If he had any intention of marrying her, he would have said so.

Sam stared at her with his lips pressed into a firm line.

"If there is anything I can help you with before tomorrow, tell me," he repeated.

"You can tell me what happened to Alexander." If nothing else, she deserved an explanation.

Sam shook his head, the hint of a smile on his lips. It was worth a try.

"Stay out here as long as you wish," he said. "I'll be sure to give you enough warning before we arrive tomorrow."

"Thank you." She turned to walk back to the cabin but stayed on the quarterdeck. This was her last night on a ship. Perhaps her last night of freedom. She looked out over the taffrail at the rippling black water, glowing under the lights from the *Seren*. On the horizon, between the water and the twinkling stars, they approached a solid black mass. Land. English land, if Sam was telling the truth. Her heartbeat quickened, apprehension and excitement pulsing through her body and competing for attention.

THE FOLLOWING MORNING, once again restricted to Alexander's cabin, Harriet watched the grassy countryside pass by, gray in the predawn light. Sam had stopped by an hour ago to wake her, but his effort had been pointless. She hadn't slept a wink. The small cottages and open fields soon gave way to the close buildings of the town. She had never seen London from this angle before, but the sight incited a sense of familiarity. The *Seren* sailed up the Thames, the motion calm and steady.

She was home.

She stayed on the bed, watching the sun rise over the river through the windows at the rear of the ship. The farther up the Thames they sailed, the slower they moved. The ship would be docked soon, but she had time to finalize the details of her plan. Boarding the *Seren* undetected had been easy enough, and she could navigate it much better now. Disembarking without drawing the crew's attention wasn't impossible. It would be best to leave as soon as the opportunity presented itself. She would figure out her next steps once she'd made it off the ship. Alexander's word she would have trusted, and she might have believed Sam if he hadn't sided with Harvey. But since the new captain had come aboard, she couldn't be certain of anything.

The one problem remaining was Shadow. He hadn't left her side in over a week, and she wasn't sure what he might do if she tried to sneak away. She lacked the confidence to pull off her plan with him in tow. All she could do was hope he would remain quiet, if only for the few minutes it took to escape.

The prospect of being home was exquisite, but that same thought also sent a bubble of nerves spiraling through her. She had been missing for weeks and was arriving hundreds of miles from where she'd disappeared. Not to mention she had been thoroughly ruined. How could she explain her way out of this? The past week of rumination had given her not so much as a plausible excuse. No matter how hard she'd tried, she had come up short with a reason for her reappearance so far from Hull.

When her family had realized she was missing, every friend, acquaintance, and servant would have been on the lookout for her. Hopefully, her arrival would bring comfort to her parents and sisters. They could cease worrying before she was banished to the countryside to live out her life as a spinster.

She laughed. That had been what she wanted, hadn't it?

The ship came to a stop, and shouts between the crew and men on the dock rang through the air. She hugged Shadow closer, making the most of their final moments together. Giving him one final pat and a scratch behind his ears, she left him on the bed. She pushed her arms through the sleeves of her coat and exited the cabin. For once, Shadow didn't bark, as though he understood how important this was.

A quick scan of the main deck revealed that the sailors had opened the lower deck to drop the gangplank. She hurried for the stairs.

The mess deck was quiet, and she made it to the gangplank without incident. Many of the sailors were already on the dock, tending to the moorings. Groves spoke to an official man off to the side. This was her one chance to get off the ship undetected, but she wouldn't make it far with so many familiar faces along the dock. She could run and hope they were too slow to stop her. That might be her only option.

She grabbed the edge of the opening and put one foot on the gangplank.

"I wouldn't do that if I were you." The voice came from the stairs behind her.

Harriet froze and forced herself to turn around. Harvey stood beside the stairs, half hidden in the shadow. Her heart leaped into her throat.

"Are you going to stop me?" she asked, her mouth dry.

He stepped into the light.

Instinct forced her to withdraw, and her back bumped against the hull of the ship. She hadn't seen him since the day he'd come aboard the *Seren*—Sam had made certain of that—but that experience alone had been enough to instill fear deep within her.

"It's six miles to Mayfair from here," he said.

Six miles? It would take her hours to walk there, and she didn't know the way. Her disguise wouldn't keep her safe from those who stalked the streets this soon after sunrise. Being found alone on the docks was a mistake she didn't want to repeat in her lifetime.

Harvey continued. "Sam has gone to hire a phaeton and will escort you home if you would wait."

She frowned. Was he trying to smile? The grimace on his face was not threatening, nor was it particularly reassuring.

"And you can take that bloody dog, too. He's not staying here with me." Harvey's grin was unmistakable this time, as was his soft chuckle.

"All right," she said. She could accept assistance from Sam.

She returned to Alexander's cabin without another word passing between her and Harvey.

Within the hour, Jacob arrived to escort her to the waiting phaeton.

She glanced around the cabin. There were no belongings to pack, no trace of her left behind. An underwhelming end to such an unexpected journey, one that had changed her life. For better or worse, she was yet to discover. She turned her back on the cabin and the memories it held, following Jacob. Harvey was nowhere to be seen.

Shadow trailed behind her down the gangplank. As they walked away, she cast one last look over her shoulder at the *Seren* towering over the dock. Groves and a few other sailors waved. She returned the gesture and turned her back on them.

A final goodbye.

Sam helped her into the phaeton and climbed in beside her. Jacob lifted Shadow onto her lap.

"Thank you again, 'Arry." Jacob said with a cheeky grin.

"Think nothing of it, Jacob," she replied, her voice catching in her throat. Despite everything awaiting her, she couldn't bring herself to regret her actions of the past few weeks. She'd been a sailor, however fleeting the experience, had made new friends, and met a man who had changed her irrevocably. She'd saved Jacob's life. Whatever price she had to pay, it was all worth it.

Jacob turned away and started back toward the ship. Her heart was heavy, beating its solemn rhythm behind her aching ribs. All these people she had come to know over the past weeks, who had befriended her and watched over her, she would never see again. The tightness in her chest settled uncomfortably, and she suspected it would stay with her for some time.

Sam shook the reins, and the horse started off. They navigated through the streets at a steady pace, and she soon appreciated not attempting the journey on foot.

"Alexander informed me of your seasickness," Sam said. "Are you well enough to increase the speed?"

"I'm fine so long as the carriage doesn't enter stormy waters," she said, smiling. "What else did he tell you about me?"

Sam's eyes narrowed, but he didn't look at her. "That you were a woman. Alexander told me on that first day, and the circumstances by which you came to be part of our crew. He had no choice. I hope you understand."

She played with Shadow's fur as they continued

through London. There was much she was still trying to understand.

"Will you tell me about Alexander?" she asked.

Sam glanced at her out of the corner of his eye. "It's not my place. He will tell you about himself when the time is right."

Hope blossomed within her. If Alexander sought her out in London, what would he say?

"You expect him to return?" she asked, failing to hide her optimism.

"Yes, but I don't know what awaits us. I wish I could tell you more, but I simply can't."

"This has something to do with Harvey, doesn't it?"

Sam remained silent, and the town buildings passed in a blur. The views of the river and fields were long gone, replaced by stone structures lining either side of the street. Splashes of color caught her eye, pink, white, and red plants spilling from window boxes.

"Did Harvey hurt Alexander?" Harriet asked.

"No." Sam chuckled. "It's nothing like that."

"Then what is it?"

"I truly cannot say." His attention was on the horse, guiding it through the streets.

"Did Alexander know he wouldn't come back to the ship that day?"

"No, but it was always a possibility," Sam said. "What we do, it isn't structured. That serves a purpose for what needs to be done. Alexander did what was necessary, and there is more to do in London."

"What do you do, exactly?"

Sam sighed. "You already know more than you ought. I don't know what Alexander told you, so it's best if I keep my mouth shut."

"Alexander told me nothing," she replied. Clearly, she wasn't going to get more information out of Sam. "Why does Harvey hate me so much? Surely you can tell me that?"

"He doesn't hate you." Sam sounded surprised. "What would make you think that?"

Wasn't it obvious? "He sent me to my cabin within minutes of meeting me, and he was particularly unkind."

"He's not used to having a woman on board, especially one who knows how to sail." Sam's answer was not satisfactory to explain Harvey's actions, but apparently it was all she would get.

"Who is the real captain?" she asked.

"Pardon?"

"Is it Alexander or Harvey? That information wouldn't be giving away all your secrets."

"We are all captains," Sam said, turning his head and glancing down an alleyway. "Alexander sails the *Seren*, but if needed, we can all captain that ship, or others."

"There's more than one ship?"

Sam clicked his tongue, and the horse's speed increased.

"What I mean to say is that we all possess the skills required. The vessel isn't the important part. We're not bound to one ship as its captain, but Alexander does own the *Seren*."

She was beginning to appreciate that trust ran deep between the three men, and she had underestimated their loyalty to each other.

"We're not far from Mayfair now," Sam said, taking the phaeton around a corner. "Once we arrive at your home, I will escort you inside."

"Did Alexander tell you about my family?"

Sam's hesitation confirmed her suspicions.

The horse's hooves clipped on the cobblestone, the familiar rhythm calming her nerves.

"Thank you, Sam, for everything." She meant it. "It would be best if I did this on my own. I don't know how my father will react to my sudden appearance. He's far more generous than anyone gives him credit for, especially with me and my sisters, but I doubt that would extend to a man who had conspired to detain me on a sailing ship." And what would he say when she told him she'd been ruined in every sense of the word?

Sam's brow creased. "Alexander gave me strict instructions to speak with your father when I brought you home."

"You may watch me to my door, but I will not permit you to come in with me. Once I am over the threshold, you may leave."

Sam's expression told her she hadn't convinced him.

She didn't give him the chance to object. "Pull into any of the side alleys you deem appropriate, and I will make my way there on foot."

"Very well." He guided the phaeton into an alleyway and alighted first. Offering a hand, he assisted her down. "I'll stay here until you're inside. I hope we meet again, Harriet." Sam's attention turned to Shadow. "You know, Alexander will be in a right mood when he sees how loyal that dog has become to you."

She beamed at Shadow and lowered him to the ground. "I know."

Chapter Eighteen

A LEXANDER'S DAYS in dark alleys would soon be over if he could help it. Without a residence of his own, he had been forced to roam the streets, awaiting Sam and Harvey's arrival. No wonder he was in such a foul mood. Biding his time in London would have been more pleasant at George's empty home, but his dratted brother was here early, doing Lord knows what.

It had not been a smooth passage from Saint-Malo on that miserable excuse for a vessel. The thing could barely be considered a boat, and it was a far stretch of the imagination for anyone to call it a ship, but the loyal crew had insisted upon it. Sailing from France to London in four days had been no easy feat, either. He hadn't slept, had scarcely eaten, and it had now been over a week since he'd had a decent wash. But he'd wanted to be here before Harriet returned. He had to see her to her door, even from a distance. Once she was home, he could focus on the task at hand.

A horse clipped past, drawing his attention back to quiet Berkeley Square. The stone wall was cold where he pressed his back into it, staying in the shadows. There weren't many people out at this hour, but he couldn't risk anyone seeing him. He kept his right shoulder curled away from the wall, still tender after his meeting with Harvey in Saint-Malo. The dratted man had been right. It wasn't broken. The phaeton passed, and Alexander glimpsed Harriet.

His breath caught in his throat. He'd known she was safe. Sam had reassured him of it repeatedly when they'd met that morning. But he hadn't stopped thinking of her since he'd left the *Seren* in Saint-Malo. The relief of seeing her home overwhelmed him.

The phaeton slowed, and Sam guided it around a corner, into another alley. What was he doing? Alexander was of two minds. If he followed them, and Harriet saw him, he wouldn't possess the ability to drag himself away despite knowing that he must. But Sam had deviated from their plan, and he wanted to know why.

The seconds ticked by, but indecision rooted him to the spot. He couldn't bring her back into this, not now. She was home, and he wouldn't burden her again until he could keep his promises, whatever they might be.

Harriet stepped into the dim light of Berkeley Square, and Shadow followed close behind. The sun had not yet risen above the buildings, and a thick blanket of fog still covered the square. She was dressed in the disguise he'd brought her, and in the middle of Mayfair, appeared entirely out of place. How would she look the next time he saw her? The idea of her in a gown was so foreign, he couldn't picture it. She crossed the square and disappeared into the Hazelby residence, taking Shadow with her.

Alexander and Sam had arranged a meeting place not far away, but they had agreed on a half-hour delay.

Alexander craned his neck and glanced down the street. No sign of Sam. He stayed against the wall, eager to get on with matters with Sam and Harvey but wanting to stay close to Harriet.

Out of the corner of his eye, a movement caught his attention. A gray shape darted out of the house. He hadn't time to groan before setting off behind Harriet, mindful of keeping enough distance between them so that he wouldn't alert Shadow to the chase. She was faster than he'd expected, though he shouldn't be surprised that she was a proficient runner as well. Was there anything lady-like about the woman at all? And could he admire anything about her more? He had to push past a comfortable running speed to keep pace with her. Where was she headed?

They turned onto a street at the northern end of Berkeley Square. The wind picked up behind him, and Shadow stopped.

Alexander froze.

Shadow had caught his scent. Alexander had few moments before the game was up, and no time to find a place to hide. Shadow spun around and raced in his direction.

"No," Alexander groaned, but that didn't stop Shadow from barreling into him. He ducked into an alleyway, pulling the dog with him and keeping an eye on Harriet. He waited for her to realize that Shadow had left, but the moment never came. She ran through the streets of Mayfair as though her life depended on it, so he followed with Shadow at his heels. They reached Grosvenor Square in record time, and at last, he ascertained her destination.

Eliza Malstern was Harriet's eldest sister, a person she trusted, but why would she prefer the house of Lester Malstern over her own family? The duke was not known for his chivalry since he'd married. No woman would put herself in his presence without dire need. What had happened at her own family home for her to run to her sister?

HARRIET TORE THROUGH MAYFAIR, her boots thudding on the cobblestone street. The rest of the family was yet to arrive at their London residence, or so the footman had told her, but they had been expected a week ago. Her sister, Eliza, was the only one in London. Had Harriet's disappearance from Hull delayed their departure?

The distance between their homes wasn't far, and Harriet was knocking on the black front door of Malstern House within ten minutes, albeit slightly out of breath.

The butler, Mr. Tombs, answered. He took one look at her and attempted to thrust the door shut.

She leaned all her weight against the door, stopping it from reaching the latch. "Mr. Tombs," she said, desperation thick in her voice, "it's me, Harriet Hazelby. I know I must look quite the sight, but I need to see my sister."

Mr. Tombs stilled, and his sharp gaze raked over her twice. His brown eyes crinkled at the corners, but the expression was one of suspicion. Not a single brown hair was out of place on his head, and his dark gray uniform was as crisp as ever.

His manner was most unimpressed when he spoke. "This way, my lady, and do mind the carpets." He ushered her inside, his gaze sweeping across the street. The door snapped shut. "I don't know where you've been, but I cannot permit you to see Her Grace in this state. I'll have one of the maids draw you a bath." He gestured toward someone out of sight and steered her farther into the house with a reluctant touch on her arm. She resisted the urge to shake him off and allowed him to guide her down the white marble corridor.

"Harriet Hazelby!" Eliza's voice was instantly recognizable, as was the tone indicating that Harriet was in *big* trouble.

Mr. Tombs retreated to the wall, leaving Harriet to face her sister alone. She braced herself and turned around.

"I thought I heard your voice," Eliza said, striding down the corridor. Her heels clicked on the marble and echoed around the corridor. Pale blue skirts fell in perfect symmetry despite the brisk movement, and her upswept hair didn't jostle. "But then I stopped to consider how that could be possible, as you are still in Hull." The rhetorical lecture, one of Eliza's best techniques.

Harriet squirmed and waited for the point to be made. It would be, *eventually*. Not before Harriet felt completely wretched.

"I briefly considered the possibility that the family had indeed arrived, yet this is not a respectable hour for a social call. Then I saw you, standing in my house, dressed"—Eliza's fierce gaze examined every inch of Harriet. She waved a hand between them, and her mouth turned down —"as though you have been working in a stable."

Harriet sensed that the time for an explanation drew nigh, but she dared not speak until Eliza asked her a direct question. It would be best to know how informed her sister was.

"This arrived last evening." In Eliza's hand was a letter that she flashed in front of Harriet. "It's from Millie, and the reason that I am awake so early. Why, pray tell, do you think she would be asking me how you and I are faring in London, when we both know that you should still be in Hull?" Eliza finished her question with a piercing glare.

Harriet's eyes widened, and she scrambled for an answer. Why would Millie think she was in London? "I don't know," she said, sticking to the truth.

"Where have you been, Harriet? I don't recall seeing you in my carriage when I traveled from Hull. Nor have I seen you here in London since I arrived."

"I..." Harriet started, a bubble of emotion rising too fast in her chest. "I..." she tried again.

"What have you done?"

The tears flowed in earnest, and she couldn't stop them. Every emotion from the past few weeks seemed to have waited until now for release.

Eliza's arms wrapped gingerly around her shoulders, and she guided her into the parlor. Black and gold blurred together in her tear-filled vision. They collapsed onto a settee, sinking into the dark cushion.

"Mr. Tombs, a light breakfast, please," Eliza said. "We'll take a small tray in here and a pot of tea."

"Yes, Your Grace," he said, disappearing through the door.

Eliza's fingers ran up and down her arm until the tears subsided.

"You need to tell me what happened, Harriet, otherwise I cannot help you."

Harriet hesitated. How much of the truth could Eliza handle? She settled on an honest version of events, excluding the finer details that might cause Eliza to have an apoplexy.

"I was on a sailing ship."

Eliza's eyes narrowed. "How? Why? Where did you go?"

She peppered Harriet with so many questions, she couldn't keep track.

"I didn't do it intentionally," Harriet said. She told Eliza about the messenger, Captain Alexander finding her below deck and tying her up, and how she hadn't freed herself until the *Seren* had sailed. Eliza's expression grew more dubious as her story progressed, and Harriet hadn't divulged the quiet moments she'd shared with Alexander, kissing him, and jumping overboard to save Jacob. Especially not what had happened that morning in Saint-Malo. That would be treading dangerously close to apoplexy territory. "We sailed into two ports," Harriet continued. "When Alexander left the ship the last time, a man called Harvey arrived and sailed it back to England. I don't know what happened to Alexander. Harvey and Sam refused to tell me anything."

"Who is Sam?" Eliza asked.

Not quite the point Harriet expected her sister to focus on.

Harriet met her sister's pale green gaze, but it gave nothing away. This response was rather tame given Harriet's story.

She answered her sister, unsettled by the calm. "Sam is Alexander's first mate. He brought me back to Mayfair this morning after we docked in London."

"Were you seduced?" Eliza's bluntness shocked her. It took every effort not to blush. She failed.

"No," Harriet answered. "Sam was incredibly kind to me. I would consider him a friend if I saw him again."

Eliza regarded her, exasperated. "I meant by the captain."

"No." Her reply wasn't convincing. The heat flushing her cheeks made it worse.

Eliza harrumphed. "You're not to speak of this to anyone."

"Not even Papa?"

"No," Eliza said. "We'll wait until he arrives and see what he knows. I'd say by Millie's letter that they all believe you have been here with me this entire time, and that is a blessing."

"Why are you here, Eliza?"

Eliza fixed her with a stern stare. "After you disappeared from your room, I called on the Duke of Ailesbury alone. I'd assumed you had gone to find Uncle Frederick or for another ride. So, I went without you. We *had* accepted the duke's invitation. While I was there, a messenger arrived with a summons from my husband. He'd been sent by the butler at Balmaine. The Duke of Ailesbury saw me on my way posthaste, and he sent a note to Uncle Frederick explaining where I had gone. They must have thought you were with me and accompanied me to London."

"Yes," Harriet mused, watching a serving maid bring in a tray and place it on the table. The buttered toast, sunny eggs, and tea held no appeal.

"It would be best if you forgot about this," Eliza said. "If it's possible that not a soul in England, save you and me, knows where you have been, it would be of the utmost importance to keep it that way."

Forget what had happened? Harriet would not speak of it to a soul, but she could not forget. The hope that Alexander would return still burned inside her. Despite not knowing what a future with him might mean, or if it were possible at all. If he returned, would her father allow her to marry him? He was a sailor, after all.

"Now, there is much to do today," Eliza said, switching seamlessly to the next item of business. "If you had been with me for weeks, we would be a lot further ahead in the season preparations. We'll begin our morning at the modiste." She paused. "On second thought, we will have the modiste visit here. No one has yet seen you in London, and they might wonder when you arrived, and if you came alone. It would be best if you stayed here until we figure out what to do."

"You don't expect me to proceed as though this hadn't happened!" Harriet protested. How could she still be presented for a season? It wasn't possible. No man would marry her now. And if they did, what would they do when they discovered another man had taken her virtue?

"Absolutely, I do," Eliza said, her voice stern and leaving no room for argument. "And you're not to leave this house at all."

And there she was, trapped all over again.

Chapter Nineteen

ALEXANDER PACED the uneven stone floor from one end of the room to the other. Fourteen paces. Not that he needed to count again. He'd only done it forty times each day since they'd arrived a week ago. Hardly a grand room, but one of the more generous in which he'd been imprisoned. The gray stone walls housed a bed, a chair, and a damn fireplace. This wing of the Tower of London was heaven compared to some places he'd been held in the past decade.

"How long do you think they'll keep us here?" Harvey asked.

Sam groaned, and Alexander did his best to ignore the pair of them.

"I swear," Sam said, "if you ask again, I'll call for the guards and tell them that, actually, I don't think you are the Harvey we were looking for. Perhaps you're an imposter and we were mistaken."

"We'll all hang if you do that," came Harvey's bored reply. He lounged on the bed, one arm beneath his head, shoveling peanuts into his mouth with the other. His right foot dangled an inch off the floor, swinging to and fro.

"Might be worth it if it means I won't have to listen to you complain," Sam grumbled. "Or *chew*."

"Will you two stop it?" Alexander asked. "Or could you take it into another room? I don't see why you need to be in here, annoying me."

The guards had kept the doors unlocked and were rarely seen. Alexander, Sam, and Harvey had been free to move around as they wished within the confines of this wing. Alexander wasn't sure why the pair of them insisted on irritating him each day. He would have been content to sit with his thoughts. Lord knew he deserved punishment, but he hadn't expected it to arrive in this form.

"We've only been here a week," Sam said, his tone placating. "The officials have probably spent most of that time summoning Lord Edington from his country home. Most prisoners spend months waiting."

Harvey groaned and threw his head back. "I'm not sure I'll last. Perhaps they should hang me and get it over with."

Alexander caught Sam's eye, and they both laughed.

"We won't hang," Alexander said. "Once Lord Edington arrives and can verify your identity, we'll be free to leave." He had to trust that would be the case. If not, he would never see Harriet again, and that was not a prospect he wanted to consider. He was determined to be released and would do all it took to be the man she needed. Sell the *Seren*? Easy. Give up sailing for the remainder of his life? Done. He'd live in London or the country, whichever she preferred. If he could only get out of this wing. If she still wanted him.

"Well, I hope the blasted man gets here soon," Harvey mumbled. "*Before* I expire of boredom."

A knock sounded at the door, and it opened without invitation.

A tall man stepped into the room, his shining black boots reflecting the low fire in the hearth.

"Gentlemen," he said, straightening the front of his gray coat. His bright blue gaze, mirroring Alexander's, appraised the room.

George.

He was not the man Alexander had been hoping to see, but his arrival was cause for thanks. Alexander could have hugged his brother if he were prone to such sentimental behavior. Now he'd have an update on Harriet, and his imagination could stop running wild.

Shadow stirred from his bed, lifting his head and offering a lazy bark.

"George," Alexander said, stepping forward and greeting his brother with a firm handshake. "It is good to see you."

Sam and Harvey both nodded in his brother's direction. The fact that neither of them bothered to stand or acknowledge his rank made Alexander smile.

"It's good to see you too," George said. "Alive. All of you." He glanced around the room again.

"No true cause for concern," Sam said, addressing George as though he were another of his own brothers.

"Perfectly healthy," Harvey added. "Though if you're not here to tell us we're free to leave, my sentiment may change."

Alexander watched his brother, but George didn't answer. He stood there, smiling.

Alexander intended to push his brother for an answer, but the question that left his mouth was far more important. "Is Harriet well?"

George's eyes narrowed, his mouth forming a smirk. So

he knew. It was as Alexander had hoped. Harriet's sister must have told George everything.

"Well?" Alexander pressed.

"She is being presented to the *ton* as we speak."

Alexander's chest tightened. He wished he could have been there.

"She will attend the first ball of the season tonight," George said. "I've heard it will be quite the event. Her sister is anticipating great interest from the available suitors."

"Why are you telling me that?" Alexander growled. "I wanted to know Harriet was well. You believe I want to think about other men swarming around her?" The thought made his stomach roil. If Alexander didn't leave this godforsaken place soon, he might be too late. Suitors would inundate her with attention. Perhaps she would be better off with one of those men. Did everything that passed between them mean as much to her as it did to him?

"Ah, Lord Edington," George said, stepping aside to let a short, balding man into the room. "I was wondering where you'd got to." His gaze moved to Alexander, laughter lighting up his eyes.

Alexander curled his hands into fists. What he wouldn't give to hit his brother right now.

"You idiot, George," Harvey said, jumping to his feet. He crossed the room and punched George on the shoulder. "You said you weren't here to let us out."

"I'm not," George said, rubbing his shoulder. "That is the role of the guards."

"I could smother you," Sam said, but his voice was light with laughter.

Alexander remained quiet while Lord Edington surveyed the room over his spectacles. His gray eyes inspected each of them.

"All is in order," Lord Edington called, and a pair of guards appeared behind him. "These men are who they say they are. You may let them go."

"Wait," Alexander said.

Lord Edington raised a fluffy eyebrow. "You wish to stay?"

"No," Harvey said before Alexander could answer. "He can do as he wishes, but I'm leaving." Harvey moved toward the door, but the guards blocked his exit.

Alexander couldn't help but laugh. "I do not wish to stay," he said, "but I do wish to speak to you before I leave."

"What is this regarding?" Lord Edington asked. Sam and Harvey echoed his question, although their language was rather more colorful.

"About ending my service to the Crown."

Eliza was a force to be reckoned with, and Harriet had been no match for her sister. Varying degrees of unpleasantness filled their week in London. When Harriet wasn't being poked, prodded, or pinned by the modiste in Eliza's dressing room, she had suffered through hours-long dance lessons or wasted perfect afternoons in the company of a withered old tutor. Always under her sister's watchful eye. The Duke of Eldon, Eliza's husband, had remained occupied elsewhere, making her stay that bit less dreadful. Few moments of solitude graced the week, when Eliza had called upon the Duke of Ailesbury, and Harriet had spent those in quiet contemplation. The whereabouts and well-being of Alexander—and Shadow, the dog disappearing from her side the morning she'd sprinted through Mayfair —occupied her mind.

"Spin," Madame Donohue ordered. The modiste had been silent for so long, her order made Harriet jump. "Again."

Harriet rolled her eyes but followed the demand, coming face to face with her sister. Eliza stood alone in the doorway of Harriet's childhood bedroom, a delighted grin revealing her dazzling white teeth.

Eliza had forbidden Harriet from returning home when the rest of the family had arrived two days ago. *It's important to maintain the charade*, Eliza had said, and she'd wanted to ensure an uneventful presentation at court before deciding how to proceed.

Presentation had passed earlier that afternoon without so much as a whisper of Harriet's disappearance. Better than they'd dared to hope. Even her parents remained unaware of her escapades. Still, Harriet could not evade her sister, who had insisted upon accompanying her to the Hazelby residence and remained a hovering presence over the evening's proceedings. Namely, her first ball.

The season was progressing as planned. Harriet's courses had come and gone in the days after she'd arrived home with only the briefest mention of laundry from Eliza. She had no need to disclose the events on the *Seren* to her family. Eliza had insisted.

"What are you so happy about?" Harriet grumbled.

"I don't want to hear another moan, groan, or mumble of refusal," Eliza said. Stern words from her oldest sister. Harriet begrudged a glance at her, but Eliza's smile had softened. "You are so lovely in that color." The compliment, though meant with kindness and hope to boost Harriet's confidence, had the opposite effect.

Harriet turned her head and regarded her reflection for the first time in days, keeping her eyes away from her face and the secrets hidden there. The gown was a delicate silver silk with an overlay of the finest lace that fell from below the bust, encrusted with tiny emeralds twinkling in the light. For a moment, the beauty of it overwhelmed her, but the delight quickly vanished. She was not the woman for this gown.

"No one will be able to keep their eyes off you." Eliza clasped her hands together and pressed them to her chest.

The statement sent Harriet's stomach into an all-too-familiar state of queasiness. Eliza's determination had been commendable, but Harriet would never be ready for the *ton*.

She shook her head. All she had to do was make it through the initial introduction. The few curious glances that came her way would soon turn to disappointment, and she could disappear behind Millie. She tried to reassure herself with little success. People *would* stare, and they would see how out of place she was beside her sisters. How she was the unnecessary third daughter who should have been a son and heir to the Earl of Selby.

Madame Donohue left the room, leaving Harriet alone with Eliza.

"What were you doing this afternoon?" Harriet asked, running a hand over her skirts. The occasions that her sister had left her alone over the past week were so rare, Harriet couldn't help but notice them. She'd rather discuss anything than the impending social event.

Eliza's cheeks turned pink. "I was with the Duke of Ailesbury."

"Again?" That would be the fourth time.

"It was a social call," Eliza replied.

Harriet clenched her teeth against her retort.

The Duke of Ailesbury and the Duke of Eldon had something of a friendship, but it wasn't commonplace for a woman to call upon a friend of her husband, was it? Four times in a week was most extraordinary. There could be only one explanation for these repeated social visits. If Eliza was planning to introduce Harriet to the duke again, she could be honest. Harriet remained as opposed to the introduction as she had in Hull, except this time, she would not attempt to escape her fate. Weeks on a ship had not condemned her to spinsterhood, but it had made her slower to act on her impulses. Besides, she didn't have to accept the man's proposal. What was the worst that could happen?

Chapter Twenty

As low as they had been, the ball exceeded all of Harriet's expectations. The room was divine, each of the silver, blue, and pink decorations impressive in their splendor. The effect was not lost on Harriet, who was overwhelmed whichever way she turned. Eliza had also exceeded her expectations magnificently, although not so positively. She'd paraded Harriet around the ballroom like a prized cow. Her mother would have been kinder and more subtle in her introductions, and any of her father's conversations would have been more compelling than what Eliza and the women of the *ton* had to say.

Harriet turned away from Eliza and the woman with whom she was reacquainting. They spoke as though there had been a mere sip of tea between conversations, rather than months spent in their respective country homes. She wished her parents had attended, but the afternoon at court had been the extent of their social activities for the day. They'd remained at home together for the evening to prepare for their own upcoming events.

Admittedly, Eliza's most recent introduction had served

as a timely reprieve from the dance floor, where Harriet had trodden on far too many toes for it to be considered endearing. It wasn't as though she was entirely uncoordinated. She had been riding since she could mount a horse, had climbed many a tree, and had survived weeks on a sailing ship. All it did was reinforce the notion that she could never aspire to make a match as highly ranked as Eliza's duke.

She walked to the edge of the balcony, searching for Millie among the crowd. A tall man entered the ballroom below, garnering the attention of those nearest him.

"His Grace, The Duke of Ailesbury," a booming voice announced.

Harriet gasped. He must be fifty years younger than she'd expected.

The duke beamed at the room, the expression set into a perfect, chiseled jaw. More than one nearby young lady swooned when he glanced their way. Eliza was delusional if she thought Harriet was a match for that man.

Harriet turned her back on him and the gathering crowd. Each of their intended introductions had been avoided thus far, but she couldn't evade it now. She took what little time she had before he made it through the throng of potential brides and up the stairs. Without any means of escape, and in a pitiful effort to delay the inevitable, she hid herself behind a small palm tree. The plant reached an inch above her head, the long, thin leaves offering little protection. She cast her gaze downward, clutching her glass of lemonade between both gloved hands.

Strong fingers wrapped around her arm and dragged her from her hiding place.

"Come with me, Harriet," Eliza said, her tone bright.

Harriet tried to shake free of Eliza's grip. "I don't want to meet the Duke of Ailesbury," she hissed.

"That's too bad." The man's response came from beside her sister.

Eliza grasped her elbow and spun Harriet to face the duke. "This is Ge—I mean, the Duke of Ailesbury."

Harriet shot a glance at her sister, who had flushed a delicate shade of pink, and returned her attention to the duke. His bright blue eyes darted between Harriet and Eliza, and a peculiar smirk played on his lips. It took her a moment to remember herself, but when she did, she dropped into a deep curtsy. Beside her, Eliza appeared more interested in the tapestries hanging on the wall than in the introduction she had not completed.

"It's a pleasure to meet you, Miss...?"

"Harriet Hazelby," Harriet finished on her sister's behalf.

He grinned. "I have heard much about you."

If Eliza planned to marry her off before she could make a mess of her first season, he'd have heard much more than Harriet would approve. Hopefully, he wouldn't ask her to dance. Stepping on the toes of other gentlemen that evening had been embarrassing enough. She did not need to add a duke to her list of unsuspecting victims. Her sister's toes, on the other hand, deserved a good stamping. That would have to wait until they were in the carriage.

"It is a pleasure to make your acquaintance, Your Grace," Harriet said, taking the duke's proffered hand.

He bent his head over her hand, and she tried to control the churning in her stomach. Meeting the person your sister had intended for you had a way of making one's insides feel like worms. She preferred the fire that ignited whenever Alexander was near.

"Might I introduce you to my brother?" he asked. The duke indicated a place over her right shoulder.

Eliza remained silent.

Harriet hadn't known the duke had a brother. She plastered a polite smile on her face and followed his gaze. Her heart leaped into her throat. She swallowed against the sensation, but it brought her little relief.

"Lord Alexander Ordell," the duke said.

Captain Alexander.

Alexander walked forward, regarding her with brilliant blue eyes. A slight yellowing colored his cheek beneath one of them. Or was it a play of the lighting? He swept her hand to his lips and brushed a light kiss over her gloved knuckles, his piercing gaze never straying from her face. The brother of a duke? It wasn't possible. He could not be Lord Ordell.

She kept her mouth closed and focused on her breathing.

"It is my absolute delight, Lady Harriet." He leaned over her hand that still rested in his. "You are breathtaking."

The Duke of Ailesbury and Eliza were watching her, along with a few others close enough to witness the interaction. The time for her to speak had long passed, but no words would come. Alexander's smile faltered.

He leaned closer and whispered words for her alone. "I haven't known you to be speechless, Harriet. Are you all right?"

She scrambled for a response, coming up short. And because she couldn't think of a more reasonable action, she swooned.

The glass dropped from her hand, shattering on the timber floor and sending a splash of lemonade over her skirts. Those nearest to her gasped, Alexander cursed, and a few hands reached for her as she fell, but Alexander's reaction was swift. Had she predicted that swooning would land her in his arms, she would never have done it. She was now tucked against Alexander's chest as he carried her through the ballroom.

His breath tickled her ear as he murmured, "I can already hear the chatter about how one look at Alexander Ordell can make the most beautiful woman swoon."

Harriet buried her face in his chest, away from the watchful eyes of the *ton*. No doubt she would be the subject of the morning gossip sheet. She grabbed a handful of his waistcoat, trying to ignore that her arm had somehow become wrapped around him *under* his unbuttoned tailcoat.

"Ow," he complained.

She had accidentally taken more than his waistcoat between her fingers, but she wouldn't relent. He already controlled too much of the situation.

"If you don't like it, put me down," she hissed.

"I can't have you fainting on me again," he said, delight clear in his voice.

"I didn't faint," she grumbled into his chest. Heat spread through her chest, and she tried to ignore her body's natural response to being this close to him.

"Of course you didn't." His voice was molten honey. "Doesn't matter, I'm never letting go of you again, Harriet Hazelby," he added in a more serious tone.

Every muscle in her body tensed. "Yes, you will."

"No," he announced, "I can't risk it."

She relaxed her hand and remained silent until they reached the end of the ballroom. A footman held the door open, and they passed into the hall. She squirmed away from Alexander, preparing to be put down.

"Will you stop wriggling, please? I've injured my shoulder, and you're not making this any easier."

He *was* hurt. A bruise under his eye, an injured shoulder... What had happened to him in Saint-Malo?

"I'm perfectly capable of walking myself, if you'd let go—"

"Not yet," he interjected, his voice cheerful again.

She stilled. Where was he taking her?

"There is no need," she said. A half-hearted protest at best. When it came to it, she didn't want him to let her go in earnest, but the longer she was with him, the worse it would be when he left. Because he would leave. She was no match for a duke's brother. All those dreams she'd had on the ship and since, now seemed ridiculous.

He ignored her protests, striding down the hall.

They made a sudden turn to the left, and a door clicked shut behind them. The din from the hall and ballroom hushed, and Harriet pulled her face away from his chest. A small crackling fire and a few candles lit the room. Leather, smoky and rich, filled her nose, giving her a brief reprieve from Alexander's delicious scent. Ginger and warmth enveloped him, and other things she shouldn't be noticing. It soon blended with the leather, and the resulting scent was a sweet and spicy combination that did things to her insides she did not want to think about.

"We should have a few moments of peace in here," Alexander said, setting her on her feet. His hands stayed on her shoulders.

"Will you stop it?" she snapped. "I'm not going to faint!" Though her knees were acting a little strangely in response to the way his eyes roamed over her. She might well turn to jelly if she wasn't careful.

His deep, throaty chuckle sent her insides melting.

"Very well, but I'll be here if you do." He stepped back, keeping her locked in his gaze. "I've been waiting for this moment for weeks. I could never imagine you like this on the ship. This gown suits you well. The designer was obviously inspired by your emerald eyes. Though, if I may be so bold and honest, I prefer you in breeches." He bent his head to the side, ogling her behind.

The many layers of her gown and petticoat kept her well-concealed, but that didn't stop the heat from rushing to her face. She swiveled her hips away from his stare, inspiring a most devilish grin to cross his face. Her neck and cheeks burned, heat creeping down her chest. She pointed a finger in his direction.

"Don't try to distract me," she said.

"If either one of us is distracting, it is you."

She stepped back and tripped on the hem of her gown. Alexander's arms wrapped around her again. Her heart stuttered, and she leaned into him.

"You are utterly hopeless in a gown," he said. "It is as I suspected. You're much better suited to breeches."

"Let me go!" She had to leave. Someone could walk in and discover the two of them alone. Alexander wouldn't want to be caught with her. Why else had he taken her so far from the ballroom? If anyone saw them together, they'd be forced to marry. Worse still, her treacherous body was moments away from giving in to him. His hands didn't leave her hips until she was standing steady again.

"I am not utterly hopeless in a gown. I've spent my entire life wearing them."

He grinned. "So, it is me?"

"You're impossible. And I am not discussing this any further. Thank you, my lord, for bringing me out for fresh air, but it is time I returned to my sister." She fluffed her skirts back into place and secured her reticule around her wrist. Where was Eliza? Harriet could have sworn she'd seen her following them out of the ballroom.

"Alexander," he whispered.

She glanced at him. "What?"

His eyes were downcast, hands clasped behind his back. The playfulness in his expression was a shadow of what had been there before. "Please, call me Alexander," he said, meeting her gaze through his eyelashes.

"How could I?" Harriet asked. "You're Lord Ordell."

"Not to you, I'm not."

Her chest tightened. "What is that supposed to mean?"

"That's what I want to explain, if you could give me a chance," he said.

She huffed. "Three minutes. Say what you must so that I may return to my sister." She held her breath and waited. Would he ask her not to expose him for kidnapping her? Beg to be released from any obligation to marry her? Whatever he said, she wasn't ready to hear it.

ALEXANDER'S MIND WAS SPINNING. Where should he start? How could he explain it all in three minutes? Not that it would matter. He'd have an abundance of time over the next few weeks to tell her the truth of his past. He tried to focus on the important details. The ones that would earn her trust enough to buy him that time.

Harriet's eyes were wide and accusing, but they twinkled in the candlelight. The sight wrenched the memories of watch duty together to the forefront of his mind. Those quiet moments he'd fought to keep himself away from her.

Her strength and subtle sensuality. That kiss on the quarterdeck. The morning in Saint-Malo...

Heat rushed through his body, pooling in inconvenient places.

"Well, my lord?"

"Alexander." He winked, then internally cursed himself. As if that would help. Why was he such an idiot around her?

Her jaw clenched, and her teeth ground together. "Why don't you start by telling me why it took weeks and a surprise introduction at the first ball of the season for me to learn that you're Lord Alexander Ordell."

Alexander swallowed and resisted the urge to close the distance between them. "I wanted to tell you. Especially when I found out who you were, but it wasn't the right time."

She scoffed. "You believe this was better?"

"Well, no, but I couldn't see you sooner. I have been busy with... things." Understatement of the century. "I wanted to ensure that it was all resolved before I saw you."

"How well do you and Harvey know each other?" Her tone had softened, and her gaze had left his, focusing on her reticule. She ran her fingers over the strands wrapped around her wrist.

He'd been expecting her questions, but this wasn't the topic he'd intended discussing. Perhaps following her line of questioning would help his case.

"We've worked together for five years," he said. He could still steer this conversation back to his main purpose.

"And do you know he had me locked in your cabin for the entire journey home?" She glanced up, meeting his eyes for a moment, but her gaze flicked away. "If it weren't for Sam, I wouldn't have been outside for a week."

Alexander blinked. He hadn't known. Neither Sam nor Harvey had said much regarding their return journey, other than that it had gone to plan. Having Harvey lock Harriet in his cabin hadn't been part of the plan.

"That seems a bit of an exaggeration," he said.

She pierced him with a glare so fierce that he stumbled back a step, bumping into the table. The candlesticks rocked on the timber top but stayed upright. Their flames flickered and reflected in Harriet's eyes, though he couldn't be sure if they were responsible for the flashes there.

He hurried to offer an explanation. "I was explicitly clear about what I would do to Harvey should any harm come to you." Had Harvey taken those threats to heart?

Her eyes narrowed. "You spoke to Harvey in Saint-Malo?"

"Yes."

Her reticule whistled through the air. He whacked it away before it collided with his head.

She stalked toward him, apparently intent on using her fists now that she'd dispensed with her only weapon. "I didn't know what happened to you when we left that port! I thought I'd never see you again."

"You cared about what happened to me?" he asked. It was better than he could have hoped.

A loud snort ripped from her, and she rolled her eyes. "Only so that I might kill you myself!" Both of her hands landed on his chest, knocking the last of his breath from him. He grabbed her wrists. Her face was so close, and it took every effort not to pull her a little closer and kiss her. Not yet.

"Do you want me to explain?" he asked.

"Fine."

"If I let you go, do you promise not to hit me again?"

"No."

That fire within her burned bright, and he was a moth to a flame. He bit back a smile, and dropped her wrists, waiting for her next move. It seemed she was unlikely to hit him again in the immediate instance.

"Two men followed me from the ship in Saint-Malo and cornered me." Her gasp made him pause, but he told her what had happened in Saint-Malo after Harvey had joined his pursuers. "Harvey has worked hard to overcome his reputation as a pirate. I sailed his ship, the *Black Witch*, and arrived in London before you. When the *Seren* docked, I met Sam and gave him instructions to get you home where I went to wait."

"So that's why Shadow left me?" she asked. "He saw you."

"I was prepared for Shadow to give me away, and for you to discover my presence. But you were in such a hurry I almost couldn't keep up. He's pining for you, by the way. So much for a loyal breed."

The corners of her mouth twitched, but her face turned serious again. "Why didn't you come to me? If not that day, any day during the past week would have sufficed."

He'd have been by her side in a heartbeat if he hadn't been locked in the Tower of London awaiting Lord Edington's arrival. An unnecessary footnote. He didn't have time to explain all of that tonight.

"I knew you were all right," he said. George would have found a way to tell him if something had happened.

"I didn't know that you were all right!"

She had worried about him, and that surprised him, so did the wretched feeling that he'd made her suffer through those weeks since Saint-Malo without word. He hadn't dared to hope that she'd care if they were not reunited.

He beamed. "I am well."

She stepped closer, touching a finger to his bruised cheekbone. "Are you?"

"It's nothing," he reassured her. "I've had much worse than a punch to the face."

She winced. "And your shoulder?"

He shrugged, ignoring the tenderness that remained there. "No broken bones. It's healing quickly." And another irrelevant topic. His three minutes were almost up. "There's a lot to discuss, but we have plenty of time over the next few weeks while the banns are read. That is if you're not preoccupied with planning, though there are no expectations. If you would prefer a small affair, or in the country..." He rambled on, unable to stop himself in his excitement.

"The banns?" she muttered.

"What? Oh yes, I apologize for my lateness in the offer, but there were things I had to address before I could ensure my dependability. I spoke to your father—"

"You did what?"

"Yes, this afternoon. I will marry you. It's the right thing to do."

An expression that he couldn't interpret crossed her face.

"The right thing to do?" she whispered.

"If anyone were to find out the truth about you being on my ship, you are as good as compromised. And I—"

"You were able to find the time to call on my father and propose to marry me, but you could not visit me in the same house?"

Alexander's stomach dropped. She'd been getting dressed for the ball. He couldn't have interrupted that.

Harriet continued without waiting for his response. "And what did you say to convince him that he should allow his daughter to marry a gentleman she had never met?" Her eyes widened. "Good Lord, you didn't tell him the truth?"

Oh, how he wished he could tell her he hadn't. Or that he could undo many things he had done in the past weeks. Alexander held up his hands, surrendering. What else could he do?

She stumbled back. Her brows knitted, and she shook her head. "I can't marry you. I—this is all—I must go."

"Harriet." He reached for her, but she dashed through the door before he could comprehend what had happened. She'd been caressing his face—a gesture full of concern for his wellbeing. It was only natural that he should discuss their marriage. Had the prospect of marrying him been so repulsive? Had he got it all wrong?

He'd been standing in a daze for a few minutes when his brother's face appeared around the door. George strode into the room, Eliza close behind him. Alexander rolled his eyes and suppressed a groan. Then he stared at Eliza. The two sisters were similar enough that he ought to have recognized Harriet as a Hazelby the instant he'd looked at her. Yet Harriet was unique, special.

"What did you do, Alexander?" Eliza accused.

"I don't understand," Alexander said. "I offered for her."

Eliza rolled her eyes. "Not well."

"Clearly," he ground out. One thing was certain: these two Hazelby sisters were as stubborn and irritating as each other. He couldn't speak for the third.

"Well, you'll need to fix it," George demanded.

"It doesn't matter," Alexander said, resigned. "I'm not going to force her into marriage. There has been enough control exhibited on my part. We both know how miserable such a situation can be." He forced a stern glare at his brother, but the words alone were enough to buy his silence. "I won't condemn her to a life she doesn't want."

"The marriage is not a requirement, then? You didn't compromise the young lady?" George asked.

Alexander's face burned. "How dare you say such a thing in front of her sister?" He ignored the question and flicked his eyes in Eliza's direction where she stood silent, averting her gaze. Had Harriet told her about that? Eliza would tell him if Harriet was with child, wouldn't she?

"I don't need to explain myself to you," George retorted.

"I must find Harriet," Eliza said. "Fix it, or I'll never forgive you for hurting my sister."

Alexander waited until the door closed behind her before he spoke again. This time, his voice was thick with emotion. "George, what do I do?"

"I am the last person on earth who should be giving advice on the topic." George had a point. His own romantic life hadn't fallen into place as he would have liked, but that gave Alexander pause for consideration.

"Would you mind if Harriet married me?" He'd known from the minute he'd discovered Harriet's identity what this would mean for George. He didn't believe himself capable of walking away, but after everything George had done, Alexander owed his brother that much. If George asked it of him, he would leave.

His brother fixed him with a solemn look. "What would it matter? My fate is sealed, as is Eliza's. That will never be, so do not let it stand in the way of your happiness, or Harriet's, if she so desires you. But please do not tell anyone. Eliza must never know I'm in love with her."

Chapter Twenty-One

THE FIRST FEW weeks of the social season had taken a different turn from Harriet's expectations. She had refused to speak to Alexander since the incident at the ball, which led to a surprising amount of attention from other gentlemen. The more they witnessed her dismissal of Alexander, the more interested they became, swarming around her like bees to honey. And while that had helped her avoid Alexander, it had also presented a host of other problems.

Despite the lessons, her dancing had not improved, and many of the gentlemen chivalrously limped away from their turn about the dance floor. She had also reached her limit for polite conversation. About her family, how many children she wanted, whether she would prefer to live in the country or London. Having her marriageability assessed so frequently was intolerable.

Necessary.

Every insufferable discussion kept her away from Alexander and his attempts to speak with her. And, *Lord*, he had tried. He'd attempted to call on her every day, and she'd refused him each time. On more than one occasion, he had tried to interrupt a dance. That had only increased the competitiveness of the other gentlemen, but she wished it weren't happening.

Her decision to ignore Alexander had not gone unnoticed, but she had dismissed Eliza's questions on the matter. The rest of her family had accepted her excuse of embarrassment after she swooned at the ball, and her father hadn't raised the topic of her unchaperoned weeks on a sailing ship, despite knowing all about it. She was only too happy to avoid that discussion. Not that she knew what to say if he asked.

On a fine Thursday morning, Harriet ventured out of the house at Millie's request. Their horses ambled leisurely through Mayfair toward Hyde Park, and Millie had remained silent beside her since they'd left the stables. Their father and uncle followed a few lengths behind, the muted tones of their conversation barely reaching Harriet's ears.

Nearing Hyde Park, they passed two gentlemen who bowed at her and Millie. The men bade them good morning, and Harriet returned the greeting with a warm smile, though the expression was forced.

"What is the matter with you?" Millie demanded as soon as they were alone again.

"Nothing."

"It is not *nothing*. You have had that miserable look on your face for weeks," Millie said.

Harriet waved a hand at the retreating men. "I smiled at those gentlemen," she said, doing her best to defend herself.

"You did this." Millie twisted her face into a grimace that made Harriet laugh despite herself.

"I was lost in thought," Harriet said, glancing at the

reins in her hand. The horse needed little guidance, keeping pace and navigating into Hyde Park without so much as a word from her.

"I know *that*," Millie said. "I want to know what you're thinking about. We've always been close, Harriet. I know when you're keeping something from me."

Discussing her journey on the ship was out of the question, and not just because Eliza had sworn her to secrecy. What could she say if she were free to speak of it?

Oh, by the way, I was kidnapped in Hull and spent a few weeks on a ship. And I made love with the captain, who happens to be the Duke of Ailesbury's brother.

There was no telling how Millie would react to such a tall tale, and no reason to find out. They would both be ruined if anyone discovered the truth. The insidious gossip from the *ton* would be enough to shun them both from society. Even Eliza would suffer the effect of it. This was her secret, and it was one she must keep.

"It's the start of the season," Harriet lied. "It has been such a whirlwind. You know I find it all overwhelming."

"No." Millie shook her head. "Granted, you have never been one for attention, but it's not that. You tolerated social events before your presentation. This is different."

"I—" Harriet started. "It's—" *Say something.* Anything but the truth.

"What did he do?"

Harriet's head snapped in her sister's direction. "Who?" Try as she might to give an air of nonchalance, she failed.

"You know very well *who*, so don't try to deny it." Millie's tone was more formidable than ever. She was beginning to sound like Eliza. When Harriet failed to answer, Millie continued. "What happened between you and Lord Ordell at that ball? I never expected you to be one to swoon at an introduction to a man, and then for him to carry you away for *fresh air*. It was hardly scandalous when the duke and Eliza followed you, but—"

"They didn't follow us," Harriet said without thinking. She hadn't seen them once she'd left the ballroom.

"Well, the rest of the *ton* doesn't know that, and considering that you are not already married—"

"Would you keep your voice down?" Harriet hissed. She swiveled back in the saddle to ensure that they were still far enough ahead of their father and uncle. "My *virtue* is not open for discussion, and I am not the type to swoon at a man upon introduction."

Millie's eyes widened and she cast an accusatory glare at Harriet. "I knew it! You met him before the ball. When? This has to do with your time in London with Eliza, doesn't it?"

So much for secrets.

It was simple enough to turn away from Millie and quicken her horse's pace, but her sister's curious stare still prickled into the back of her neck. She wasn't about to give in and divulge her story, but Millie wouldn't let the subject rest now.

Harriet scanned the park, glancing at the path ahead. Her stomach clenched.

Alexander lounged under a tree ahead of them, tossing a ball across the grass. No matter how much she'd tried, she could not make herself think of him as Lord Ordell. He threw the ball again for Shadow, who tore after it, his long fur pressed to his body as he raced into the wind. The sight made Harriet smile.

She bowed her head and tilted her face away, but any hope that they would make it past without him noticing soon disappeared.

"Harriet!" Alexander called.

Her attention went to him, and she cursed herself. His brows pulled together, and he pursed his lips. He glanced at the few people who could have heard him call her so informally and closed the distance between them.

"Lady Harriet," he said, dipping his head.

A ground out, "Good morning," was all she could manage. She tugged at the reins to keep her horse moving around him.

"Harriet, please," he begged. "I wish to speak to you."

Her horse stopped, and Harriet stared at Alexander, who appeared to be placating it with a sugar cube—or four!

Shadow raced up beside him and was poised to jump onto the horse with her until Alexander stopped him with a quick order. Shadow whined at Alexander's side, his short fluffy tail wagging furiously.

"Don't move, Shadow," Alexander ordered.

The dog's eyes were wide, that lopsided grin gracing his face, and his body trembled from head to tail. Harriet beamed at Shadow, triumphant that he still showed loyalty to her.

Millie moved her own horse along but stopped well within earshot.

Harriet turned her glare on Alexander. "Well?"

"I'm sorry for surprising you at the ball. It was extremely thoughtless on my behalf."

It had been a most tremendous surprise. But that hadn't been the most outrageous part. It was the proposal of marriage. Though one could hardly call it that. A presumption of marriage more likely. He believed she was his responsibility. Well, she wasn't. Marriage to a duke's brother would place her much more centrally in society than she cared for, but she could have learned to live with that. His responsibilities as captain of the *Seren* would have seen her remain in England, alone and awaiting his return. She might have managed that, too. But a forced marriage? One bound by duty and responsibility, as dictated by society? She couldn't be with him if his only emotion toward her was guilt.

"We need to talk," Alexander said.

"We are talking," she replied, her tone flat. Neutral.

He stared back. "Somewhere more private, perhaps?"

"No," she said, willing him to move along.

"Harriet, tell me what I have done, so I can remedy it."

She scoffed, but the sound was forced and painful. It wasn't what he had done, rather what he couldn't do, and telling him so wouldn't change that. She couldn't make him love her. And without that, she'd prefer to remain unmarried.

"My offer of marriage was in earnest, and it still stands," he said.

His sincerity was stark. It struck deep in her core, awakening the ache she had been trying so hard to bury and ignore. She swallowed back the lump that rose in her throat. He would do it, but she couldn't allow it. She'd been a burden on her parents enough. A third daughter, an unnecessary addition for a family in need of an heir. As unladylike as they came, and without a hope of securing a match as well as Eliza had done. She would not transfer that burden to Alexander. He would grow to resent her for it.

"Thank you, but it is not necessary." She lowered her voice. "There has been nary a whisper about me since I returned to London, except for that unfortunate incident at the ball, and there were no consequences of our... relations." Her courses had come and gone twice since the morning they'd shared on the *Seren*. "You are no longer responsible for me. Now, if you could please stop feeding my horse"—*Where was he hiding all those sugar cubes?*—"I'd like to be on my way." Her emotions were close to the surface, and she would rather not let him witness them, especially in the middle of Hyde Park.

"Harriet, I—"

"Do not call on me again, Alexander." She yanked her horse's nose away from his hand and pushed past him without looking back.

ALEXANDER PACED BACK and forth in his brother's study, flexing his fingers and curling them into fists. His attempt to speak with Harriet that morning was a spectacular disaster. He hadn't expected to see her in Hyde Park, but he couldn't convince himself that preparation would have helped his case. She didn't want anything to do with him.

"I'm leaving," Alexander announced, stopping in front of the fireplace. He told himself that Shadow's groan from the chair by the fire was a coincidence.

George's head shot up from the stack of paperwork, and he leveled Alexander with a disapproving stare. "What do you mean, *you're leaving?*"

Alexander held up his right hand and inspected his fingernails. He couldn't let George see how much Harriet's rejection had hurt.

George studied him, and Alexander kept his face impassive—as best he could.

"I thought you planned to stay?" George asked.

"I did." He let out a sigh that hopefully sounded exasperated. The alternative was far too embarrassing. If his brother caught him *yearning*, he'd never hear the end of it. Sam and Harvey were bad enough. "Things have changed. We will resume work and plan to sail a week from Tuesday." Perhaps if he said it enough times, he could accept it himself.

"Absolutely not," George said in his most irritating and assured ducal tone. "No brother of mine runs away from his problems."

Alexander slammed his fist against the mantel. "I'm not running away," he snapped. "My *problem* has told me where to go, and I'm listening. I caused enough trouble for Harriet. She won't see me. She doesn't want anything to do with me."

George stood, his eyes narrowed. "Well, you can't blame her. You left her on a ship in a foreign port while you sailed back to England, let her go weeks without knowing whether you were alive or dead"—George held up his finger, stopping the protest that Alexander was about to start—"and instead of having a calm and private conversation with her, you surprised her at her first ball *ever*, with all the *ton* as witness."

Wonderful, a thorough list of his failings. How could he possibly feel worse?

George crossed his arms, his stern stare boring into Alexander's. "And this all started with you kidnapping her."

Alexander squirmed under his brother's intense gaze as he'd done since they were boys. "I am perfectly aware of the wrongs I have committed against Harriet," he replied. "But I stand by what I did in Hull. There's no telling what might have happened to her if I let her go." The possibilities were too devastating to consider, and he had considered them in detail. "When I finally realized who she was, I was more certain of that decision. The least I can do is respect her wishes after everything I put her through. She deserves a say in her own future, does she not?"

"You must have some idea what you've done to offend her."

"I did a great many things…" The end of his sentence drifted off as he recalled all the horrendous things he had done. George had only scratched the surface of it. Kidnapping, yes. He had also forced her to work, allowed her to live among sailors, withheld the truth from her, and he had been so angry. None of it was her fault. Then he'd kissed her, and he'd kept kissing her, unleashing a desire that he couldn't restrain. He'd taken her virtue, and he wanted Harriet far more than he ought, but he had to live with the reality he repulsed her.

"What kind of things?" Shock colored George's words, pulling Alexander back to the present.

Alexander's cheeks heated despite himself. "Not *those* things," he insisted. George didn't need to know what he'd done. If Harriet forged forward with her life, she didn't need his brother knowing that Alexander had properly compromised her.

Alexander cursed. The color in his cheeks must be the cause of George's smirk. He ignored his brother and pushed on. "On the ship, I believed Harriet reciprocated my feelings. What I cannot comprehend is that nothing made her despise me so much until we returned to London. I know the ball was a bad idea *now*, but I had already waited too long to see her. I couldn't wait another night. All I can think is that she realized I am not the man she wants. She doesn't trust me, and for good reason, as you have so thoroughly noted. This is all going as wrong as possible, more than I ever imagined." Alexander thought aloud, covering his eyes with his hand. He didn't care if George kept up.

"Have you told her that you love her, Alexander?"

"*What?*"

"Good Lord, do not tell me you are so thick. It's as plain as day. You can't be in the vicinity of her without everyone present seeing it. I thought Sam was exaggerating, but he wasn't at all. And Eliza, well, she knows that Harriet's confidence is slim. She compares herself to her older sisters in such an unfair light. But even Eliza thought—"

"Of course I love her!" Alexander yelled, filling the small space of his brother's study with his emotion.

George cleared his throat before he spoke. "Have you told her that? You might consider a gentler approach if you do." His gaze was mocking, and Alexander could have hit him. "You spent weeks trying to sort out this business with Harvey, and now that you have, you're going to leave? Without telling her anything?"

"I couldn't tell her any of that until I was certain I could be the man she needed. Now she refuses to see me. And my feelings shouldn't have any bearing on her decision. I've told you I'm not going to force her into a marriage she doesn't want." He sank into the chair opposite George. "What do I do?"

"I can't tell you that."

Alexander frowned at his brother. "Never stopped you before."

"Well, you are the captain of your own ship, so you *might* like to delay sailing. As for the rest of it, you'll need to work it out for yourself."

Chapter Twenty-Two

Harriet sat in the parlor at Malstern House, a book open in her lap. Ostentatious gold and black decorations aside, it was far more peaceful at her sister's residence. It was the fifth time that week that she'd had to escape. She had been receiving a preposterous number of callers at home and she'd had enough. Mr. Tombs had been tremendous at his task of fielding the few inevitable callers who arrived. The one time Alexander had tried to call, Mr. Tombs had turned him away before he'd had the chance to say his name. That had been four days ago, and he had not come again.

Mr. Tombs entered the parlor, standing beside the over-large black door. "There you are, my lady."

She glanced up from the book she'd been pretending to read and smiled. "How can I help?"

"I have two gentlemen in the drawing room who are determined to speak with you."

"Who are they?" she asked.

"They won't say but said they know you."

"I don't want to speak with any callers today," she said,

returning her attention to the book. "Thank you, Mr. Tombs."

"I know, Miss, that's what I told them. But they're insistent. Since Her Grace is not here to deal with them, I thought I'd check with you before I call for Cook to help me escort them from the premises."

Harriet frowned. Who would be that desperate to speak with her? They mustn't be ordinary callers.

"I will accompany you if you want to send them on their way yourself," the butler said. "They don't look like they could kill a fly between them if I'm honest."

That made her chuckle. She trusted the shrewd butler's character evaluation. He wouldn't allow her to meet with unknown men if she was at risk.

"I can handle them," she said with a wink.

Harriet rounded the corner into the drawing room with Mr. Tombs hot on her heels. She stopped dead in her tracks at the sight of the men, and Mr. Tombs bumped into her back. He jolted away, repeating his apologies. Her gaze darted back and forth between the two men, and she was unable to get a word out.

Sam, she immediately recognized. Neat, combed hair and clean-shaven chin aside, it was still the kind face of a man she had come to know and trust. He was dressed smartly indeed in a dark blue jacket and cream breeches and did not look as out of place in a London drawing room as she might have expected. He must have a connection to another member of high society, as Alexander did.

Beside Sam stood Harvey, dressed in similar attire, except for his deep red jacket, and a respectable haircut. His smile was not the wicked one full of too many glistening white teeth that he'd had at their first meeting. This smile was small and apologetic. He didn't seem comfortable here, standing next to Sam. She could throttle them both for arriving unannounced. Had Alexander sent them in his place?

Mr. Tombs, who had regained his composure, looked as though he might beat her to it. Curiosity got the better of her. She rested a hand on the butler's elbow, stopping him from edging forward.

"Lady Harriet," Harvey said. He bent in a stiff bow.

"Miss Harry." Sam greeted her with a wide grin and dipped his head.

"What are you doing here?" she asked, directing her question to Sam.

"May we speak to you in private?" Sam asked. He cast a glance toward Mr. Tombs, and then his warm brown gaze fell on Harriet once more.

"Over my dead body," the butler replied. He shook Harriet's hand off his arm and stepped around her, putting himself in the middle of the room as a human shield.

"There's no need for that, old boy," Harvey quipped.

Mr. Tombs grumbled something unintelligible and stepped forward. His hands balled into fists at his sides.

Harriet intervened. "There's no need for *that*, either." She glared at Harvey, feeling far braver with the butler standing between them. "If you cannot be courteous, you can leave." She spoke to Harvey, refusing to blink until he acknowledged her with a nod. "Why are you here?"

"It's Alexander," Sam said.

Her stomach dropped, and her pulse raced into a frantic pattern. "What happened? Is he all right?"

"Nothing like that," Sam said. "He's well. It's just that he plans to sail again in two days."

"We had to speak with you before we left," Harvey added.

"Why would that matter to me?" she asked. Though the ache deep in her chest told her it mattered a great deal.

"We have some explaining to do," Sam said, stepping forward. His palms were outstretched in a gesture of surrender. "I know Alexander has tried to speak with you and that you won't receive him."

"So, he sent you to do his bidding?" she asked, peering around Mr. Tombs.

"No, he doesn't know we've come," Harvey said. "We would like a chance to explain ourselves."

Harriet stepped around the now quavering butler, touching a hand to his arm again.

"It's quite all right, Mr. Tombs. I want to hear what they came to say. If you'd be more comfortable staying, I won't ask you to leave."

"I'll not leave you alone with them for a minute." Mr. Tombs bowed without taking his eyes from Harvey and stood by the door. He remained there, glaring at the men triumphantly.

Harriet hid her grin, and she faced Sam and Harvey once more.

"First," Harvey said, "I'd like to formally introduce myself. Harvey de Lyle." He bowed low.

Sam followed suit. "Samuel Wethering," he said, smiling.

Neither name was familiar. She curtsied and waited.

Sam spoke first. "Do you remember what brought you onto the *Seren*?"

"I was given a message to deliver. *The change of tide will be reflected in the orange moon.*" The phrase had lingered in her mind, though it still made little sense. "What about it?"

Harvey and Sam exchanged a glance.

"The orange moon refers to me," Harvey said. His hands

were clasped behind his back, but his arms made slight movements. Was he nervous?

"And the tide was a metaphor for mine and Alexander's fate," Sam said. "Which depended on finding Harvey and bringing him back to London. Something none of us were aware of until you came aboard with that message."

"Was the messenger trying to help you?" she asked, glancing between the two men. That didn't make any sense. Alexander had said the man would kill her if she returned to the docks that day.

Sam shrugged. "It is a slim possibility. We don't have any connections in Hull, save Alexander's brother. We didn't know who gave you that message, or why, and we still don't know. Alexander did what he believed to be right at the time. He was trying to protect you by bringing you with us."

"Why didn't he tell me what it meant?" she asked.

"I tried to tell him that it would be better if you knew," Sam said. "But he was adamant you weren't to know any more about it while a risk to you remained. We didn't know if we would find Harvey, and if we returned to London without him, we would have been hanged for murder. The less you knew about any of that, the better off you would be, and the easier we could extract you from the situation."

"Did you say murder?" she asked, her voice rising an octave.

Harvey cleared his throat. "There was an incident involving me, and I had to disappear. Sam and Alexander dropped me off in Rotterdam. It was an easy place to lie low."

"Why did you need to disappear?" Harriet asked, though she suspected the answer. Taking an involuntary step back, she put another foot between her and Harvey.

Who had he killed? She glanced at Sam, his eyes and smile a clear attempt to reassure her. Had he killed people too?

"The work we do is rarely dangerous," Harvey said. "We transport cargo between countries—France and Spain, mostly. Between our three ships, passing things inconspicuously is easy."

"You work for the Crown?" Mr. Tombs asked.

Harriet jumped at the butler's question. She had forgotten about him standing behind her.

"I cannot confirm that," Harvey replied.

"Well, that just about does," Mr. Tombs said. "Though it doesn't sound very structured for such important operations."

Harvey's eyes rolled heavenward. "That's the point, old boy."

The butler cursed but didn't move from his position.

Harvey continued. "The time of the... incident, I was delivering a small parcel. The man I intended to meet had been killed. Whoever did it had already left."

"What happened to the parcel?" Harriet asked.

"Harvey still had it when he returned to the ship," Sam said. "We expected our superiors to suspect Harvey of the murder. Double-crossing is common in our line of work. We still had the parcel with us when we returned to Hull and had planned to sail back to London to find someone to deliver it to. It was finally delivered last week."

"What was in the parcel?" Mr. Tombs asked.

"That's not part of the job," Harvey said.

"So, you ferry these items wherever you are told, implicitly trusting that it's the right thing to do?" The butler's tone hid none of his disbelief.

"Do you trust your employers?" Harvey asked.

"What sort of question is that?" Mr. Tombs asked,

clearly taking offense that anyone would question his loyalty to Eliza and her husband.

"Exactly," Harvey replied. "We complete the tasks assigned to us, and we don't ask questions. How else could we keep getting work? I never knew what was in that parcel, and I still don't. It's not the most important part of the story, is it?"

"Well, it must have been rather important for a man to lose his life," Mr. Tombs said.

Harvey shrugged. "It was a dark alleyway in a rather unsavory part of London. It's not an unusual place for a man to die."

Sam spoke again, seemingly unaffected by Harvey's bluntness. "The man Harvey was due to meet had come across the body not long before us, and he'd assumed that it was Harvey's dead body. So, by taking Harvey to Rotterdam, we all but admitted to murdering him ourselves and going on the run. Our assumption that Harvey would be blamed got us into more trouble than if we had stayed in London in the first place."

"How butchered was the body if none of you could recognize it?" Mr. Tombs asked.

Harriet's stomach flipped and turned queasy. "Please don't answer that."

Harvey, whose mouth was open and on the verge of a reply, snapped it shut and grinned sheepishly.

Harriet glanced between Sam and Harvey. "I don't see what any of this has to do with me?"

"Given the circumstances, we weren't sure why that man gave you that message. Alexander couldn't guarantee your safety if you returned to Hull. That's why he kept you on board with us. We owe our lives to you for bringing us that message." Sam finished with a heavy sigh.

Harriet couldn't believe what they were saying. She'd saved their lives? "Why wasn't I told any of this on the journey home, or when we arrived in London?"

"There were no guarantees about anything when we returned," Harvey said. "Alexander and I discussed it before we swapped ships in Saint-Malo, and we agreed that things would be better for you that way if it didn't resolve in our favor. Imagine if we had returned and been unable to clear our names. What would the truth have meant to you if you watched Alexander hang? He wouldn't allow it."

"He was trying to protect you, again," Sam said. "Besides, we were in the Tower of London that first week back. None of us could have told you the truth if we wanted to."

The Tower of London? Why hadn't Alexander mentioned that? She did her best to pierce Harvey with a sharp glare, but she was warming up to the man. "Why were you so cruel when we sailed from Saint-Malo?"

He flashed an apologetic smile. "I am sorry about that. Alexander swore he would have my head if I let anything happen to you. He told me all about your *swim*, and I wasn't prepared to have a repeat of that. The last thing I wanted to do was explain to Alexander that the woman he—"

"*Ahem.*" Sam cleared his throat and shook his head, frowning at Harvey.

Harriet glanced between the two of them and frowned. What were they still keeping from her?

"Right," Harvey said. "Anyway, I wasn't going to be responsible for anything happening to you while you were in my charge, and I didn't know how else to keep you in your cabin. He's right, you are a little spitfire." He frowned but the expression was less severe.

"What is the point of telling me all of this?" she asked. "I'm sure it's not purely to appease my curiosity."

"Alexander has been a miserable sod since he surprised you at that ball, and you refused to see him," Harvey grumbled.

"We thought you might reconsider if you heard the truth." Sam sounded desperate.

The truth. A relief to understand at last, but not what she'd been hoping to hear.

"If I might comment, my lady, there is no need for you to go anywhere you don't want to go. There has been enough of *that*," Mr. Tombs said with a huff. "We must wait for Her Grace to return home. I shan't be answering to her for why I escorted you to the docks to see the ruffian."

"That's not necessary, Mr. Tombs. I will not be going." Alexander's guilt would cease once he resumed his work. He'd forget about her soon enough. All she had to do was make it past Tuesday. "Please see these gentlemen out."

Chapter Twenty-Three

"Papa," Harriet called through the solid wooden door of her father's study.

Philip Hazelby's answer was muted. "Come in, Harriet."

How did he always know? One word was all it took for him to recognize which of his daughters called to him through his study door. Not once in her life had he got it wrong.

She inched open the door, and her father smiled from behind his oak desk. Dark green eyes mirrored her own, glittering with knowing.

"I know you're busy," she started. She knew better than to disrupt him when he had work to do.

"I'm *never* that busy." He reassured her with the same phrase he had used since she was a child. His tone still brought warmth and calmness to her. "What is it?"

The words sat on the tip of her tongue, but that wasn't what came out. "Millie and I are going for a ride. Would you like to come?" she asked.

Coward.

Nothing in her father's expression showed that he

believed her. "Are you certain that's what you came here to ask? You look as though you might run at any moment. I've never seen you that anxious to get on a horse. Has one has thrown you off recently and you haven't deigned to tell me?"

"I haven't fallen off a horse since I was a girl." She defended herself. "But you're right, that's not why I'm here." The things she hadn't deigned to tell him.

"Well, if it's not that, you had better close the door and start at the beginning. And can you please stop wringing your hands? I can't bear to watch if you take skin off."

She froze and glanced down at her hands. They were clasped in front of her waist. She released them and forced them to her sides, her fingers aching as she stretched them out.

Her father rose from his seat and walked around to the front of his desk. He leaned back against it and held his hands out to her. Gray morning light filtered through the cream gauze curtains, illuminating his figure.

Harriet closed the door and walked to him, clasping his hands. Warm air filled her lungs, and she exhaled it through pursed lips. Her father's solid and reassuring presence calmed the knot that had been twisting away in her stomach. She could do this.

"I can't help you if you don't tell me what happened," he said.

She chewed on her lip. "I don't know that there's anything you can do to help," she said. "I haven't been completely honest with you, Papa."

Her father's eyebrows climbed close to his hairline. "Of that, I am certain."

Silence hung in the air between them, and Harriet tried to arrange her thoughts. She glanced around the room, but the words wouldn't come. A fire burned low in the grate, heating the small study. She returned her gaze to her father, who watched her expectantly. Patient as ever. Nothing would make him speak before she did. The best way to get the whole truth from someone was to speak as little as possible, so he had always told her.

"I didn't travel to London with Eliza." It was all she could manage. One small piece of information at a time until the whole story was out. It might take her all day.

A small smirk tugged at the corners of her father's lips. "I know that."

"Oh, yes, Alex—Lord Ordell already spoke to you."

"Perhaps you should tell me the whole story, your version, so that I might be in a better position to understand what is going on." He gestured to the two wingback chairs beside the fire.

She settled into one and took a steadying breath. "The morning after we arrived in Hull..." she began.

To his credit, her father remained silent while she relayed the story of her journey, and not a detail was spared. Except for the morning in Saint-Malo. She would take that to her grave. Instead of the embarrassment she'd expected, an overwhelming sense of relief washed over her after sharing the ordeal. And yet a heavy sensation settled in her stomach.

"Well, that was only slightly more interesting than the version I got from Lord Ordell," Philip said.

Her face flushed. "What did he say?" She hung on her father's every word. Had Alexander also withheld the details of Saint-Malo?

"Lord Ordell called on me the day of your presentation, much to my surprise as I am sure you would agree. We had never met before. He proceeded to tell me much of the same story, although with a few less details." Her father gave her a look that made her cheeks burn. "He asked for my blessing to marry you. He was certain of your acceptance and didn't want anything to stand in the way when he offered. I said no."

"You denied him? He didn't tell me that."

Philip made a sound that resembled a scoff. "I know better than to speak on behalf of my daughters, especially the most outspoken of you."

She gave him a shy smile.

"My blessing could wait until you had accepted his offer. If you had accepted, I would not have withheld it, and that's what I told him. I said that if he wanted to marry you, he must ask you, which I expected him to do as soon as he could. He was so enamored of you." Philip gave a mock shiver and fixed her with a wide-eyed stare. "Fancy bringing a sea captain to his knees! I should have never expected anything less from you, I suppose." He patted her hand. "But if the marriage is not what you wish, and you can assure me there was nothing more than a few kisses"— he rolled his eyes—"I will trust you. On the other hand, if he did not propose or needs to be held accountable for his actions, I will see to it immediately."

Alexander was enamored? Of her?

When she didn't speak, her father continued. "This has something to do with your early morning visit to my study, doesn't it? When you ran from the ball and refused to see him, I assumed he had offered to marry you, and you had declined. You do not need to tell me your reasons, only to assure me that it is what you wish."

"Alexander didn't propose marriage," she said. "He stated it as though it were an inevitable event. He told me it was because I was compromised and that he'd already spoken with you. That was more than enough informa-tion." Her father had read the situation all wrong. Her shoulders stiffened, and she raised her chin. "He is not enamored of me. He couldn't be."

"Why do you doubt it?"

Tears welled in her eyes. "It is *me*," she whispered. It was idiotic and embarrassing to her core to admit it out loud.

"You are your own harshest critic, Harriet."

"Even you said I am the most outspoken of the three of us. That is not a redeeming quality in a woman."

"I disagree. At times, your outspokenness is one of your most redeeming qualities. When you are not arguing with me." He winked. "More often, though, it is your subtle beauty, for which you can thank your mother. I will take all the credit for those eyes. And you are incredibly kind. I could not count how many times you have helped someone in need without any consideration for yourself. You have little cause to doubt his love for you."

"He never told me he loved me. All he did was kiss me." She clamped her mouth shut. Never in her wildest dreams did she expect to have such a conversation with her father.

He responded with a small chuckle. "Some of us aren't adept at sharing our deepest feelings. Have you ever asked your mother about our courtship?" He gave another shiver, one that was very sincere. "It took me far too long to tell her I loved her, even though I was certain of it the moment I met her. I almost lost her because of it. At times, we *all* need a little push to realize what is happening." His pointed gaze held her still.

She considered everything that had happened between Alexander and her on the ship, and at the ball. It wasn't love. It couldn't be.

"Alexander doesn't love me," she said.

"Do you love him?"

"I... well..." Words failed her.

Her father waited, his smile reaching his eyes.

"I do," she whispered. "That's the problem."

"Why is that a problem?" he asked.

"I couldn't let him marry me. It's not right. I can't spend the rest of my life with a man whom I love, when he does not return it." She had never dreamed that she could love anyone this deeply. But she did, and Alexander didn't reciprocate.

"Have you not listened to a word I said? The man is in love with you. How can you not see it?"

"You're saying that because you must."

"I would not knowingly put you at risk of heartache. Why don't you speak with him? Listen to what he has to say, and then you can decide what to do."

Tears streamed down her cheeks before she could stop them. "It's too late. They sailed this morning. He's gone and there's nothing I can do."

Philip stood and pulled her against his chest. "I'm sorry, Harriet."

Her sobs grew louder, and her tears fell onto her father's waistcoat.

"Harriet." Millie's urgent whisper made her jump. "We need to hurry."

Harriet wiped the remaining tears from her eyes. She studied her sister in the dim light of the hall outside her father's study. How much of the conversation with their father had Millie overheard? Did it matter who else knew at this point?

"Hurry where?"

"To the docks. They haven't left yet."

Harriet remained cautious. It wouldn't do to get her hopes up. "Who hasn't?"

"Lord Ordell. The *Seren* isn't due to sail until eight o'clock this morning." Millie might have overheard her conversation, but she couldn't know that much about the situation.

"How in the world do you know that?"

"Sam told me," Millie said, betraying no emotion.

Harriet's mind was already reeling, but that was too much. "How do *you* know Sam?"

"Does that matter right now? We have less than thirty minutes before they're gone."

"It would take that long to get the horses ready, and it's a twenty-minute ride to the docks. There isn't time." Harriet's heart leaped at the possibility regardless.

Millie's cheeks turned a deep shade of pink. "There are two horses ready to go. I saw to it this morning, and I would have talked to you sooner, but I couldn't find you."

Harriet stared at her sister, unable to verbalize her questions. What else did Millie know?

Millie seemed to appreciate her confusion. "Sam called here yesterday while you were out. He begged me to get you to the ship before they sailed. I didn't need to overhear the end of your conversation with Papa to confirm what I already suspected."

"And what is it you suspect?"

"That you're in love with Lord Ordell."

"How could you—?"

"Oh, please. You have been moping around the house

since I returned, and you got worse after you saw him at that first ball." Millie grabbed Harriet's hand and tugged her along the hall. "I knew there had to be more to it. No way you had recently met the man. Nor did I believe you had met him on a social call in London."

"How much did Sam tell you?" Harriet asked.

"Enough to know that Lord Ordell is likely in love with you too. If he's anything like you, and it sounds as though he is, his sulking has been enough to match yours and forced Sam to act. While I do loathe the idea of a brother who is as stubborn as you, I'd prefer that to living with you in this mood for the remainder of the season and into the summer. You're going to sort it out this morning."

Harriet chewed her bottom lip. What if he'd changed his mind? She'd given him reason enough to reconsider his offer over the past few weeks. Or worse, what if he insisted upon marrying her solely for her virtue and protection? A third possibility was almost too good to consider. Could he love her, too? Her father had believed so. As had Sam.

"What are you waiting for?" Millie asked, a frantic edge to her question. "Let's go!"

The grooms had two horses waiting for them outside the stables.

"How cross do you suppose Mama will be that we didn't change into riding habits?" Harriet asked.

"I'm sure she'll forget about it as soon as we tell her that we rode to the docks unchaperoned at daybreak for you to tell a captain you're in love with him."

Harriet let out a nervous giggle. "This is mad," she whispered, to herself or Millie, she wasn't sure. Millie didn't reply as they mounted.

The slow trot through Berkeley Square was torture. Harriet gripped the reins, turning her knuckles white, and fought the urge to quicken the pace. What if they arrived at the docks and in time to watch the *Seren* sail down the Thames? She shook her head but could not dispel the image from her mind. They must get there. She couldn't miss this chance.

With one hoof off the pavement of Berkeley Square, she gave her horse the nudge it needed, sending it into a canter. Buildings passed in a blur, and soon they were well out of Mayfair. They reached the part of town that was unfamiliar, but Millie raced ahead without missing a beat. How did she know which way to go? They shared a similar sheltered and restricted knowledge of London outside of Mayfair. Neither of them should know the way to the docks.

Sam. He had told Millie what she needed to know to get them there in time. They might make it.

Chapter Twenty-Four

ALEXANDER GLANCED out at the river and the few small boats that sailed before them. It would be a sunny morning once the fog cleared and a decent breeze blew east. Perfect weather for sailing. He hauled the rope over the taffrail.

Shadow let out a booming bark right in his ear. The sound was desperate, like nothing he'd heard from the dog before.

Alexander glanced at Shadow, ensuring that his fur wasn't caught in the rigging. "Cut it out, Shadow!" he ordered, wincing and rubbing his ear.

"What's his problem?" Sam called across the deck.

"I'm not sure." Alexander reached down and tried to placate the dog with little success. Shadow escaped the loose embrace of his arms and shot across the deck to Sam, then back to Alexander again. He jumped at each of them, then lunged for the taffrail.

Alexander's arms shot out to stop him from flying overboard, and Sam came running, but Shadow stopped with his front paws on the taffrail. He barked at something below, his tail wagging. Alexander followed the point of Shadow's nose, down onto the docks.

Harriet.

And her sister.

"That woman is going to be the death of me," Sam said with a sigh, reflecting Alexander's thoughts with incredible accuracy.

"Undeniably," Alexander replied. "What is she doing here?" He didn't wait for a response before interrupting the crew's preparations and directing them to moor the ship again. The gangplank, often the last thing to leave the dock, was still fixed in place.

Harriet had already dismounted her horse, and she walked toward the ship.

"I'd say you're about to find out," Sam said.

"Someone must know she was with us on the ship," Alexander said, looking at Sam. Why else would she be here right before they were due to sail? The only people who knew they were leaving were... He frowned. "What did you do?"

Sam averted his gaze. "I don't suppose you would accept nothing for an answer?"

"Most certainly not," Alexander muttered. He gripped the railing, and his heart pounded.

"Then I shall wait to hear what she has to say before I admit how guilty I am." Sam inclined his head toward the gangplank. "Shan't have to wait long."

Alexander turned as Harriet stepped onto the deck. Pink cheeks, windblown brown hair, and those deep green eyes. She was the picture of determination. Exactly how he liked her. Her blue dress swished around her legs. How had she ridden all the way here in that, and was still perfection embodied?

Shadow pattered over to Harriet, sat at her side, and opened his mouth in a big grin. Alexander watched Harriet fight her own smile as she stooped and scratched behind the dog's ears.

"Traitor," Alexander hissed at Shadow, quirking a brow. "Harriet." The decision to forgo the formalities had not been a conscious one, so he rectified the mistake. "Lady Harriet," he said, bowing his head.

She rose from petting Shadow, and drew in a deep breath, straightening her back. She was preparing herself. For what?

"I'm sorry to delay your departure today, my lord," she said, not meeting his eye.

"Will you please, for the love of all that is holy, call me Alexander?"

"Alexander," she replied, smiling. That surprised him and eased his bubbling nerves, but not enough.

"What is it?" he asked. "Has someone said something? Do you need my help?"

Harriet twisted her head, looking back at the docks where her sister waited with the horses. She faced him again, this time with tears in her eyes. Whatever—whoever—had caused those tears deserved every punishment in the world, and he would ensure they received it.

Her shoulders lifted, and she sighed. "Yes. I mean, no. I don't need your help. I only wanted to speak with you before you leave." Tears rolled down her cheeks. She swiped at them with the back of her hand.

Alexander longed to close the distance between them and wipe away those tears, but he was reluctant to take those few small steps, aware of the many eyes on them. Most of the sailors were still on the main deck where he had stopped them in the middle of preparing to depart.

"All hands on deck," Alexander called, "far away from here, now. You too, Sam."

They all obliged, and soon he and Harriet stood alone on the main deck.

"My apologies," she said, "this was a terrible idea. I shouldn't have come. You need to sail before you miss your chance." She turned away. If she thought she was leaving without a proper explanation, she had the wrong idea.

He reached for her arm, stopping her. "I'm not sailing now," he said. "Whatever brought you here this morning requires my presence in London. We won't leave today, so you might as well say what you came here to tell me."

She hesitated, and then slowly pivoted back to face him. She glanced at his hand, and he dropped it to his side.

"First, I must beg your forgiveness for the way I acted over these past few weeks," she said.

"Forgiven," he said. "Go on," he added, still concerned with what brought her to the ship.

"Oh, well, thank you."

If he had delayed sailing for an entire day to listen to her apologize for not receiving his calls, he would toss himself overboard.

"Let me say," she continued, "that I have no expectations of you. There is no reason for you to marry me, and I wouldn't want that because polite society dictates it. I couldn't bear to be bound to you under some misguided notion of duty or honor on your part." She stared resolutely into his eyes and held his gaze. "I am not a burden that you must bear."

Good Lord, it was worse. He had to listen to her apologize for not wanting to marry him. It wasn't too late to send her off the ship.

"What is it you need me to do, Harriet?" Resignation filled his voice, and an ache spread deep in his chest.

"Nothing." Her brows knitted, and she pursed her lips. "There is nothing you *can* do." She drew another breath. "As a child, I watched how happy my parents made each other and dreamed of such a marriage for myself. But I didn't grow into the beauty that my mother and sisters are, and I have starkly different interests and pursuits than other ladies. I was content with helping my father with his estates and trying to ignore my responsibility to find a husband. After Millie endured two social seasons without an acceptable proposal, I realized I wouldn't stand a chance, even if I had wanted one."

He tried to take it all in. What was she saying?

"Then I met you, and I—well, it was *different*. You made me so angry, but being near you did other things, too. What I felt defied my own logic. I began to believe that there might be a chance for us to love as my parents do, that you might come to feel that way about me. But I cannot force you to love me. Marrying you to fulfill a vow that you swore regarding my protection, that would be even worse." She paused, wringing her hands in front of her waist. "So, I, well, I'm in love with you. I wanted you to know before you left, in case I didn't get another chance to—"

"You love me?" he whispered. Oh, he'd had it all wrong. Again. What an absolute idiot. He stepped closer. That intriguing mint and gardenia scent was so much better than the lingering memory that had teased him in his dreams. He took her hands in his, thinking it might ground him. It did not. Neither did losing himself in her eyes. Their depth seemed infinite. How could he convey all his love with mere words? He had to make her see.

"How could you not know?" His voice was a hoarse

whisper. "I didn't offer marriage for reputation's sake. That you believe so reflects my poor communication. I love you, Harriet. I fell faster than might be deemed reasonable, and much sooner than you could ever guess. I am not the same man you met in the shadows of the orlop deck." He squeezed her hands. "From the moment I met you, I was changed. You plagued every waking thought, and my dreams, too. I tried to fight it, believe me. The more time I spent with you, the stronger those feelings became, but too many things happened to you that were out of your control. I made a vow to protect you, but I also swore that I would never act against your will again. When you sent me away and refused to see me, it was torture, but I wouldn't stay if you did not want me. I had no idea it was the same for you. Why did you send me away?"

Her eyes were wide and still wet with tears, but they glittered in the rays of morning sunshine peeking through the fog.

"It never crossed my mind that you could love me," she said. "Not until Sam and Harvey came to see me."

"Oh?"

"What's important is that they made me see a side of this whole situation that I hadn't before. It made me believe there could be more, but I was too afraid to take the risk. I spoke to my father this morning, and he seemed convinced there was more to your feelings than responsibility or protection. I didn't think so many people could be wrong about it. I had made assumptions without listening to you, and I couldn't bear to let you go without finding out for myself. I still can't believe you love me." She tugged her quivering bottom lip between her teeth.

"Harriet, how can you be so blind?"

"You believe now is a good time to insult my eyesight?"

She sniffed, but the corners of her mouth curled into a small smile.

"When it comes to you doubting yourself, or my love for you, any time is a good time. I don't know how you cannot see what a wonder you are, but I will spend the rest of my life trying to show you, if you'll have me." He wanted to kiss her, but not here. "I want to show you something." He led her toward the stairs. "Sam," he called, "would you escort Lady Hazelby home?"

Sam emerged from below deck, a puzzled expression on his face.

Alexander laughed. "Not this one." He gestured to Harriet's hand clasped in his. He could take her home soon enough. Alexander motioned at Millie, who was still sitting atop her horse. "*That* Lady Hazelby," he said, still not convinced that Sam followed along.

Sam grumbled an answer. "Fine."

"Don't worry, we're not leaving without you. We're staying in London."

Sam looked like he'd been slapped with a wet fish. Alexander didn't have time to dwell on that. His priority was taking Harriet to the orlop deck.

"All hands!" Alexander called. "Shore leave. Effective immediately until further notice." He turned to Harriet and gave her a wink.

At that moment, Harvey appeared, coming up from the gangplank. "What in the blazes is taking you so long?" Harvey demanded, his eyes landing on Harriet.

"Change of plans," Alexander said. "You're on watch duty, Harvey. From the docks. Take Shadow with you. Sam can join you when he returns, and perhaps you'll think twice about meddling in my affairs." It was a poor excuse, considering their meddling had been advantageous indeed, but they needn't be rewarded at this moment. He wanted to be alone with Harriet as soon as possible.

"You know that I am a captain, too," Harvey retorted.

"Not on this ship," Alexander replied, grinning. He didn't wait for the crew to leave before leading Harriet down the stairs. Soon they were alone on the orlop deck, hidden in the dark. Their breaths, and water lapping against the hull, filled the silence.

"What are we doing here?" she asked.

"You'll see in a moment."

If it weren't for her hand in his, he might have believed this was a dream. Regrettably, he had to let go. He lit the lamp that now hung on the post next to the stairs. Harriet had inspired that permanent addition to the orlop deck.

He turned back to her, smiling. "This might be the most orderly orlop deck I have ever seen."

"I took my task seriously." She crossed her arms, but her eyes sparkled and a smirk graced her lips.

"Much more than anyone else I've ever tasked with it."

"Is that why we came down here? You want to praise my rope-tidying skills?"

"No." He pried one of her hands away from her chest and tugged her off the last step and onto the deck. "I have something for you."

"How did you know I would come back?"

"I didn't," he admitted. "Did Eliza tell you we were supposed to be introduced the day we met?"

"No." Her astonishment was clear. Realization washed over her features. "I thought she was taking me to meet the duke. It was you?"

"Yes, but I wasn't going to be there, and George was furious when I told him. We had a tide to catch, you see." He winked and enjoyed the blush that crept into her cheeks.

"I wasn't keen on the prospect of marriage at the time. I was incensed that he'd had the audacity to arrange an introduction on my behalf. He wouldn't tell me who the introduction was to. I wonder what might have happened if we had met that morning."

The blush in her cheeks deepened. "I would not have been there," she said. "I was infuriated at my sister's meddling and had left the estate before she could drag me to the duke's residence. I was a little preoccupied elsewhere by that time."

Alexander beamed. How had he been so lucky?

They reached the chest, and he withdrew the key from his pocket and unlocked it. He shuffled through the envelopes and loose papers and wrapped his fingers around a small box.

"This belonged to my mother." He opened the box and held it out to Harriet.

Set on a small square of black velvet was a gold ring. A round emerald, the darkest he had ever seen, was surrounded by tiny diamonds that shaped it into a delicate flower.

"It's exquisite," she whispered.

Like her.

"George gave it to me the morning we sailed from Hull. He told me that he was unlikely to marry, and if he did, he was certain that it wouldn't be with someone to whom he would want to give this ring. We were both devoted to our mother, but especially me. This was his latest attempt to convince me to return to London. He has been insistent on my finding a wife for years. It had been the bane of my visits with him, which have been less frequent of late for that reason."

"It looks like—"

"Your eyes," he finished. "I thought the same thing when I first saw you." And every time he had come back below deck to look at it since. He lifted her hand and slid the ring onto her finger. "A perfect fit," he said, not at all surprised. He had ceased believing that anything was a coincidence when it came to Harriet. As soon as he'd stopped fighting himself, and accepted that he was hers, it had all become so clear.

"Are you certain?" she asked.

He glanced from the ring to her eyes. They glittered with tears that she attempted to blink away. He took her face in his hands, wiping a single stray tear from her cheek with his thumb. "More certain than I have ever been of anything."

Chapter Twenty-Five

Harriet couldn't believe her luck. She'd made it to the *Seren* in time, confessed her deepest love for Alexander, gambling on the chance that he returned it, and he did. Now he clasped her face in his hands, as though he worried that she might slip away if he let go.

He loved her. She could have shouted with glee. Instead, she wept.

"What is it?" he asked.

"I'm so happy, I—"

He cut off her words with a soft kiss, a mere whisper against her lips. Weeks had passed since he'd held her, but her body responded instinctively. The fibers of her being seemed to sense that nothing stood between them this time.

She sighed, and his lips curved into a smile against hers. She fingered the collar of his shirt, tugging him closer. His fingers buried into her curls, but he only brushed her lips again. She took a tiny step forward, pressing her body against his. His warm ginger scent overwhelmed her senses, and she relished in it. Their lips met again, but she didn't let him tease her a third time. She wanted more, all of him, right now. To be his.

"No," he whispered, pulling away.

"What?" she breathed, opening her eyes. Her grasp tightened around his collar and she stepped with him.

"Not here." He kissed the corner of her mouth, then his hand moved to hers, loosening her grip on his shirt. The lamp extinguished with a hiss between Alexander's fingertips, plunging them into darkness once more. Though they both knew the way, he guided her back to the stairs and off the orlop deck. The groan and creak of the ship swaying in the water accompanied them.

Morning sunshine welcomed them back onto the main deck, the fog dissipating during their short time below. Her hand was still wrapped in Alexander's as he gestured for her to enter his cabin first. Excitement and anticipation thrilled through her, making her giddy.

The door clicked shut, and Alexander stood behind her, hands resting on her shoulders. His breath tickled her neck as he grazed his teeth along her earlobe. Her eyes closed, and she leaned back against the warmth of his body. His hands slid down her arms, and he took hold of her wrists. She shivered and was delighted by his responding sigh.

"Harriet, are you certain? We can wait." He let go, and her answering groan was heavy with displeasure.

"Don't you dare," she murmured. "You might possess the control of a saint..." *She* did not.

"I can assure you," he whispered in her left ear, sending gooseflesh down the entire side of her body, "that I possess nothing of the sort."

He grasped her hips, and waves of desire washed over her. He slid his hands up her stomach, reaching her breasts, and she cried out. She cursed the layers of her dress and corset for getting in the way.

He groaned. "I want to see you."

She spun around, but he shook his head.

"More than your lovely face."

"I'm all yours," she replied, smiling.

The rumble that came from deep in his throat was a guttural sound, one that melted her insides and stirred them into a desperate whirl. One hand moved to the small of her back, and he buried the other in her hair, pulling her against him for a kiss.

Her dress loosened, and he guided it over her shoulders. She did her best to shimmy off the rest of it and with a swish of his hands, it was gone. His fingers returned to her back.

"Not so tightly bound in your corset today?" he asked, his lips brushing hers.

"A thoughtless omission, I'm sure," she whispered, struggling to focus when his lips did such things down her neck... her chest... along the top edge of the corset.

"Negligent, really," he murmured against her skin. "Look at what trouble it has got you into." With that, his fingers slid through the remaining loops of ribbon, and the corset came loose. He cast it aside, and it landed on the floor with a soft thump. "You are beautiful," he whispered, without taking his eyes from hers.

Before she could respond, his mouth moved to her breast, taking her nipple with a swirl of his tongue. The sensation was exquisite through the thin material of her chemise. Her head thrust back, and she arched against him. The hard line of his body pressed along her, his hands splayed across her back. He guided her backward until she was against the wall and held her there. His mouth moved to her other breast, and he seemed intent on bringing her closer and closer to the edge of... of what, she wasn't sure, but she wanted to find out. This was different to the last time.

Her lips parted, and she let out an involuntary sigh. Twisting her fingers through his hair, she pulled him closer. She was rewarded with his answering moan, the sound vibrating against her chest. Warm hands covered her breasts, squeezing and kneading in all the right ways. She breathed him in, savoring every touch.

She slid her hands down his sides, eliciting a shiver from him that ran along the length of her body. The curve of his muscled torso was strong under her hands. She squeezed his hips, as he had done to her, to test if her touch was as powerful. His mouth crushed against hers and erased any thought of what she might do next as he explored her with his tongue. Oh, she wanted more of this.

The soft linen of his shirt filled her hands, and she tugged it from his breeches. Beneath it, his skin was smooth and firm. She ran her hands over his chest and reveled in each gasp that he made in response to her touch. What else could she do?

She took his lower lip between her teeth. Then she wrapped her leg around one of his, testing the hold she had over him. His response was instant. One hand left her breast, and for a moment, she regretted challenging him, but he hooked it under her knee and brought it to his hip, wrapping her leg around his waist. His fingertips trailed over her ankle, and up her calf. A gentle caress of her thigh turned into a desperate hold—one that she needed as much as he. The fleeting pressure of his erection against her sex was delicious.

He snatched up her other leg, bringing it around his

waist. His big, rough hands cupped her bottom, and he held her to him. He was so close to the delicate skin where her own desire pooled, and she wished he would touch her there.

ALEXANDER LAID Harriet on his bed, needing all his control, wrapped around him as she was. He rested on his knees between her legs, taking in every inch of her and wishing he'd had the sense to remove her chemise before now. Light spilled through the windows and onto the bed, lighting the threads of gold in her hair. He lifted his shirt over his head and tossed it across the cabin. Kicking off his boots, he let them thud onto the floor. He spent more time tending to Harriet's boots, untying the laces and slipping them off her feet. He liked that she'd been wearing them instead of slippers beneath her dress.

Alexander raked his gaze over her again.

Intentionally.

Possessively.

She was perfection. From the brown hair sprawling over her shoulders to the tips of her stockinged toes.

"Mm," he murmured. "Stockings on, or off?"

She lifted her foot from his hand and placed it on his chest. The motion caused her chemise to slip off her knee, giving him a full view of her. The deep rumble in his throat surprised him for a second time. Her tongue ran over her bottom lip, which she took between her teeth. He groaned again. The woman would have him expire in an untimely manner without so much as a sigh. That couldn't happen. He'd waited weeks for this moment.

He traced soft patterns on the outside of her calf up to

the band of her stockings. Untying her garters, he let the ribbons slip through his fingers. He slid her stockings down and traced his fingertips to her inner thigh. Beneath the chemise, where the material was most translucent, her nipples formed soft pink peaks. He brought his mouth down to one, and then the other, appreciating her sighs of pleasure. He lifted her hips off the bed and yanked the chemise out of his way, nestling between her legs.

His lips left her breast, and she groaned. The frustrated sound echoed his thoughts. He couldn't bear not to touch her now, even for a second.

"Do you know what you want?" His voice was dark with a desire that reached his core.

Her eyes stayed closed, and she bobbed her head up and down.

"What is that?" he asked.

"More," she whispered.

Oh, he would give her that. They had all the time in the world, and this time, he was determined to do it right.

He pushed the chemise over her head and tossed it over his shoulder, stopping to take in the beautiful sight of her naked body. "Can I touch you like this?" His fingers found the sensitive place between her legs, and she cried out, nodding. He kept his movements steady, tracing the lines of her silky skin and paying intimate attention to her response. If he moved his fingers like this, she would sigh. But if he did that, then her back would arch off the bed and she'd press herself into his hand.

Harder.

Softer.

Each touch evoked a different reaction, and he was having trouble deciding which one he liked best. He brought his mouth down over his fingers and stroked her with his tongue. The way she nearly bucked off the bed made him chuckle against her skin, and that elicited a long moan that came from deep within her. She was close.

More purposeful now, he kept the rhythm constant as she rocked beneath him. The soft skin of her bottom filled his other hand, and he kept her from instinctively arching away.

All too soon, she let out a loud cry, and her legs trembled.

He sat back, soaking in the sight of a spent Harriet. Her hair had become a tangled mess where she'd tossed her head in the bed sheets. The blush that adorned her cheeks had spread to her breasts, and she was a lovely pink color. She opened her eyes, and he grinned so broadly, the edges of it might have reached his ears.

"What. Was. That?" She took a breath between each word.

"That was only the beginning."

He jumped off the bed and removed his breeches. Climbing back into bed, he settled once again between her legs. The warmth of her fingertips trailed up his arms and he shivered with pleasure.

"I'm ready," she whispered, with the hint of a smile on her lips.

Alexander slid inside her, moving inch by tortuous inch. Her tight, wet heat was glorious, and he fought against every instinct to thrust hard and fast. That effort was for naught.

Harriet raised her hips, the action swift, taking his length in one move.

Buried deep, her muscles tightened around him. Curse it, he couldn't make this last. She felt too good. Moving his hand between them, he found her sensitive bud and rubbed small circles. Each of her exhales turned into a moan, until it became one long sound, and her inner muscles clenched.

One final rock of his hips brought them crashing into oblivion together.

He nuzzled her neck, inhaling the sweetness of mint, gardenia, and passion. Of Harriet.

ALEXANDER WOKE SOMETIME LATER, still lying on top of her. *Lord,* she would be crushed. He pushed himself up and made to get off her, but she stirred and tightened her arms around his neck.

"No," she murmured her protest.

He settled back onto her and kissed her, the intensity of his desire building again.

She broke away. "Is it too soon?"

His head tilted to the side and he frowned. "For what?"

She answered his question silently, taking one hand from his neck and wrapping it around his erection.

He spluttered a response and then tried again. "Uh, no." He coughed. "It isn't too soon."

She brought her lips to his ear and whispered, "Perfect."

"I, uh, need to check the time." He reached over the edge of the bed for his breeches and pulled the watch from his pocket. Sunlight still streamed into the cabin. It couldn't be too late, not yet midday.

"And?" she asked.

He barely heard the word and had forgotten to pay attention when he'd looked at his watch. Her hands gliding up and down the length of him had driven him into a frenzy. He mumbled something unintelligible but nodded.

She slowed down the words. "Do we have time?"

"Don't know," he huffed. "Don't care." He kissed her fiercely, tangling his fingers in her hair. Her hands were all over him, leaving a trail of fire in their wake. He burned for her, and every touch, every stroke, ignited him further.

He wasn't as gentle this time, but she matched his rhythm with enthusiasm. Soon, they were a flurry of arms and legs, tangled in the bed sheets. Her cries grew louder, as did his own, until they reached their release together.

As they lay there, panting, he wrapped his arm around her shoulders, and she traced patterns across his chest with her fingertips. Bright daylight shone through the windows that ran the length of the stern wall, soaking them in warmth and casting shadows across the cabin.

"We should be going," he said reluctantly.

She sighed.

"I don't *want* to go, Harriet. I wouldn't move from this bed for the next month if I didn't need to. But if I don't take you home soon, I'll wager that your family will come looking for you. Besides, you must be as hungry as I. All that food in the galley is no good without a cook."

Her stomach rumbled at his mention of food, and they both laughed.

He climbed over her and out of bed and gathered her clothes. With his back to her, he plucked up his own clothes and dressed hastily. The urge to let his gaze wander over to her was impossible to resist. He wanted to take her to bed again, and he'd meant what he'd said about staying there with her for the month. There was nothing for it, he would need to wait for her outside. The cool morning air would do his head some good.

He stepped out of the cabin and waited for her on the deck. Down on the dock, he spotted a hackney waiting.

Excellent.

The door creaked open behind him, and he turned back as Harriet stepped out of his cabin. She had dressed quicker than he'd expected and was not quite as disheveled as she ought to be after two sessions of lovemaking. He'd be sure to remedy that when next he got the chance.

He raked his gaze over her, and she blushed a delicate shade of pink. If he didn't stop staring, he'd need to turn around and take her back to bed. But they still had the hackney, and that would provide another thirty minutes alone with her. He took her hand and led her to the gangplank. She followed behind him, and Alexander couldn't stop the Cheshire grin spreading across his face.

Harvey and Sam waited for them on the dock, both wearing expectant looks.

"Do you know how long I've had this hackney waiting for you?" Sam said. "It has cost me a small fortune—"

Harvey cut him off. "I don't know if it was that long, Sam." His eyes danced at Alexander. "Leaves something to be desired for the young—"

"Not another word from the pair of you," Alexander begged as he passed them, leading Harriet into the hackney.

Chapter Twenty-Six

ALEXANDER COULDN'T WIPE the smile off his face. He'd cursed George's insistence that a special license would not do for the brother of a duke. *Four weeks wasn't so long*, George had said. Four weeks had been torture. After the morning he'd shared with Harriet on the ship, Alexander hadn't had one respectable thought about her without being interrupted by a stirring of need that stretched against his breeches. The dreams had kept coming, too, and with his intimate knowledge of her body, they were something else entirely. But the insufferable delay of having the banns read had been forgotten the moment he'd seen Harriet standing at the end of the aisle. Now he sat across from her in one of his brother's carriages as they trundled away from the church.

They were married, and Harriet loved him. He was the luckiest man on earth.

Her face was tilted away from him, and she watched the buildings pass by the window, smiling to herself. He'd never known beauty or the true meaning of it until that first night of watch duty together when he'd suspected that he might fall in love with her, not realizing that he already had.

He took the opportunity to study her while the carriage rocked through the London streets, taking in every detail. The way her hands folded in her lap. The profile of her nose and lips. Sunlight shone into the carriage, highlighting the golden strands that weaved through her thick brown curls. And that familiar hint of her mint and gardenia soap swirled around his head. Her wedding gown was light green, a pale reflection of her eyes, and had flowed and danced around her ankles as she'd walked down the aisle. The memory—still fresh in his mind—did wondrous things to the bulge in his breeches that he was presently trying to ignore.

"This may be my new favorite Harriet outfit," he murmured.

She turned, her smile widening. "And I made it the whole way down the aisle without tripping over."

"Or swooning," he remarked, before he could help himself.

"See, I can manage in a gown." Her eyes glittered playfully, but more lingered there.

"Stop looking at me that way, right now." He shifted in his seat and stared out the opposite window.

"Looking at you how?" she asked, surprise coloring her voice.

"You know perfectly well what I am talking about." He darted a glance her way out of the corner of his eye.

"I do not! I was only sitting here, thinking about..." She trailed off, and her gaze roamed around the blue upholstered carriage until her eyes went unfocused. A small, satisfied smile appeared on her face.

He groaned, loud enough to bring her awareness back

into the carriage, and her cheeks blushed his favorite shade of pink.

"I will not consummate our marriage on the floor of a carriage," he announced.

"I didn't ask you to."

"Not so explicitly. But I know what you're thinking."

"No, you don't," she said. "And there's nothing innocent about the way you're staring at me either." So, she had noticed.

He slid forward in his seat so that their knees brushed together. The slightest touch had him hungry for more. He reached for her face, turning her chin toward him and brushing his thumb over her lips. She parted them with a soft sigh, and her eyelids fluttered closed.

"You're thinking about the time I touched you like this," he said. He trailed his fingertips down her neck and across the embroidered flowers on the neckline of her gown. She shivered. He dipped a finger between her breasts, hooking it under her bodice, and tugged her toward him. "I was thinking about the same thing," he whispered.

He leaned over and kissed her. How had he made it through four weeks of chaperoned visits? In his opinion, he'd been a veritable monk.

She withdrew, her dark gaze holding him rapt.

"What about the bench?" she asked, her voice husky.

"What are you talking about?"

"You said not on the floor of the carriage, but there's always the bench."

The growl that escaped his lips came from a place of deep desire. "Since you insist on looking at me the way you do, and saying things like that, I have no choice."

Without giving her a chance to respond, he grasped her waist and pulled her across to his side of the carriage. She landed on his lap, and he fell back onto the bench with a low chuckle. He reached over to each window and yanked the curtains across.

He couldn't waste any time removing her gown, so he slid a hand to cover her breast. His other hand twisted in her hair, and he guided her down to kiss him. The bounce of the carriage had an exquisite effect on the way her bottom moved over him. He longed to be inside her, to feel her tightening around him.

She interrupted that delicious thought. "We must be almost there?"

"I instructed the driver to take the longest route possible if I gave the signal," he admitted, knocking twice on the roof of the carriage. Nothing wrong with being prepared, even if he'd had the best intentions. "But now I'm not sure if it will be long enough."

She responded with a long, hard kiss. He could sense her desperation and his own raged within him. He pushed her skirts up around her hips. She straddled his lap, and a devilish grin spread across her face. Her deft fingers moved to his breeches, unbuttoning the fastenings and grazing his erection. Not enough time... There would be time to spare at this rate. She guided him inside her, as ready for him as he was for her.

"I have been waiting weeks for this," she whispered in his ear.

He thrust his hips upward, and she tossed her head back. Her long brown curls went tumbling over her shoulders. His lips went straight to the hollow of her throat, over her rapid pulse. Her inner muscles tightened around him.

It was over before it had begun, but he wasn't embarrassed. Quite the opposite, it was a testament to Harriet's beauty and sensuality that he had even made it inside her.

It had been four *very* long weeks.

He returned her to the other bench and fixed his breeches, tucking his shirt back into place. Taking his handkerchief from his pocket, he handed it to her.

"Sorry," he said, "I don't have anything better right now." He was a cad, but he couldn't have brought a pot of water into the carriage without his brother's notice.

"Thank you." She set about righting her gown.

Alexander glanced out the window while she straightened her underskirts. He might have survived four weeks of chaperoned visits, but watching his wife now would unravel his remaining self-control. They must be nearing her family home, and he needed every moment to prepare himself for the wedding breakfast.

"How do I look?" she asked.

He took in her tousled hair and red, slightly swollen lips, and pulled his lips into a firm line between his teeth, fighting a chuckle. "Positively ravished," he managed. "Entirely inappropriate for a wedding breakfast." As was he.

She reached over and slapped his chest playfully. "Help me!"

He did his best to rake his fingers through her hair, but all that did was make him hard again. "Dammit," he said.

"What?"

"If you want to get out of this carriage without looking as though you've made love at least twice, I recommend you fix your own hair. I'll give you directions from over here." He scooted to the farthest edge of the carriage.

"At least twice..." she murmured. "I rather like the sound of that."

He did his best to ignore her, and it was a good thing he did. Minutes later, the carriage slowed, stopping in the middle of Berkeley Square. There would be plenty of time for *twice* later.

HARRIET CLASPED her fingers over Alexander's as they danced across her thigh. He'd been doing it under the table right through their wedding breakfast, and she couldn't focus on anything else, no matter how much she tried to study the dark green walls of her parents' dining room. Millie sat opposite her, beside Sam, but Harriet hadn't caught her sister's eye once.

"Alexander!" George's cheerful call came from the end of the table. George had insisted that Harriet use his first name since her betrothal to Alexander had been announced. She was still getting accustomed to being on such friendly terms with a duke. The conversation along the table hushed as her family looked at Alexander.

His fingers stopped fighting her grasp. "Yes?" he replied. With a quick wink at her, he brought his hands together above the table. His thigh brushed against hers, sending a jolt through her body, and interrupted the moment of reprieve. She did her best to ignore him. The corners of his mouth curved up. He was enjoying himself a little too much. Well, two could play at that game.

"Have you given any thought to what you're going to do now?" George asked.

Harriet's hand was in her lap where Alexander's fingers had left hers. She inched closer until her hand hovered above his leg.

"I—" He choked on his words as she dropped her hand onto his upper thigh and slid up to the fastenings of his breeches.

"Are you all right?" she asked, letting sweetness drip from her voice.

His eyes narrowed before he composed his features into a smile. "I have no plans beyond the next few weeks, which I will be spending with my wife."

Harriet was sure she imagined the emphasis on the word *wife*, but the quiver in her core was very real. In the brief moments of solitude they had shared over the previous weeks, Alexander had told her in exquisite detail what he would be doing with her.

To her.

His whispered promises had sent shivers down her spine, and tingles everywhere else. Recalling them made her insides coil in anticipation.

"Excellent." George interrupted her thoughts not a moment too soon. "Lord Hazelby and I have been in discussions with Frederick."

Harriet glanced between her father and uncle, both of whom beamed back. She had avoided any discussion with Alexander about what would follow their few weeks together but presumed she would reside in London while he sailed. That's what sailor's wives did, and she doubted she could stowaway again. Alexander would be sure to check every possible hiding place on the *Seren* or make her stand within his sight on the dock while he left. Her brows pulled into a frown. She didn't want to think about this on her wedding day.

"What have you been discussing?" she asked hesitantly, keen to get past the conversation.

"You," her father answered.

"Where you will live," Uncle Frederick continued.

She looked at her mother, who cast a warm, encouraging smile her way. What did they know that she didn't?

"There is a cottage on a secluded part of my estate in Hull," George said. "I arranged for it to be made ready for you both to enjoy a quiet, private honeymoon. If you would like to leave today, it will be ready by the time you arrive."

"That is kind of you, brother," Alexander said. Then, in a murmur meant only for Harriet, he added, "It was my mother's. You'll adore it."

"It is yours if you wish," George said, "as a temporary residence, or a retreat. It's on a small plot of land with which you may do as you see fit."

"Temporary?" Alexander echoed her thoughts, though why would he be surprised? It could be her permanent home, and his when he returned from sea.

"Yes," Uncle Frederick said. He closed his hand over Aunt Amelia's on the table, and they both turned their attention to Harriet. "Balmaine is unentailed, and one day it will become too much for us. We decided that you will inherit it, but you are welcome to learn the ins and outs of management whenever you are ready."

Harriet's eyes welled with tears of gratitude for her family. "I'm not sure I'll be able to manage it on my own while Alexander is away," she admitted.

"Away?" Alexander asked, returning his gaze to her. "Where am I going?"

She tilted her head to the side. "Won't you be sailing?" The rest of her family had been informed of her voyage soon after her betrothal, so she could speak freely in front of them.

"No." Alexander said. "I'm not sailing again."

"Why not?" she asked.

His eyebrows inclined. "I can go if you wish."

"No!" she exclaimed, blushing at the volume of her objection and Alexander's answering smirk. "I don't understand. When I came to find you on the ship, you were ready to sail. I assumed you delayed long enough for the banns to be read and the wedding." And those few promised weeks together that she needn't bring to anyone's attention. "Is there not somewhere you need to be?"

It was Alexander's turn to blush, something she hadn't seen before and delighted her.

"No," he said. "I have nowhere else to be except beside you. If you're willing." He flashed a hesitant smile, and her cheeks warmed again. "A week after we arrived in London, and once Sam, Harvey and I had clarified what had happened, I did what I could to extract myself from it all so that I could offer you stability. I'm ashamed to admit that the voyage you stopped was nothing more than me running away. You wanted nothing to do with me, so I was leaving without so much as a plan. I'm sorry I didn't tell you before now."

She could sense that everything she wanted was within her reach, and she dared to hope that it would be true. "You don't want to sail anymore?" she asked.

"The only place I want to be is with you," he replied.

"We could sail together," she suggested.

Alexander shook his head. "I have no desire to spend our marriage being so distracted by work. Life on a ship is hard, and I've done it for long enough. I'd been thinking about stopping for a while, investing in the merchant trade and naming someone else as captain. The only reason I hadn't was George's insistence that I attend the London season." His cheeks turned pink again. "I've been using it as an excuse to run away a little too much. Honestly, it would be nice to spend more than a few days on land each year."

Her chest swelled. She would never need to say the goodbye she had been dreading.

"What will happen to the *Seren*?" she asked.

Alexander shrugged. "Harvey will take it, and along with Sam's ship, it will be the start of our fleet. We've already found work in trade and will see how it goes. I'll remain a partner and manage things from here. Or Hull."

Harvey's objection came from the other end of the table. "I still don't see what's wrong with the *Black Witch*. Why does she need to be the one to go?"

"Besides the fact that it's a known pirate ship?" Alexander asked. "The thing is falling apart. I barely sailed it back across the Channel. You can't take it into open waters in that state."

"Plus, it's *tiny*," added Sam.

"It is not," Harvey defended.

"Excuse me." George interrupted the argument before it started in earnest. The room fell silent, and everyone's attention returned to him. In the short time she had known George, Harriet had recognized his ability to command any situation.

"What do you think, Harriet?" her father asked. "Would you be happy living at Balmaine?"

She would be very happy indeed, but another thought niggled at her. "What about Millie?"

Her sister looked up from her plate, eyes wide. "What about me?"

"Why am I the one to inherit Balmaine? Where will Millie live?" Concern for her sister filled Harriet, and she glanced between her father and uncle.

"There are other unentailed properties in my estate," her father said. "We thought Balmaine would best suit you and keep Alexander connected to the ships. If you would prefer somewhere else—"

"No," Harriet interrupted. "Balmaine is perfect." She

hadn't considered other unentailed properties for her sister.

Philip spoke again. "You can rest assured that I had plans for each of you if you did not marry."

Millie rolled her eyes, a small smirk playing on her lips. "Besides, it is only the start of the season. I am twenty and not yet on the shelf. I may find a husband this year or next."

Harriet beamed, content that her sister was capable of looking after herself.

THERE HAD BEEN a distinct lack of conversation since Harriet had left her family's home for the first time as a married woman. Long glances between her and Alexander filled the silence in the carriage. The arrangements had been made after their wedding breakfast, and they were already headed for Hull.

Harriet broke the silence first. "May I ask you something?"

"Anything," Alexander said, smiling.

"Your mother's cottage?" she prompted, unsure of the precise question she wished to ask.

Alexander sighed. "It was a retreat. She went there to paint and to escape my father. He was not a kind man. She would take me often when I was a boy. The place holds many happy memories. I remember her singing or reading to me, teaching me cards, and never letting me win until I had earned it." His eyes glazed over. "It had the most beautiful garden."

"I like to garden," Harriet whispered.

He focused on her face again, and his eyes shone. "I can't wait to see what you do with it. It makes me happy to think of you there. My mother was a wonderful woman. Did I tell you that I named the ship for her?"

"You didn't," Harriet said.

"She died when I was seventeen. Her name was Serena. *Seren* seemed fitting—it is a Welsh word meaning star. I wish you could have met her. She would have adored you."

His words warmed Harriet, and the way his gaze raked over her did exciting things to her insides. There would be plenty of time for *that* soon enough.

"Will you tell me more about the week in London?" she asked. "Before you surprised me at the ball."

He shrugged. "What more is there to tell?"

"How did you—what was the word you used?—*extract* yourself from your work with Sam and Harvey?"

He hesitated, and for a moment, she thought he wouldn't tell her.

"The three of us spent the week in the Tower of London, as you know."

She nodded.

Alexander smiled. "It wasn't as bad as you're imagining. And it's not the first time we've been held in that wing."

"How many times have you been imprisoned there?" she asked. What else had he been accused of?

"I've lost count of how many times I've been in and out of the Tower, or other dungeons. In London, it's usually while we wait for a contact to confirm our identities, same as this time. You'd think they'd have painted a portrait of us by now. Sam and I have been doing this for a long time, over ten years."

"Then you must have been—"

"Fourteen," he finished. "We ran away from home together and joined the first crew that would take us. It was foolish, but we were desperate. Sam's family life wasn't much better than mine, and we were not missed by our fathers. We were hired to a ship for a specific purpose. Not only were we small, we could dress well and speak with enough eloquence to pass in certain circles that most sailors can't. We rose quickly through the ranks, and when our captain retired, Sam took over captaincy of that ship. We must have been eighteen or nineteen at the time. By then, the wrong people knew who we were, and it was becoming difficult to perform covert operations together. That's when we bought another ship, the *Seren*."

She frowned. "How could you pay for another ship?" She hadn't considered Alexander's income while he was sailing.

"I was out of the inheritance at that point. I hadn't seen my father since I left and had only risked seeing my mother on brief occasions. That will always be my biggest regret. I wish I'd done more, spent more time with her before she died." Alexander's gaze was unfocused again as he stared over her shoulder. He shook his head and glanced at her, smiling. "We were paid handsomely for a long time and had enough sense not to gamble it all away or partake in the normal port activities. There's a lot of money in covert operations for the Crown—if you don't get killed."

She gasped, but he was safe now. "Where does Harvey come into all of this?"

Alexander laughed. "I'm sure I don't need to tell you that Harvey has an ability to present himself as an unsavory sort, but that is not his true character. We met him in Saint-Malo. He *was* a pirate at the time."

Her eyes widened. "At the time?"

"I don't believe he has a single pirate bone in his body, but he is the roughest of the three of us. He didn't have the same upbringing. No one ever suspected that we worked together, so that made it easier to continue what we were doing. He had connections in France that Sam and I never dreamed of having."

"Until ..." She paused.

"Until he was accused of murder, and we were going to be blamed for his murder, yes. Am I making sense?"

She smiled. "I'm keeping up."

"Well, that brings you up to date. The next thing I know, I had a vexing mystery woman on the orlop deck of my ship, telling me that she had a message to deliver and consequently upending my entire existence." His eyebrows rose, and she stifled a giggle. Upending existences had been a mutual achievement.

"How were you allowed to stop doing all of this to marry me?" she asked.

"I have done my service, and some. I was never contractually obliged. We continued because we wanted to. All I had to do was ask. George has been begging me to stop sailing for years, but I had no reason to, until I met you. Stepping away was the easiest thing I have ever done."

Silence filled the carriage again, and Harriet's mind turned to other matters.

"What are you thinking about?" Alexander asked, reaching across and taking her hands in his.

"How long is the journey to Hull?"

Alexander cast her a quizzical look. "Haven't you made this journey every year with your family since you were a child?"

"Yes," she admitted, a warmth rising in her cheeks. "I didn't know how else to ask if we had time for *twice* now."

He groaned, pulling her across the carriage and onto his lap.

And Harriet was home.

Epilogue

ONE YEAR LATER

ALEXANDER HAD SEARCHED EVERYWHERE for Harriet. They'd come to Balmaine that morning for breakfast with her aunt and uncle, but as usual, estate management had distracted him and Frederick. By the time they'd arrived at the dining room, Harriet had finished and left. Shadow was also gone, which was no consolation. The footmen recalled last seeing her headed toward the stables, but she wasn't there. If she had gone for a ride, he would have no choice but to tie her up for the next five months. He couldn't risk her or the baby's safety.

Alexander rushed through the gardens, slowing when a faint groan near the gardenias reached his ears. It was early summer, and they had recently blossomed. He stilled, taking a deep breath of the sweet smell that always reminded him of Harriet. Then he glimpsed her through the bushes, leaning forward against the garden wall, her back to him. The pale cream muslin dress cinched at her waist.

She didn't look pregnant at all from behind yet. Until her whole body seized and she dry retched over the wall.

Long ground-eating strides took him through the garden, but he was forced to stop out of arm's reach.

Shadow stood his ground between them, growling at Alexander. His loyalty had swayed further in Harriet's direction recently. All for good reason, but Alexander wasn't a threat.

"Harriet." His voice was a blend of relief at finding her and utter terror as he considered the possibilities of what could be happening.

"Shadow," Harriet murmured, "it's all right."

Shadow reacted instantly to her subtle command and withdrew to sit beside her. His eyes did not leave Alexander when he reached down to pat him. At least Alexander was allowed into the protected space now. That wasn't the case a few weeks ago.

As soon as Alexander was close enough, he wrapped his hands around Harriet's hair, pulling the loose strands together over her back. He held the mass in one hand and traced circles over her back.

"What is it?" he asked. "Is it the baby?"

"The baby is fine." Another long groan undid her feeble attempt to reassure him.

"Harriet." This time, his tone was serious.

She twisted her face toward him, and her emerald eyes glittered in the sunlight. "I needed fresh air."

"That's not what it sounds like. Come inside and I'll call for the doctor to examine you." He wrapped an arm around her shoulders and attempted to guide her back to the house.

She waved him off with her hand and frowned. "I told you the baby is fine. And I'm not going inside."

"Then what is it?" What had happened in the half hour he'd been preoccupied with Frederick?

"Apparently there has been a disagreement between us over my decision to have eggs for breakfast." She gave him a weak smile, her pale pink lips pulling tight.

He didn't follow. "Between whom?"

"The baby and I," she said, as though it were the most obvious answer and he was the fool for not following along. "I was overcome by such a desire to eat eggs this morning that I had four." Her throat bobbed on the word *eggs*.

Was simply thinking about them doing this to her?

"Four?" he asked. "I've never seen you eat more than one."

"I know, and that must be the limit for this little one." Her hands caressed the small bump of her abdomen. "I've managed to keep it down, but the baby isn't happy."

"This is pregnancy sickness?" he asked.

"Yes." She patted his cheek with one hand, the other still on her belly.

"You're not in early labor?"

"No," she said, her voice a placating and patient coo.

"This is normal?"

"Yes." She smiled. "That's what my mother reassured me in her last letter."

He blew out his breath. She was all right. He placed his trembling hands over hers. Over their little one. Their baby was safe.

"What can I do?" he asked.

"I don't think there's anything you *can* do. I'll be all right, but don't let me eat that many eggs again." She gagged again on the word.

"Oh, no!" Alexander exclaimed. "The last time I stood

between you and food, you almost tore my head off." He shivered, the movement involuntary.

"That happened *before* I realized I was pregnant."

He shook his head. "That doesn't change anything. I won't make the same mistake again, and I doubt anyone else will risk it, either. You frightened the butler that day."

The corners of her mouth twitched.

"There must be something else I can do to help." As he spoke, he wrapped his hands around her wrists, pressing a finger into each of the pressure points. It was the only thing he could think of trying.

Her eyelids fluttered closed, and she sighed. Her chin lifted to the warmth of the sun and sunlight danced on her eyelashes. If she hadn't been so unwell, he would have given her a chaste kiss on the cheek, but he doubted it would help.

"Well, now you need to follow me around like this all day," she murmured.

"There is nowhere I'd rather be," he replied. "But in the interest of your comfort and independence, it might be worth considering ginger."

"Of course," she said. "I hadn't thought of that."

He made to leave, but her desperate groan stopped him.

"Please don't let go. I feel so much better already."

The footman, who had searched with Alexander, had remained at the edge of the garden. Alexander gestured for him without letting go of Harriet's wrists.

"A piece of ginger from the kitchen," Alexander said as soon as the man was close enough.

The footman turned on his heel and set away at a brisk walk.

"I hope it works," Harriet said.

"I see no reason it shouldn't. It worked well for you on the ship."

The footman soon returned with a tray, a single piece of ginger sitting in the middle looking quite absurd. Harriet laughed, and Alexander joined her. He moved his hand with hers as she took it from the tray, and the footman retreated. She bit into the ginger and chewed. The muscles in her jaw clenched and unclenched, and he allowed his gaze to wander down to the much-too-enticing neckline of her gown. He returned his gaze to her face. She raised an eyebrow.

"Sorry," he muttered.

"You are not."

"You're right," he replied with a grin. "How do you feel?"

"Much improved."

"I'll request that the cook make biscuits or cakes with it. That ought to be more palatable."

She wriggled her hands free of his grasp and wrapped them around his neck. "That sounds lovely."

He pressed his lips to hers, but he wrinkled his nose.

"What is it?" she asked.

"I don't like the ginger. It overpowers the scent of you."

"That's funny."

"How so?"

"I love it," she said. "It was one of the first things I noticed about you. I was intrigued."

"Is that all you were?" he whispered against her neck, then moved his lips further down to her collarbone.

"You know it isn't," she whispered back, taking his earlobe between her teeth.

"If you're feeling well, might we reschedule our

morning commitments so you can tell me more about your first impressions?"

"I can show you if you like."

He'd like that very much.

The End

Loved this book?

Enjoyed reading Harbored Desires?
    I would love for you to leave a review
    Amazon Australia: https://books2read.com/u/4jONqk
    Amazon: https://a.co/d/002lyvtc

Wondering how Millie and Sam know each other?
    The Hazelby Sisters book two is coming soon. Sign up to Shannon's newsletter, The Drawing Room Whispers, for updates!

Acknowledgments

I wouldn't be a writer if I didn't spend pages thanking everyone who has helped me bring this book to life. And there's a lot of you!

Endless thank you to:

Ryan, you keep it together when everything is unravelling around me and consistently nudged me toward my goal of getting published. You are the voice of strength and reason when I need it most. Your sarcastic comments might inspire my favorite scenes, but your belief and support get me through. It's cliché but I truly couldn't have done it without you. Also, you promised you would read this when it finally went to print and I intend to hold you to that.

H. When my maternity leave coincided with the release of Bridgerton, it began an unstoppable journey. From binge reading and listening to audiobooks to me finally realizing my childhood dream of becoming an author. Having those early years with you gave me so much space to be creative, and I would never have found that side of myself without you. I could have done with more sleep, but we made it.

My mum and dad. Thank you for the freedom to grow into my true self, while being there when I felt lost. You have always believed in me and encouraged me to pursue things that brought me joy. Bet you didn't think it would be writing kissing books.

My dad, brother, and sister-in-law for your knowledge of all things ship related and indulging my questions.

Constance, you've been there since this story was just 900 words of absolute drivel. You encouraged me to keep writing and taught me so much. Harriet and Alexander (and the rest of the Hazelby family) wouldn't exist in such a vibrant world without you.

Hannah McCarthy, I'm so grateful to have someone as supportive as you who I can trust to alpha read anything I write. You always give me the boost I need to start the next round of revisions and the confidence to let other people read my work. I live for our daily reel exchanges and chats.

Selina Shapland at Empowered Words. You have read many of my stories and formatted this one, but it's our regular calls and check ins that really keep me going. I'd have given up many times without your support.

All the people who beta read one or more versions of this story. Your honest feedback helped shape this book into what it is, and I appreciate you all so much: Kirsten, Hilary, Karen, Ali, Michelle, Kiarnie and Sandra. I hope you'll come back for the next ones.

Dar Albert at Wicked Smart Designs for bringing the cover to life better than I could have imagined.

Lesley Marshall at Editline for providing a developmental edit that helped this story flow beautifully and for making me write the scenes I'd been too lazy to think about, they really do need to be there.

Dannielle Line for the best copyedit I could have asked for, your skills brought such a shine to my writer voice and gave me the confidence to take the next step and publish.

Susan Mackie for your mentorship as I learned about indie publication. Your knowledge and encouragement have been invaluable, and I couldn't have done it without your guidance.

Romance Writers of New Zealand, especially the Pacific

Hearts contest. Winning that award gave me the courage to imagine myself as an author.

Romance Writers of Australia and the Aspiring eLoop where I have met so many incredible writers and made wonderful friends. The information shared within this group has been fundamental on my journey.

And finally, you, the reader. Thank you for taking a chance on Harriet and Alexander, and on me as well. To know you read this story brings me such joy. I hope to find you here again soon.

Shannon x

About the Author

Lover of historical romance, Shannon Frances James is forever falling for regency gentlemen, but it's the independent heroines who truly capture her heart. She adores a heroine who brings a hero to his knees. Her award-winning stories are filled with romantic tension, charm, and a dash of humor – steamy scenes guaranteed.

She lives in Queensland, Australia, with her wonderful family and has reached the age where birds are cool again. She can't drink caffeine without having a panic attack so relies on a healthy dose of sarcasm to get through. Her free time is filled with family activities, camping, and enjoying the outdoors.

Sign up for Shannon Frances James's newsletter, The Drawing Room Whispers, to stay in the know about upcoming releases.

~

www.ingramcontent.com/pod-product-compliance
Lightning Source LLC
Chambersburg PA
CBHW021234060726
47590CB00005B/1763